Maya Banks is a No. 1 *New Y...* whose chart toppers have includ... suspense, contemporary romance, and Scottish historical romance. She lives in the South with her husband and three children and other assorted babies, such as her two Bengal kitties and a calico who's been with her as long as her youngest child. She's an avid reader of romance and loves to dish books with her fans and anyone else who'll listen!

She very much enjoys interacting with her readers on Twitter @maya_banks and facebook.com/AuthorMayaBanks. For more about Maya's books visit www.mayabanks.com.

Praise for the sensational novels of Maya Banks:

'Incredibly awesome . . . I love Maya Banks and I love her books' Jaci Burton, *New York Times* bestselling author

'Maya Banks writes the kind of books I love to read!' Lora Leigh, *New York Times* bestselling author

'Quick-paced . . . plenty of smoldering explicit sex, delivers a satisfying one-two punch of entertainment that will leave readers eager for the next book' *Publishers Weekly*

'Maya Banks . . . really dragged me through the gamut of emotions. From . . . "is it hot in here?" to "oh my god" . . . I'm ready for the next ride now!' *USA Today*

'A deeply emotional, highly satisfying, edge-of-your-seat read . . . Compelling and cutting-edge romance' *Joyfully Reviewed*

'A cross between the *Bared to You* or Fifty Shades series and the Wicked Lovers series by Shayla Black' *Book Savvy Babe*

'A must-read author . . . her [stories] are always full of emotional situations, loveable characters, and kick-butt story lines' *Romance Junkies*

By Maya Banks

The Surrender Trilogy
Letting Go
Giving In
Taking It All

Maya Banks

Giving In

headline
ETERNAL

First published in the United States of America in 2014 by Berkley,
a member of Penguin Group (USA) LLC.
A Penguin Random House Company.

First published in Great Britain in 2014
by HEADLINE ETERNAL
An imprint of HEADLINE PUBLISHING GROUP

1

Cataloguing in Publication Data is available from the British Library

ISBN 978 1 4722 2112 4

Offset in Palatino by Avon DataSet Ltd, Bidford-on-Avon, Warwickshire

Printed and bound by CPI Group (UK) Ltd, Croydon, CR0 4YY

Papers used by Headline are from well-managed forests and
other responsible sources.

MIX
Paper from
responsible sources
FSC® C104740

HEADLINE PUBLISHING GROUP
An Hachette UK Company
338 Euston Road
London NW1 3BH

www.headlineeternal.com
www.headline.co.uk
www.hachette.co.uk

For Sandra,
the mother of my heart.

ONE

"YOU look like hell," Jensen Tucker said bluntly from the doorway of Kylie Breckenridge's office.

Kylie shot him a look that would have withered a lesser man. But Jensen was frustratingly unaffected by her icy demeanor around him. He acted as if he didn't have a clue that he bugged the shit out of her. But no, she imagined he knew exactly how much he bothered her, and he just chose to ignore it. Stubborn, impossible, completely overbearing man. Precisely the kind of man she avoided at all costs.

Only he was her boss. That put another sour expression on her face. Carson had been her boss, he and Dash. And then when her brother had died three years ago, Dash had become her only boss and she had liked it that way.

Jensen should hire his own damn personal assistant, but he seemed perfectly content to dump his workload on Kylie and annoy the piss out of her in the process.

"Gee, thanks," she said in a tone to match her glare. "Nice to know I pass muster around here."

Jensen strolled into her office, uninvited. But then he'd never come in here if he waited for an invitation. Kylie had made it clear she didn't want him anywhere near her. Another thing he chose to ignore.

He took a seat in one of the chairs in front of her desk, and she made a mental note to get rid of them. They were unnecessary. Jensen and Dash did all the entertaining of their clients. There wasn't a need for anyone to ever enter her office. She did her job quietly and efficiently, never drawing attention to herself. Only for some reason, Jensen seemed determined to invade her personal space. A fact that had increasingly frustrated her in the weeks since he'd joined Dash in their consulting firm.

"You aren't sleeping," he said in that same straightforward tone he'd used to tell her she looked like hell.

His gaze penetrated her, raking over her features, and she knew what he saw. What she saw in the mirror every morning. Eyes haunted with the past. Deep shadows seemingly permanently etched underneath her eyes. She knew what she looked like. She didn't need this arrogant asshole to point it out to her.

"I wasn't aware that my appearance or sleep habits in any way interfered with my duties here."

Her sarcasm was wasted because Jensen just let it roll off him, much like he did everything else. Never once had she seen him express any sort of emotion. He didn't get upset or angry but neither had she ever seen him express happiness or excitement. Nothing but that steady gaze that saw too much. Peeling back the layers of her skin—and her mind. She hated it. She felt like a bug under a microscope. She wouldn't put it past him to know when she went to the damn bathroom.

He was a man who nothing escaped his notice. He was quiet, observant. He stood back and observed others. It suited him well for the career he'd chosen. But it discomfited her. He could save his scrutiny for the consulting jobs he and Dash took on.

Those companies needed his unbiased and discerning eye. She sure as hell didn't need it or want it.

"You do a damn fine job, Kylie. I don't believe I've ever given you reason to doubt my confidence in your abilities. If I have, then I apologize. Dash and I would certainly be lost without you."

She blinked in surprise over the unexpected praise, and unwanted color washed into her cheeks, warming her skin. She didn't want to acknowledge the brief surge of pleasure his veiled compliment had brought.

"When was the last time you slept?" he asked pointedly, still staring at her, studying intently.

"Last night," she said lightly. "Just like I do every night."

"Bullshit."

Her eyes widened at the growl in his voice.

"If you're even getting a few hours of sleep I'd find that hard to believe. Why don't you take some time off? Go somewhere. Relax. Take a vacation. Dash says you've never once taken off. Only when Carson died."

Kylie flinched, unable to temper the surge of grief that hit her square in the chest.

"You can say it," Jensen said in an almost brutal tone. "He's dead, Kylie. Joss has moved on so why can't you?"

She slapped her palms down on her desk and stood, staring him down, not giving a single inch.

"He was my family," she hissed. "My *only* family. He was all I had left in the world. He was the only person who loved me, who protected me, and now he's gone. If you think I can just blithely forget that and go on about my life like his death didn't affect me, you can go to hell."

"There. Finally some emotion, Kylie. Even if you're spitting mad. But at least you're not acting like some goddamn robot working on autopilot. Would it kill you to be human like the rest of us? Shit happens. You deal with it, pick up the pieces and move on. Just like everyone else in the human race. You aren't special. You aren't the only person who's had a shitty past and who's lost someone they love."

Fury clouded her vision, making the room go hazy. Anger tightened every one of her features and for a moment she was paralyzed, unable to respond around the knot in her throat choking her.

"How dare you?" she raged. "Who the hell are you to judge me? You don't know a goddamn thing about me. Get the hell out of my office and don't come back. If you want or need something, you can damn well e-mail me, call me or text. But do *not* come back into my office."

He didn't react to her outburst. To her astonishment, a faint smile glimmered on his lips.

"I know a hell of a lot more about you than you think. But you're right. I don't know everything. But I plan to change that. Starting now. You and I are going to be working very closely over the next few weeks because Dash and Joss are going on their honeymoon. We're trying to land a contract with Simpson & Gerrick Oil and it's a big one. They're downsizing and they want to cut the fat. Get rid of the unproductive workers. Rearrange duties. Decide who goes and who stays. And that's going to fall on you and me."

Kylie's eyes widened. "I don't have any experience in handling that. I work in the background, Jensen. You know that. I run the office. You and Dash are the cutthroats."

"And you don't have the heart for it, do you, Kylie?"

She flushed. Admitting her weaknesses wasn't on her top-ten list of things to reveal.

"You act the bitch. You come across as abrasive, even to the people who love you. I wonder why? Are you so afraid of loving someone, of getting close to someone and losing them like you lost Carson? Because you don't fool me, Kylie. Not in the least. Underneath that tough-as-nails exterior lies a vulnerable, big-hearted woman and she's who I want to pull out. And I will. Take it to the bank, sweetheart. You and I are going to be seeing a lot more of one another so get used to it."

"Get out," she said through clenched teeth. "I don't have to put up with this in my own office."

He shrugged. "Doesn't matter where it's said. It doesn't change what will be. And what will be is you and me, Kylie. I go after what I want and I don't fail. Ever."

She snorted, her blood pressure rising, her breath hitching in her throat. His words terrified her and yet there was something about them that made her pulse kick up several notches.

Jensen Tucker was everything she didn't want in a man. Not that she wanted any man. But especially not a dominant, alpha, overbearing male. There was no way in hell she'd ever put herself in a position of vulnerability again and no matter what woman was with Jensen, she'd definitely be vulnerable. Hell, she'd be eaten alive. Jensen would chew her up and spit her out in ten seconds flat.

"Don't hold your breath," she said in a frigid tone. "It will never happen. And so help me, if you ever even hint about this again, I'll slap a sexual harassment suit on you so fast your head will spin."

He grinned, surprising her with his reaction. He stared lazily at her, his gaze stroking up and down her body, making her feel as though he'd just undressed her.

"Something else you should know about me, sweetheart. I

love a challenge. Telling me *no* is like waving a red flag in front of a pissed-off bull."

"I'm not your sweetheart. Save it for a woman who gives a damn because I'm not her."

His grin got bigger and she swore this was the first time she'd actually seen the man smile. He was always so quiet and brooding. He didn't frown, but he didn't smile either. He always wore an inscrutable expression that drove her crazy because she never had any clue what he was thinking.

Only now she got the distinct impression he'd been thinking about her. A lot.

She mentally went through every single one of her favorite four-letter curse words and added a few with extra syllables for good measure.

"Let me make this simple for you since you love a challenge. I'm not a challenge, Jensen. I will never be a challenge because you don't have a chance in hell with me. You're out of your goddamn mind anyway. What the hell would a man like you see in me? According to you I'm scared of my own shadow. I'm timid, apparently I look like hell and have as many issues as *People* magazine."

He rose, ignoring her outburst, which only infuriated her more. He seemed utterly unfazed by her cutting remarks. Then he leaned over the desk so they were nose to nose. To her surprise he traced one finger over the dark smudges under her eyes.

"Get some help, Kylie," he said softly. "Go to a doctor. Get something to help you sleep. See a shrink if that's what it will take. You can't keep up like this forever. Sooner or later you're going to crack. And then you're going to fall apart and shatter. If you won't do it for yourself, do it for the people who love you and are worried sick about you."

And then before she could respond to that particular bit of nonsense, he turned and strode out of her office, closing the door with a soft bang.

She sagged into her chair and dropped her face into her hands, suddenly so weary that she couldn't even hold her own head up.

He was right and that pissed her off even more. She was walking a very fine line between sanity and insanity. She wasn't sleeping. Her sleep was too fractured by nightmares. Of the past. The demons of her past and how they still controlled her present.

But see a shrink? Ask her doctor for sleeping pills? That would be like admitting defeat and she was not a quitter, damn it. Not her. She'd survived hell and she was past that now. Wasn't she?

Or was she every bit the prisoner now that she'd been as a child? Her father's abuse was as recent as yesterday in her mind. Because she couldn't forget. She couldn't just get over it. Couldn't make peace with her past.

She closed her eyes, another wave of fatigue nearly flattening her. Sleep. She just needed one night without the nightmares that visited her so frequently. Maybe she'd stop on the way home and get some over-the-counter sleep aids at the pharmacy. Then there would be no embarrassing, *weak* trip to the doctor and certainly no visits to a damn shrink where she'd lie on a couch and bare her soul.

Oh hell no. Hell would freeze over before she ever allowed anyone to know her torment and shame.

WHAT was it about the woman that drove him to the brink of insanity? Jensen was absorbed in his thoughts as he stalked back to his office. He had a mountain of paperwork, contracts to look over and sign, if no changes were necessary. For the next two weeks, he was solidly at the helm while Dash took Joss away on their honeymoon.

Dash was happy. Disgustingly so. Now that he'd made up for his fuck-up of monumental proportions. Joss was a good woman. The best. Dash was damn lucky to have his heart's desire. A beautiful, submissive woman who'd granted Dash everything. Her trust, her love and her complete surrender.

In other words, the complete opposite of the woman who preoccupied so much of Jensen's thoughts lately.

Kylie Breckenridge was as prickly as a cactus and yet every time she sent him one of her withering gazes, he got a hard-on from hell. He wanted her so damn much that he couldn't breathe around her. And that pissed him off.

She was a woman who was strictly off-limits to him. The complete antithesis of the women he liked to fuck. And he said *fuck* because that's what it was. His heart was certainly never involved. His need for control precluded any warm and fuzzy thoughts.

It wasn't that he was a bastard to the women he dominated. He made certain they were cared for, provided for and that they were sexually satisfied.

But Kylie?

Hell. A dominant, alpha male was the very last thing she wanted. If she wanted any man at all. Not that he could blame her. Dash had told him of Kylie's childhood. It made him shake with rage that she'd been so abused, so shattered by the one person in her life she should have been able to trust for absolute protection. Her father.

But when he looked at her, he saw past that abrasive exterior and what he glimpsed made his heart soften to the point of aching. It made him want to hold her, cherish her, show her how it could be with a man who had her best interests at heart. A man who cared about her.

Hell, *did* he care? That was the million-dollar question. He cared, but to what extent? Was she, as he'd said, simply a challenge? Something to conquer before he moved on to the next? He was a man who thrived on challenges. It was what had made him successful at a very early age. So just how much did he care about Kylie Breckenridge? Because she wasn't a woman to trifle with. She'd had enough hurt for two lifetimes, and he damn sure didn't want to be yet another man who destroyed her.

He didn't fool himself into thinking he could "fix" her. No one could do that but her. But she had to *want* to be fixed, and so far she'd shown no signs of doing it herself. Which increased his desire to step in, take over and push her.

The urge to dominate was powerful. It beat like his pulse, strong with anticipation, even as he knew Kylie was not a woman to dominate. She wasn't a woman who'd submit. Ever. Not physically. But dominance was so much more than the physical trappings that often accompanied such a relationship. Emotional surrender was much more powerful, and perhaps that was what he craved when he looked into those shadowed eyes of hers.

She needed a man who'd cherish her, protect her from any and all hurts, provide shelter for her. A place of refuge from the rest of the world. She needed a man she could turn to and trust unerringly in his ability to shield her from any threat. Even those that weren't physical, but emotional, because those were hurts far worse than physical ones.

She was infinitely fragile. So very vulnerable. He watched her. He watched her a damn lot, and when she didn't realize others were observing her, she lost the icy façade and he got a glimpse of the frightened young girl behind the ballsy exterior.

She was complex, a puzzle, one he had every intention of figuring out. But how?

His normal method of operation certainly wouldn't work with her. There was no approaching her, taking control, laying down the law according to him and telling her the way it would be. He'd attempted to do precisely that just moments ago and it had been like hitting a brick wall.

She'd remove his balls with a rusty knife if he pushed her that way again and, well, he wouldn't be able to blame her.

She had no reason to trust him whatsoever, but damn if he didn't want to get behind those carefully erected barriers she threw up. It was only with the people closest to her that she let her guard down and he got a taste of the real Kylie.

Soft. Sweet. Fiercely loyal and protective of her loved ones.

He wanted to teach her that not all men were bastards. He wanted to show her that dominance did not equal pain or humiliation. That dominance was so much more. Emotional surrender was the most powerful of all, but it also made people so much more vulnerable. And that would absolutely frighten her as much as the more physical aspects of dominance and submission.

This was a woman he'd have to tread very lightly with. His old approach would have to be thrown out the window and he'd have to come up with something new. She was, as he'd said, a challenge. One that he had every intention of overcoming. The *how* hadn't occurred to him. Yet. But he wasn't a quitter. He'd been absolutely serious when he'd told her that he went after what he wanted and he didn't fail. Ever.

There was a first time for everything, or so the saying went. But he'd be damned if his first failure would be Kylie Breckenridge.

TWO

"KYLIE, can you come into my office?" Jensen said over the intercom.

He knew the summons would annoy her, but she'd been clear about wanting him to stay out of her office—her space— and so he'd make her come to him. Not an unreasonable request from a boss to his personal assistant.

"Right away, sir," she said in a crisp tone that made him smile.

She was so determined to keep their relationship, if you could even say they had a relationship, strictly impersonal and confined to boss and employee.

He knew she hated that Dash was out of the office for an extended period of time because Dash usually acted as a buffer between Jensen and Kylie. Most of the requests came from Dash, even ones that involved Jensen, because Dash sought to protect her.

But enough was enough. If they were to work together long-term, and he had every intention of doing just that, Kylie had to learn to deal with Jensen. And he planned to push her. She was extremely intelligent. She had an MBA and, in his opinion, that degree was wasted in her current position. It was one she was comfortable in, and he knew she liked it that way.

She liked nothing that pushed her out of her comfort zone. She liked routine—a trait they shared, though it would annoy her that the two of them had anything in common.

But in fact, they had far more in common than Kylie knew or would admit to. They were both disciplined people who liked control. He was fully prepared to be involved in a battle of wills, a battle he intended to win. He just hoped he didn't push her to the point of her walking away from her job.

A moment later, Kylie appeared at the door, her features locked and impassive as she stared coolly at him.

"You wanted something, sir?"

"You can drop the *sir*," he said dryly. "You don't call Dash sir. My name is sufficient. Call me Jensen or call me nothing at all."

Her lips thinned and he sighed.

"Is everything going to be a battle with you, Kylie? It was a simple enough request. Say it. Say my name," he challenged. "It won't kill you."

"You wanted something . . . Jensen?"

His name came out strangled-sounding, as if she'd had to force it from her lips. It was a start.

He motioned her to the seat in front of his desk. Reluctantly she walked over and then perched on the edge of the chair, her hands folded primly in front of her, but she had the look of an animal prepared to bolt at the first sign of danger. He doubted she knew that she telegraphed her fear so broadly. Her eyes were wide, her nostrils flaring, and he could see the pulse beating a rapid staccato at her neck.

"I'm not going to leap across the desk and attack you," he murmured.

Her eyes narrowed in annoyance. "I'd kick your ass if you tried."

He threw back his head and laughed, and her eyes widened in surprise. She looked . . . shocked.

He sobered and glanced curiously at her. "What was that look for?"

She immediately dropped her gaze and remained silent.

"Kylie?" he prompted.

She sighed and then lifted her head, her stare rebellious, her chin thrust upward.

"It's just that I've never seen you laugh. Or smile, really. In my office earlier was the first time I've seen you look anything but mildly interested. You don't show your emotions much. No one can ever tell what you're thinking."

His eyebrow quirked upward. So she had been studying him. She knew enough about him for him to realize she'd spent a lot of time observing him and his reactions.

His features relaxed into a smile, as he noted again her surprise.

"I've been accused of being an emotionless, uptight bastard by more than one person," he said in amusement. "Perhaps you draw out another side to me that no one else sees."

She looked disgruntled by that suggestion.

"You wanted something?" she prompted, obviously anxious for the meeting to be over.

He had no such plans for her to scurry back to the safety of her office where she shut the rest of the world out. He knew she went straight home every day. Didn't have a social life unless you counted her lunches with Chessy and Joss, her two best friends. In fact, their circle of friends were the only people Kylie had any sort of a connection to.

It had to be a lonely life and he hated that for her. Hated that her past had shaped her future—was still shaping her future—

and that she didn't seem to be able to shake off the bonds of her childhood.

He shuffled the stack of papers in front of him.

"I want you to study up on these profiles. As I said in your office, S&G Oil is downsizing one of their refineries. They need to cut one hundred million in expenses so they're looking for ways to combine jobs. They want to eliminate at least thirty positions and cut nonessential expenses, and they want us to find those for them."

She was clearly flabbergasted by his request.

"But Jensen, I know nothing about this sort of thing. I'm an administrative assistant."

He smiled again, watching her reaction to his expression. She wasn't indifferent to him and that likely pissed her off all the more.

"I want you to learn," he said gently. "When Carson was alive, he and Dash were looking to take on a third partner. They certainly had the business. After Carson died it was too much for Dash to handle, and he had to work his ass off to keep the business solvent until he brought me in. There is still a need for a third partner and you have the credentials. All you lack is experience."

Her mouth dropped open and she was speechless. He felt smug over causing that anomaly. The woman was never short on retorts.

"You want me to be a partner?" she squeaked.

"I can't promise that," he said smoothly. "Consider this your trial by fire. It won't happen today or tomorrow or even over the next few months, but there's no reason to seek out another partner when we have a perfectly capable person working with us already. You know everything that goes on in this office, Kylie.

Every single piece of information is passed through you. You know all our clients. You schedule our meetings. You absolutely know the ins and outs of this business. There is no reason you shouldn't have the opportunity to be promoted."

She glanced down at the papers he'd shoved across his desk to her. The information she'd collected and organized for him and Dash. She was certainly acquainted with the process.

He could swear excitement flared in her eyes, but it was gone almost before it fully registered.

"What do you want me to do?" she asked huskily.

"We have a meeting with the CFO of S&G in three days' time. I want you to accompany me. You have three days to familiarize yourself with their business. The positions, salaries and duties of each employee listed. Their overhead and every single penny they have in expenses. I want you to draw up your own plan and present it to me in two days. I want your ideas and then we'll discuss before you and I meet with the CFO."

She gaped incredulously at him. "You'd trust this big of a contract with me?"

"I didn't say that I'd agree with your ideas," he said mildly. "Merely that I want to see them. We'll put our heads together and see what we agree—and disagree—on, and then we'll put together a plan that incorporates both our ideas before we attend that meeting."

"I didn't expect this," she murmured.

But he could see the spark in her eyes. She loved a challenge every bit as much as he did. He hadn't been wrong. She was wasted in her position as an administrative assistant. It was too safe. She could do that job in her sleep. She needed this. Something to get her blood pumping and remind her that she was alive.

"I have faith in you, Kylie. Can you say the same about yourself?"

This time fire shone in her eyes and he held back the grin of triumph. Oh yes, she loved a good challenge, and perhaps she hadn't been challenged in such a way ever. Dash had been far too easy on her. Not that he expected Dash to be a flaming ass-hole, but he'd wrapped Kylie in cotton after Carson's death, and from all Dash had said, Carson had wrapped her in that same cotton when he was alive. Neither man wanting to do anything to hurt this fragile woman.

But her fragility disguised the intelligent, fiery woman underneath that shell and Jensen intended to draw her out. Dash would likely kick his ass if he knew what Jensen was doing, but for the next two weeks, Jensen was in control and Dash would be completely oblivious to anything business related—as he should be. And Jensen intended to make the most of those two weeks.

"I can do it," she said, resolve tight in her voice. "When do you want to meet to go over my proposal?"

"Wednesday night. Dinner at Capitol Grill. I know you and the girls like the Lux Café, but I want something quieter and more intimate if we're to discuss something confidential. I can arrange for a table in a quiet corner where we won't be over-heard."

Kylie's brow furrowed into a frown and he could literally see the wheels spinning in her head.

"What would be more private than here in the office?" she asked. "Certainly dinner isn't necessary."

"No," he agreed. "But it's what I want."

She had nothing to say to that, though he could see she had no liking for the idea of them having dinner together.

"I'll make a reservation for seven," he continued, as if he were oblivious to her discomfort. "I'll read your proposal beforehand and we'll discuss it over dinner. I'll prepare the final analysis before our meeting with the CFO. I'll pick you up at your house at eight Thursday morning and we'll ride together to meet with S&G's CFO in his office."

He could tell she was caught in an epic battle with herself. She did not want to have dinner with him or even meet him outside of work, nor did she want to ride with him to their meeting, but neither did she want to pass up the opportunity he'd presented her with.

She bit her lip in consternation, and he'd never wanted something so badly as to reach across the desk, thumb her lip free and then kiss away the damage she was doing to the tender flesh. His dick reacted to that image, and he was glad he was seated behind his desk where she couldn't see his physical reaction to her. She'd tuck tail and run for the hills, and she'd very likely tender her resignation within the hour.

He sighed, silently commanding his dick to behave. Not that it did a bit of good because the woman just did it for him and he couldn't even explain why. Challenge. She was a challenge. That had to be it. Because he simply couldn't resist a challenge. Even as he reasoned away his inexplicable attraction to a woman who in no way returned it, he knew he was a goddamn liar.

She riled every single one of his protective instincts. She made him want to treat her gently, cherish her and protect her from anything that could ever hurt her, physically or emotionally.

Damn it, he wanted to show her that not all men were assholes. That not all dominant men were focused so solidly on the more physical aspects of dominance. Emotional surrender was what he was after with Kylie. He'd never mark her, never tie her

up. Never take a flogger to her tender flesh. He'd never do anything to frighten her or make her feel as vulnerable as she'd felt
in the past in the hands of a monster. He'd never do anything to
remind her of her past abuse. He'd die before allowing that to
happen. He too had demons he fought, and it would have made
him physically ill to ever do anything to a woman that could be
construed as abuse.

He just wanted . . . her.

"All right," she finally said in a husky voice that made him
go even harder. Because there was capitulation in her voice. Not
quite submission, but it was close and it fired his blood, made it
sing through his veins, because just this once, he'd won.

"I'll meet you at the restaurant at seven," she said.

She lifted her gaze challengingly to his, as if to dare him to
argue with her statement. He merely smiled back. He'd allow
her this small victory because the bigger one was already his.
Dinner. Just the two of them. Yeah, they'd talk business, but he
also planned to delve deeper into this intriguing woman. Figure
out what made her tick. And he'd pick her up the next day and
drive her to their meeting. Which meant she was dependent on
him the entire day.

He liked that idea. Liked it too damn much. Her dependent
on him. The hell he'd ever let her down or make her regret her
grudging trust. Oh, he knew she didn't trust him yet. That
would be the biggest hurdle to overcome. Baby steps. Take it one
small victory at a time.

"Seven it is," he agreed.

She was surprised. It showed on her face. She had already
been bracing herself for an argument, her shoulders squared
and chin thrust upward in defiance. Even that aroused him,
almost violently.

He might like submissive women, but submissive didn't mean being a doormat. He loved an independent woman perfectly capable of making her own choices. Submissive women, or at least the ones he'd been with, *chose* to submit. *Chose* to offer their surrender into his keeping. And that was a very powerful thing indeed.

He wanted a strong woman. Someone who didn't *need* him and what he offered but *wanted* it. That made all the difference to him. He wanted someone who could stand up for herself and not back down. Who would go toe-to-toe with him and meet him halfway.

In return? He'd lay the world at her feet. She'd never want for anything he could give her. He'd pamper her, utterly adore her, worship her and cherish her.

He ached to do that for Kylie. Had ached for that since the very first time he'd met her when they'd had dinner at Dash's that night. He'd seen the shadows under her eyes, had seen the torment she hid from the world. And he wanted nothing more than to be a balm to the agony she'd endured and still endured to this day.

But it would require infinite patience on his part. Patience had never been high on his list of good qualities, but for the right woman? He could exert the patience of Job.

She gathered the papers, already scanning the contents. He could see her mind working furiously, taking it all in. He knew well she was an extremely intelligent woman with an eye for business. Just as he knew she was wasted in her current job. Even if things never worked out for them the way he intended, she'd still make a valuable asset as a partner one day. If he didn't frighten her away first.

"If that's all," she said absently, still absorbed in the paperwork, "I'll get back to my office and start going over this. I'll have my ideas ready by our dinner Wednesday night."

He smiled again, taking in her adorable features. For just one moment, the shadows that seemed a permanent fixture in her eyes had been removed and a determined fire had replaced them. He could sense her excitement, her anticipation. She wanted to prove herself. She was rising to his challenge beautifully and he couldn't wait to see the results.

He knew she wouldn't let him down. That she was far more intelligent than either Carson or Dash gave her credit for. It wasn't that either man belittled her or didn't believe in her abilities. They were just too emotionally involved and their instincts were to protect her. He understood it, even agreed with them to a certain point.

But they'd done her no favors by sheltering her so vigorously. She needed more of a challenge. Needed an outlet for her analytical mind and intelligence. A trained monkey could do her current job. Answer phones, schedule appointments, ready contracts for signature and run the office.

But he was offering her a hell of a lot more.

Equality.

And when in her life had she ever felt she was an equal to anyone else? She'd lived her life as a victim. With good reason. But it was time to move beyond being that victim and become a survivor. A survivor who rose above her past and kicked the present's ass.

If he could have any part in that at all, whether they entered a relationship or not, he'd be fiercely proud of her.

THREE

SHE couldn't believe she was following through with this lunacy. Kylie rolled to a stop in front of the Capitol Grill and the valet opened her car door to assist her out. After collecting her ticket she headed inside the darkened interior.

The restaurant screamed *rich old farts*, or at least it catered to that crowd. The furnishings were very masculine and portraits of rich old farts even dotted the walls. She glanced down self-consciously, wondering if she was dressed appropriately for this joint. The other women in the waiting area all wore cocktail dresses and plenty of expensive jewelry with elegant, upswept hairdos.

Kylie had worn her hair down. It was either that or a ponytail, and even she wasn't gauche enough to sport a ponytail to a restaurant like this. But she'd worn a simple black sheath with no sparkles or adornments. It fell to her knees with a gentle flare, giving her room to at least walk, unlike some of those skintight hip-hugger jobs that one had to take teeny tiny steps in or face-plant.

And her shoes were flats, though they did have some sparkle to them. Sparkly shoes were her one weakness. Anything with a heel? No. She'd embarrass herself trying to walk in them. But blingy sandals or flip-flops? She had a closetful. She wore a different pair every day to work, and her other weakness, thanks to Joss, was wearing her toenails painted. A different color every week, but her favorite was hot pink. There was something mischievous about having hot pink toes and it was as daring as she ever allowed herself to be.

The rest of her wardrobe was a study in trying not to attract attention. Specifically male attention.

Jensen appeared seemingly from nowhere, melting from the shadows to stand right in front of her. She swallowed, her mouth suddenly gone dry, because while his dress code at work was business casual, usually meaning a button-up shirt—without a tie—and simple slacks, tonight he was dressed in a black suit that screamed wealth and privilege, and the darkness of his clothing only enhanced what she already knew to be true. That this was a man not to be trifled with. He was someone who could crush her like a bug without any effort whatsoever.

But then he smiled, transforming the harsh lines, the almost cruel beauty of his face, so that he became someone more approachable. Someone who wouldn't eat her alive. Maybe.

She was a fool for even thinking that. For relaxing her guard even for that rare smile from him. She needed to remember that he was a natural-born predator. Strong. Implacable. And so easily capable of hurting her.

"Glad you made it," he said easily, cupping her elbow as he steered her farther into the darkened interior.

They walked by larger tables, filled with various business types and others dressed more formally. Couples having intimate dinners, waiters hovering with expensive wine to refill glasses. This was Carson's world—a world he'd created for himself. But it had never been hers, even if Carson had been determined to share it with her.

He'd been determined to rise above his circumstances and go in the opposite direction from their childhood. And Kylie? She seemed to be in a holding pattern, one she recognized even in her denial.

She'd never stepped fully into the present or even tried to embrace it. She was still too firmly rooted in the nightmare of her past, paralyzed and unable to move past it.

That Jensen had nailed her so precisely on it in her office two days ago only made her more uncomfortable with his scrutiny and those eyes that saw far too much.

Jensen courteously seated her, pushing her chair forward once she'd settled into it, and then walked around to the chair directly across from her. At least he hadn't taken the seat catty-corner to her. But now she'd be required to actually look him in the eye and meet that intense gaze.

She glanced hastily around, noticing, to her discomfort, how intimate they appeared. A cozy corner in a dimly lit restaurant, no other people occupying the tables nearest to them. It was, as he'd promised, a spot where they wouldn't be overheard. Had he arranged it so no one else would be seated near them or had he simply gotten lucky?

But no, he wasn't a lucky sort of man. He wasn't someone who'd leave anything to chance. He'd arranged this as he did everything else in his life. To his liking and his specifications. A delicate shiver snaked down her spine at the raw power emanating from him. It—and he—scared the holy hell out of her.

Yes, this was supposed to be a business dinner, and by resolving that in her mind, she'd been able to make herself go through with it. But now, sitting here across from him in a decidedly intimate setting, she knew damn well this could have been done just as easily in the office.

She hated that he made her so nervous. Hated admitting that weakness to herself. She'd spent her entire life being weak, though she disguised it by being abrasive and even bitchy. She wasn't proud of those things, but it was far preferable to ever showing vulnerability to another person.

"Relax, Kylie," Jensen said, drawing her gaze to his.

She saw warmth in his eyes and pondered that oddity. It wasn't that Jensen was some heartless, cold bastard. But he'd perfected the look. Anyone would think twice about crossing him. Usually his eyes were impenetrable, showing nothing of whatever emotion he was feeling, if he even had them.

But now? There was an odd tenderness in his eyes and it seemed to be directed at her. It was one beat off of sympathy and that got her back up because the very last thing she wanted from this man was pity.

"Did you just scowl at me?" he asked, his lips twisting in amusement.

"No. Yes. Maybe," she muttered.

"Relax," he said again, his tone growing as gentle as his eyes had been just moments ago. "I'm not going to bite you. Unless you ask me to. Nicely," he added with a grin.

Her scowl deepened before she realized he was merely yanking her chain. Something he did with more frequency ever since coming to work with Dash.

"Maybe I'll do the biting," she said with a sardonic smile, not even realizing the sexual connotation until it was too late. She'd envisioned snapping at him like a ferocious dog. Not biting him . . . *sexually.*

But it was obvious that was the way he took it because his eyes suddenly smoldered with a fire that made her shiver again. Yes, this man was dangerous. Far too dangerous for her to bait.

It was better to ignore him. And only speak about work. The reason they were here in this damn restaurant to begin with.

Thankfully he didn't respond to her ill-thought-out remark. But that look . . . It was still there in his eyes, his gaze positively glowing, almost as if he were imagining her biting him and taking much pleasure in the act.

Gah, she had to stop this train of thought and push the conversation to the topic at hand.

"So you've read my analysis," she said in a crisp, business-like tone. "What do you think?"

He paused a moment and then evidently decided to let her have her way. Again, something she was certain was rare for him. He appeared to her to be a control freak. Was she surrounded by them? Tate, her best friend's husband, she knew to be in absolute control. Chessy had relinquished it willingly in their relationship. But Dash . . . She still shook her head over that one. Only recently had it come to light—at least to her—that he was every bit as dominant as Tate, and more shocking was that it was what Joss had wanted.

Her head-in-the-sand approach to life likely made her unaware of a lot, and she was happy that way. Wasn't she?

So much was changing around her, in her very small circle of friends. Dash and Joss married. Happy. Jensen coming on board, replacing Carson. And only Kylie was the same. Predictable, dull, scared-of-her-shadow Kylie.

She grimaced her disgust and Jensen's eyebrows rose.

"You think I hated it?"

She shook her head. "Sorry. Was thinking of something else."

"Care to share? It must not have been very pleasant."

"Just reflecting on what a coward I am and how I live my life with my head in the sand."

Her frank admission shocked her. She couldn't believe she'd just blurted it out. She never did things like that. It appalled her that she'd just broadcast her weaknesses to a complete stranger. No, maybe he wasn't a complete stranger, but he certainly wasn't someone she'd ever seen herself confiding in. And she couldn't even blame it on alcohol since they weren't drinking wine.

"You're too hard on yourself, Kylie," he said gently.

She shook her head, waving her hand in a dismissive gesture. "Please. Let's just forget I said that. I can't believe I did. We're supposed to be talking business. What *did* you think of my analysis?"

He sent her one of those searching looks, one that told her he could see beyond her prickly exterior to the heart of her. The timid, freaked-out heart of her. And that was never a person she wanted anyone to see. Ever again. Only Carson had ever seen her that way. He and their father.

She had to call back the shudder that even thinking of that monster evoked. It took everything she had to sit there, looking at Jensen expectantly, calm and collected, when her insides were a seething, writhing mess.

"It was very thorough," he said. "And dead-on. I admit, especially when you said you didn't have the heart for this sort of thing, that I thought you wouldn't be objective and wouldn't go right to the heart of the matter when it came to cutting positions."

Her cheeks warmed under the praise. Her hands trembled and she dropped them into her lap so he wouldn't see the effect he had on her. As though she needed or wanted his approval.

She shrugged instead, giving him the impression his words had no effect whatsoever.

"I looked at areas where they could reduce costs, and honestly, there was a lot there that is completely unnecessary. They could reduce employee perks, the things that don't really matter, and not have to reduce benefits, the things that *are* necessary."

He nodded his agreement. "I too saw a lot of unnecessary expenditures, and by focusing on those areas, it will eliminate the need to cut some of the positions, though there are those that could easily be absorbed into other jobs."

She stared thoughtfully at him a moment. "You don't like cutting jobs. I mean, they aren't just nameless, faceless people to you, are they?"

She wasn't at all certain what had given her that flash of insight into his character. It was something in his tone though, and the brief glimmer, almost a grimace, that had registered in his eyes. Perhaps he was more human than she gave him credit for.

"Of course I don't," he murmured. "I'm not an unfeeling asshole, Kylie. Those people have families to support. Children to feed and put through college. They need their jobs, however unnecessary they may be to the company's survival."

She winced at the guilty stab that tightened her chest. She'd as much accused him of being just that directly to his face. He made her antagonistic and at first she hadn't known why. Their first meeting had left her off-balance and it wasn't until later that she'd understood her reaction to him more clearly.

He scared her. Not on a physical level. But on a feminine one. Scared her as a woman. He frightened her. Riled her self-preservation instincts. Ones she was well acquainted with. And she hated that feeling, had sworn no one—no man—would ever make her feel vulnerable and afraid again.

"If I implied you were heartless, I apologize," she said quietly, hoping he could hear and see her sincerity.

She'd lifted her hands from her lap and rested them on the table and Jensen reached for one, surprising her with the speed of his capturing it before she could withdraw. Almost as if he'd anticipated such a reaction.

"I didn't think you implied anything. No offense was given or taken."

She went utterly still as his hand continued to cover hers. He didn't tighten his fingers around her hand. She couldn't really even consider it holding hands, but his hand blanketed hers, warm, heavy. Thankfully, her wrist was not facing up or surely he would be able to feel how rapidly her pulse beat.

Desperate to keep the topic to business, she casually pulled her hand away, reaching for her glass of water as if she only wanted a drink and wasn't breaking free from his grasp. The quick flash of amusement in his expression told her he hadn't been fooled for a moment. Did nothing escape this man's attention?

As if conceding to her thoughts, or perhaps because her desperation *showed*, he leaned back and resumed their conversation.

He studied her intently, his gaze more professional than before. This dynamic was one she was more comfortable with. Boss and employee. Not a man and a woman sharing an intimate dinner. A date for God's sake. She hoped to hell this didn't qualify.

"I've incorporated many of your ideas into my final proposal, as they align with my own. I'll have the completed analysis for you to look over on the drive to the meeting tomorrow."

She'd nearly forgotten that they'd already ordered and this was in fact a dinner when the waiter arrived with their entrées. Silence descended as their plates were set, glasses filled with wine, the bottle left on the table at Jensen's request. Then the waiter silently departed, leaving the two in seclusion once more.

She stared down at the filet and lobster she'd ordered. They looked succulent. Perfectly cooked and yet she was so unnerved by . . . Jensen. It was him. She'd certainly had dealings with other men. It wasn't as if she'd avoided any and all contact with them in her adulthood. But none of them had ever made her feel as starkly vulnerable as Jensen did. And he was absolutely the kind of ruthless man who'd exploit any weakness, take advantage and swoop in like an avenging god.

She mentally rolled her eyes. *God, Kylie. Dramatic much? You're a flaming moron. You flatter yourself to even imagine he has any interest in you whatsoever. He just likes pissing you off and you're an easy target. Eat your damn food and quit pretending this is a date and not the business matter it is before you really freak yourself out.*

After chiding herself, something she seemed to do with more frequency since meeting Jensen, she dove into the delicious-smelling food. The flavor burst over her taste buds and she hummed her pleasure before she could call back the sound.

"Good?" Jensen asked.

She glanced up to see his gaze fastened solidly on her mouth. Following the up and down motion of her jaw as she chewed. His eyes glittered predatorily and for a moment she couldn't swallow.

Finally forcing down the food, chasing it with wine she couldn't even taste, she nodded.

"It's wonderful," she said in a husky voice she didn't recognize.

God, she was acting like they were out on a date. Making cute and feeling awkward over the sudden absence of conversation.

"I'm glad it meets with your approval," he said. "It's one of my favorite places to eat."

She actually did roll her eyes then. "That somehow doesn't surprise me."

He arched one dark eyebrow in question. "Why would you say that?"

She shrugged. "It suits you. Very . . . masculine. Your kind of crowd."

He pinned her with an imperious look. "And what crowd is that?"

"Powerful," she said after giving a moment's contemplation. "Wealthy. When I first walked in I thought, 'This is a place that caters to rich old farts.'"

He laughed, startling her with the rich, vibrant sound that rumbled from his throat. She would have never imagined laughter to be beautiful. Laughter was alien to her anyway. But coming from a man who rarely smiled, it sounded almost magical. She wanted to hear it again. Savor the sound for the brief pleasure it gave her.

"You think me a rich old fart?"

She grinned then, teeth flashing, and she hoped she didn't have any food in those teeth. How embarrassing would that be?

"Definitely not old."

"So a rich fart then. I feel so much better," he said dryly.

"You have to admit, everything about this place caters to wealth and power." She gestured to the walls. "How many restaurants do you know of that hang portraits on their walls of older men who look like judges or politicians or bankers or some other guy who founded some corporation and has loads of money?"

His lips twitched and he took another sip of his wine, licking his upper lip to remove the excess moisture. Her breath hitched and she yanked her gaze away from his mouth.

"I know nothing about the whims of the proprietor, or whom he wants to cater to. All I know is that they serve a damn fine steak and their service is impeccable. I'm easy that way, though."

"You like your creature comforts. Fine food and being waited on hand and foot."

She didn't intend it to be an insult, and she hoped he didn't take it as such. It was merely an observation spoken aloud, though perhaps it shouldn't have been. She didn't want to encourage anything more than a strictly professional relationship with him. She had friends—good friends—and she wasn't looking to broaden that small, intimate group. But she might have no choice since Jensen would surely be included in more of her friends' get-togethers.

He shrugged. "Who doesn't? Life is short. I choose to enjoy life's pleasures, even the little ones."

She sucked in her breath, pain sharp through her chest. He was certainly right about that. Why couldn't *she* be as simple as he? She, more than anyone, knew she should move on, quit living in the past, grab onto the *good* in life. Let go of the bad. The bad was behind her, wasn't it? She'd moved way beyond her past. And yet? She was stuck much like a truck in the mud, buried to the bumpers. Still allowing her past and fears to rule her present.

Weak. She was weak and she was so damn tired of feeling that way. Acting strong didn't make her so. It just made her an abrasive, standoffish bitch, and she wasn't proud of that. Thank God her friends—the people who loved her—accepted her, warts and all. She couldn't even contemplate her life without them. That unconditional love and support.

She'd very nearly botched things royally with Joss. She'd said unforgivable things to her sister-in-law. Things that had hurt Joss and had made Kylie feel an inch tall. But Joss was . . . Well, she was Joss. A sweet and loving heart incapable of holding a grudge or withholding her forgiveness. Kylie wished with all her heart that she could be more like Joss.

"That's a very good philosophy to have," she said, able to admit it even if she wasn't able to practice it. Yet. But she was determined to get there. One day. And *soon*, damn it.

He nodded. And as she suspected he would do, he said, "One you should adhere to."

"We were talking about you, not me," she said lightly, directing the conversation away from her. Always away from her. Anything beyond the superficial pleasantries with her was strictly off-limits. She'd already allowed him to see far more than anyone ever should.

"Would you care for dessert?"

She blinked at the abruptness and his instant acceptance of her diverting attention away from herself. It would seem he had at least some give to him. Who knew?

Then she glanced down at her half-eaten entrée and smiled ruefully. "No. I'd much rather fill up on the rest of my steak and lobster. It's delicious and there'll be no room for anything more. Besides, we should be going soon. Early morning for us both tomorrow."

She forced the same lightness into her tone so it wouldn't seem as though she was in a hurry, dismissing him. But again, that gleam in his eyes told her he saw far more than she was comfortable with. She was beginning to think he was a damn mind reader with extrasensory perception.

"Finish then, but take your time. Tomorrow morning is no

earlier than any other business day for us. I know well what time you're in the office every morning and it's certainly not eight."

Of course he would know. She punched no time clock. She was salaried and Dash had always been absolutely flexible with her hours, though she never took advantage of that. It had been easy to lose herself in work after Carson died. It kept her occupied, an outlet. At work she could blank out her grief and desolation. At home, she didn't have any distractions. And at home, she was alone. Achingly alone. So she was always in the office between six thirty and seven each morning. Normally before Dash ever came in.

But with Jensen's arrival, to her annoyance, he often beat her in and was in his office when she entered her own.

She was nearly finished with the succulent feast before her when she glanced up and saw a man walking from the far right of the restaurant toward a table in the back. Not very far from where she and Jensen sat.

She froze, the food she'd consumed now sitting like lead in her stomach. Bile rose and her hand shook so badly that she dropped the fork, the noisy clang startling in the silence.

She knew her face had drained of blood. She was utterly paralyzed and she couldn't breathe. Couldn't force much-needed air into her lungs. Her chest constricted tighter and tighter and her throat followed suit until she was well into a full-blown anxiety attack.

Perspiration beaded her forehead and upper lip. The desire to flee, to run as fast as she was able and to get as far away from this place as possible seized her. But she couldn't make her legs obey. Couldn't even manage the simple act of breathing, much less acting on her desire to get away.

And then Jensen was right in her face, kneeling on the floor next to her chair. His hand jerked her chin so she was forced to look at him and away from the man who was now seated, alone, several tables away from theirs.

"What's wrong?" he demanded sharply. "Damn it, Kylie, breathe. You're going to pass out if you don't start breathing now."

She tried to obey the forceful command even though it humiliated her beyond measure that he was witnessing her falling completely apart. But her lungs were frozen, her chest so constricted she hadn't a hope of breathing.

An anxious-looking waiter immediately appeared, offering his assistance, asking if she needed help. Jensen turned on him, his face a black thundercloud.

"Leave us," he barked. "She'll be fine."

Would she? She didn't feel fine. She didn't feel as though she'd ever be fine. A wave of despair hit her and the room swayed around her. She knew she was precariously close to blacking out.

"I have to go," she croaked out. "Now. I have to leave. Now," she said again, with more emphasis.

The words were hard to form around her starving lungs, the knot in her throat making her voice hoarse and raspy.

Jensen did a quick scan of the room, following the direction of where she'd been staring when she'd freaked out. Shame rolled over her, wave after humiliating wave.

"Who is he?" Jensen asked in a menacing tone. "What the hell did he do to you?"

The barely controlled violence in his voice made her shudder. Black spots danced in front of her eyes and she tried again to pull in a breath, anything to ease the horrible pain in her chest.

"No one," she croaked. "He just looked like . . ." She trailed off helplessly and to her further horror, tears slipped down her cheeks. "He reminded me of someone. Please, can we just leave?"

"The hell I'm letting you drive home in your condition."

He got up, tossed several bills onto the table, then pulled her to her feet, instantly propelling her toward the entrance, not stopping until they were outside, fresh air blowing over her like the most soothing balm.

Some of the tightness eased. Her horrific fear began to subside, leaving stark embarrassment in its wake.

"Breathe," Jensen ordered even as he barked an order to the valet to get his car.

She sucked in breath after breath, gulping at the air greedily until finally the tightness eased and the spots receded. The world had stopped its sickening swaying, but as she tried to step away from Jensen and his hold on her, her knees buckled, and with a muttered curse, he hauled her right back up against his side, his arm anchoring her there so she couldn't move.

His warmth bled into her icy cold skin. Permeated the arctic layer surrounding her.

"My c-car," she stammered. "I can't leave my car here."

"Fuck your car," he said rudely. "You aren't driving anywhere tonight. I'm taking you home. We'll get your car tomorrow after the meeting."

FOUR

THE drive to Kylie's house was strained and silent. Jensen cursed a blue streak every time he glanced sideways to her pale face and tortured eyes. She sat rigid in her seat, hands clenched together in a ball in her lap. Her gaze was directed forward, like she was in some trance, not even taking in his presence.

She'd scared the fuck out of him in the restaurant. And then his fear had quickly turned to rage when he realized that the man seated several tables away had scared the holy hell out of her. He'd wanted to go beat the man into a pulp, but then she'd said he only *reminded* her of someone. Since the man was older, he could well imagine just who he'd reminded her of and he swore all over again.

His instinct was to take her home. *His* home. Where he knew he could protect her from anything that could possibly hurt her. But she wouldn't take that at all. She'd likely dissolve into another panic attack, and the one had already put a vicious strain on her.

So he'd take her home. To her home. But damn if he was leaving her in this state. She wouldn't want him there, but too fucking bad. No way he was leaving her to endure her private hell alone.

Kylie needed someone, though she'd never admit that. She saw it as a weakness, and she was a woman who'd die before allowing others to see her perceived weaknesses. Damn it, didn't she realize that everyone needed someone at some point in their lives?

And he wanted to be that person she needed even though he knew he was all wrong for her. He wasn't the man she wanted, that much was obvious. But she did need him. He knew it as well as he knew anything else. Unwavering certainty.

He just had to crack those walls and peel back the layers to the vulnerable, fragile woman behind that iron façade.

It wouldn't be easy. He wasn't stupid enough to ever assume that. But nothing good or worth it was ever easy. And he knew in his gut that no matter how crazy it might make him, she was worth it.

He had to tread lightly though, and consider doing something he'd never been willing to do before. Especially for a woman. Let go of his tightly held control and hand over that control—or at least the semblance of control—to her.

It was a new experience for him. One he wasn't altogether sure was to his liking. It would be hard for a man like him, used to being in control over every aspect of his life. But Kylie needed security. She needed . . . confidence. She needed to be able to trust him, and if he was going to gain that trust, he was going to have to do the bending for them. Because she wouldn't. She'd refuse to bend until she finally broke. And she was nearing that point with every passing day and every sleepless night. Because if she was sleeping then he was a monkey's uncle.

He'd be willing to bet everything he owned that her past intruded on her dreams on a nightly basis. He'd seen the evidence far too many times. The bruised shadows in her eyes and under them. Her paleness. The fatigue that beat relentlessly at her, that he could sense with her every breath.

Tonight she'd sleep and she'd sleep knowing she was safe. Because he wasn't leaving her in this state. No way in hell.

And so he readied himself for the ensuing confrontation, knowing she'd object to his presence in her home. Her space. Perhaps the only place she truly felt safe. But no, that wasn't true either, because in sleep, even in her closely guarded sanctuary, her dreams tortured her.

Not tonight. Not if he had any damn thing to do with it.

When they pulled into her drive, he got out before she could say anything at all and walked around to open her door, not waiting for her to accept his outstretched hand. He simply reached in, gently took hold of those icy cold fingers and pulled her from the car.

Her gait was unsteady and so, as he'd done outside the restaurant, he pulled her into the safety of his side, tucking her underneath his shoulder as he walked her to her door.

He knew she expected to brush him off once they reached the door. Issue a stiff, polite good-night and perhaps even a stilted thank-you for his help. But then she'd retreat inside and back to her private hell, shutting the door, barring him from her domain.

Fuck that.

He plucked the keys from her hand and unlocked the door, ushering her forward, making sure he was with her the entire way, and only then did he close the door and lock it.

"Jensen," she protested. "I'm fine. Thank you, but I'm okay now. It was stupid. And embarrassing. But I'd rather be alone right now. I'll see you in the morning."

"You'll see me right now," he said grimly.

Even as he spoke, he directed her toward what he guessed was her bedroom. Her house, as he'd suspected, was the picture of tranquility. Her haven. Not a single thing out of place. A study in calm and peace.

She resisted when they reached her bedroom, turning, a fierce, stubborn glint to her eyes.

"You can go now, Jensen." No trace of her earlier panic attack was evident in her eyes.

But it was the tight lines around her lips. The strain in her forehead and the paleness of her face that told him otherwise.

She wasn't okay and he wasn't leaving.

"Get dressed for bed while I fix us both a drink. Is your bar stocked? I think something strong is called for."

She paled and then shook her head. "Only wine, and I rarely indulge. Usually only when I go out with Chessy and Joss or if I'm over at one of their houses."

"Then wine it is. You need something to relax you. You have five minutes to change if you don't want me walking in while you're getting undressed."

After that directive, he strode out of her bedroom, closing the door so she would be assured complete privacy. He purposely took longer than five minutes because he knew she likely spent the first several minutes arguing with herself and forming all sorts of ways to tell him to go fuck himself.

He shrugged. He'd had far worse said to him. And he had already discovered her bark was far more ferocious than her bite. Underneath the tough exterior lay a soft heart and an even softer soul.

He poured them both a glass, though he had no desire for the drink. His thoughts were too consumed with Kylie and the episode he'd witnessed at the restaurant. Whether she wanted to or not, she was going to explain to him exactly what the hell had spurred that panic attack. He had a good idea, but he wanted to hear it from her. Wanted her to trust him enough to open up and perhaps talk about things she never spoke of to anyone else.

It was an unrealistic expectation, but it didn't prevent him from wanting it.

When he shouldered his way back into her bedroom, she was sitting on the edge of the bed, pale, shaken, dressed in very modest pajamas, long sleeved, covering every inch of her delectable flesh.

It was in the unguarded moment when she hadn't yet registered his presence that he saw beyond the façade she presented to the rest of the world.

She looked infinitely fragile and so very vulnerable. She looked . . . *lonely*. Sadness clung to her like a fog, surrounding her with such heaviness it made his heart ache. Then she glanced up, eyes startled as she realized she was no longer alone.

And just as quickly, the barriers were back up, her face becoming impenetrable. But he'd already seen beyond it. Knew what was underneath.

"This really isn't necessary," she protested when he shoved the glass of wine into her hands. "I'm okay, Jensen. It was very kind of you to bring me home, but I feel foolish. It was stupid of me and now I'm just embarrassed."

Jensen ignored her protests and settled onto the bed next to her, their thighs nearly touching.

"Who did he remind you of, Kylie?" he asked gently.

She went pale and immediately averted her gaze. She took a long swallow of the wine, gulping at it almost as if she needed the liquid courage it would bring to even dwell on the earlier episode.

"My father," she blurted.

She immediately squeezed her eyes shut, regret etched in her forehead. She shook her head in bewilderment, obviously asking herself why she'd confided that much.

"Is he still alive?" Jensen asked.

She nodded.

"And does he live here? Do you ever see him?" he prodded.

"I don't know," she whispered. "And no, I don't see him. Ever. I have no desire to. I wish he were dead. I wish it had been him and not Carson. It's not *fair*."

Tears thickened her voice and slid down her cheeks. She seemed embarrassed by them but he didn't move, didn't react. He didn't want to draw any more attention to the emotion she tried to hide from him. He wanted her to continue. To speak of the demons that haunted her. He wanted to understand every aspect of her pain and fear so he would know how to help her.

"Why did Carson have to die?" she said on a sob. "He was so good. Never did anything to hurt anyone. He loved and adored Joss. He loved and protected me. He's the only one who ever protected me. And yet he died and our father lives. It's unfair," she said again, anger seeping through the grief.

Jensen gently took her hand, curling it into his much larger one, stroking her knuckles with his thumb.

"Life isn't fair, baby. And you're right. It isn't fair that the son of a bitch that fathered you is alive and well and Carson was killed. But little in life makes sense. We have to deal with the cards we're dealt."

"I hate that I can't move on," she whispered. "I hate it, Jensen. I hate being so weak. Do you understand that? I *hate* it!"

He squeezed her hand, offering his reassurance, when what

he wanted most was to take her in his arms and simply hold her. Nothing else. Just hold her.

"You aren't weak," he denied. "I don't pretend to know everything you've gone through, but I know enough to recognize you are a survivor. You didn't allow yourself to be beaten down. You're stronger than you give yourself credit for."

She leaned into him, and whether it was conscious or not, he wasn't complaining either way. Taking a chance, he let go of her hand and wrapped his arm around her, pulling her more firmly into his embrace. She rested her head on his shoulder and he could feel the exhaustion tugging at her. The need to simply rest without fear or memories of the past intruding.

How long had it been since she'd truly slept? One night where her mind was blank and she gave in to complete and utter rest.

"At times I don't think I survived at all," she said in a voice so low he had to strain to hear. "And I wonder if he didn't win after all. I used to think I'd beaten him. That what he did didn't damage me, but that's not true, is it? He *did* win because even now, when he isn't any part of my life, my present, he's still there, just as if he was standing in front of me. And no matter what I do, I can't get rid of him or the memory of all he did."

He kissed the top of her silky hair, unable to prevent himself that small indulgence. She stiffened and he cursed under his breath. Because whatever slip she'd made, a small moment where she'd been able to surrender to the need to turn to someone, it was now gone and she was very aware of the fact that he was in her bedroom and she was in his arms, his lips pressed to her head.

She pulled away, unable to meet his gaze, but he could see

the shame and embarrassment in her eyes and it gutted him. Because he didn't want her to feel that way with him. He wanted her to feel comfortable enough with him to let those barriers down and let him into the heart of her.

"You should go now," she said in a quiet, tight tone. "I've taken up far too much of your time already."

"I'm not leaving you tonight," he said bluntly.

Her head whirled around and shocked, wide eyes met his gaze. Surprise was evident, yes, but what slayed him was the abject terror in those huge eyes. He could see another panic attack was imminent and that was the last thing he wanted.

"You c-can't s-stay here," she stammered out.

"Yes, I can," he said calmly. "And I am."

She shook her head, panic spreading over her face.

He put his hand on her shoulder, feeling the violent trembling she tried so hard to control.

"I'm not leaving you, baby," he said in a tender voice. "I get that you're freaked out and afraid. But I swear to you that you have nothing to fear from me."

Her mouth dropped open and she swallowed as if she couldn't even come up with a response.

"I don't need you to stay," she protested.

He put a finger to her lips and simply shook his head. "You don't *want* me to stay," he amended. "But yes, you do *need* me to stay. And that's the difference."

"You don't understand," she said desperately.

"Shh, baby. I understand far more than you realize. Don't you think I know how frightened you are of me? How much that guts me and how much I wish it were different? The very last thing I want is for you to fear me, and no matter what it takes, Kylie, I'm going to prove to you that you are absolutely safe with me. Safer than you'll ever be with anyone else. I will never hurt you. Never."

Tears gathered in her eyes. "I don't *want* to be afraid of you."

His entire heart softened at her admission. No, she didn't want to fear him, but fear was irrational. It defied explanation, and the simple fact was that it wasn't personal to him. She'd fear any man being this close to her. In her bedroom, sleeping in her bed. But before the night was over with, she'd know that there was nothing he wouldn't do in order to ensure she no longer feared him.

"I'm sleeping here tonight. With you. In this bed," he said in a calm voice as if they were discussing the mundane.

Terror blistered through her eyes and her breath quickened. Her pulse stuttered and panic slammed into her. He could see her struggling for breath, her nostrils flaring with the effort.

"Listen to me, Kylie. I understand you far better than you think. You value control in all things, because you once had that control taken from you. I'm going to give that back to you. Tonight. I'm going to sleep here, with you, so that you know you're safe. I want you to rest. One night without dreams, or at the very least someone to comfort you when the dreams torture you. And so you are in absolute control and so you know you have nothing to fear, you're going to tie my hands to your bedpost so that I am, in effect, helpless."

FIVE

KYLIE stared at Jensen in complete astonishment. "That's crazy!"

It was more than crazy. It was absolute insanity. Tie him to the bed? Despite the fact that this was a man she'd never imagine putting himself in a vulnerable position with anyone, particularly a woman, the idea of tying *anyone* to her bed was just nuts!

"Would it make you feel safer?" he asked mildly, as if he hadn't just proposed such lunacy. "Think about it, Kylie. You would have complete control. Nothing to fear. I would, in effect, be utterly helpless. But I will not leave you alone tonight. So your only two options are to trust me enough to share your bed with me or tie my hands to the headboard."

Her head spun. Her thoughts were a jumble of chaotic mess. The sheer selflessness that such an act involved was overwhelming.

Without waiting for her response, he abruptly got up and left her room. Maybe he had decided that he'd experienced a brief break from reality and was now getting the hell out. She didn't know if she was relieved or disappointed.

No matter how much she protested the idea or how much

her instincts screamed that this man was dangerous to her, the thought of being alone tonight, like so many other nights, was more than she could bear.

She'd just about decided he *had* run for cover when he returned, striding through her door as though he belonged there, a pair of handcuffs in his hand.

Handcuffs.

Her eyes bugged out as she stared openmouthed at him.

"Who the hell carries handcuffs around with them unless they're a cop?" she demanded.

The corner of his mouth quirked upward. "Never know when one might need them."

Her eyes narrowed. "Are you into kink? That dominant stuff Dash and Tate are involved in? Are you like them?"

His gaze was level and he seemed unruffled by her suspicion.

"I can assure you I am not like them. I'm me. Jensen. I don't need or have any desire to model my desires after another or to emulate others. What Dash and Tate do is their own business, between them and their partners. Just as what I do, what I need and desire, is my own."

"You want me to use those. On you," she said in a voice barely above a whisper.

He sat down beside her, his fingertips grazing the skin from her shoulder to her elbow. Even through the material of her pajamas the heat from his touch scalded her.

"What I want is for you to feel safe," he corrected. "And if this enables you to feel safe. With me. Then yes, that is exactly what I want you to do. Handcuff me to your bed."

Did it make her a raving lunatic to give consideration to his bizarre proposition? But she didn't want him to leave. She didn't want to be alone. She'd been alone for so very long. Just one night she wanted what he promised. Peace. A respite from fear and the agony of her dreams. A source of comfort, one he was selflessly offering her. Would she be a fool to refuse him?

"Perhaps just one hand," she murmured. "I wouldn't want you to be too uncomfortable."

His eyes gleamed, the only outward sign of his triumph. He remained still and silent, almost as if he were waiting for her to change her mind and back out. She wasn't a coward and she was trying damn hard to stop being so weak. It was one night. And he'd be handcuffed to her bed. Even so, she didn't believe for a single minute that he'd ever harm her. Her heart knew that, but her mind was firmly entrenched in self-preservation. Her mind was screaming at her to make him leave. Her heart and mind were at constant odds when it came to this man. An unusual occurrence since they normally were in perfect alignment. Trust no one. It had long been her mantra. Only now, her heart was sending different signals than her brain and the battle was exhausting.

"Do you have anything to wear?" she asked awkwardly.

"I can sleep in my clothes."

Her brows furrowed. "But what about tomorrow? The meeting, I mean. I know how important it is. I don't want to screw it up for you, Jensen."

"I'll get up early enough to go home and shower and change and then I'll come back by to pick you up," he said easily.

"Uhm . . . okay," she finally conceded and then closed her eyes, wondering what had possessed her. Maybe she was finally losing what little of her sanity she'd retained.

He kicked off his shoes and then unbuttoned the neck of his shirt and slipped his belt off, tossing everything to the side. Then he motioned for her to slip underneath the covers. He moved to the other side, careful to keep distance between them even as he slid underneath the covers with her. Then, facing her, he lifted his left arm and extended the cuffs to her with his right hand, motioning for her to secure his wrist to the headboard.

Dear God, had it really come to this? That she couldn't have a man in bed with her without handcuffing him so he was no threat? She wished she was brave enough to tell him it wasn't necessary. The rational part of herself told her it was exactly what she should do. And not return his generosity and his care of her with mistrust. But the irrational part that controlled so much of her thoughts and actions told her she'd be a fool *not* to ensure her safety.

Carefully she cuffed his wrist to one of the slats of the headboard and then leaned back, biting into her bottom lip.

"It doesn't look comfortable," she said in consternation.

"I'll survive," he said dryly. "I've slept in far worse conditions."

"I'm sorry," she said softly.

He glanced curiously at her, reaching out to touch her chin with his free hand. "What are you sorry for, baby?"

She closed her eyes. "That I'm not brave enough to let you sleep here without the handcuffs. That I'm too much of a coward to refuse your unselfish gesture. I'm the selfish one, Jensen. I'm sorry I'm not as strong as you."

His expression gentled as he cupped her chin, brushing the pad of his thumb over her jaw.

"It's a start that you're even allowing me in your bed, with or without handcuffs. I'll take that gift, no matter how it's given."

She flushed at the promise in his voice. The promise that he'd be there again, that there would be another occasion and that this wasn't a freak occurrence. No, it wouldn't happen again.

She wouldn't let it. She'd agreed to this lunacy in a moment of weakness. The weakness she loathed so much. Because she didn't want to be alone for just one night.

But she *wouldn't* allow it again.

"Ready for lights-out?" she asked lightly.

He nodded, his gaze still on her like a warm blanket.

She reached behind her to turn off the lamp and then turned back, snuggling under the covers, trying not to focus on the fact that Jensen was mere inches away. She could hear his soft breathing. Could feel his warmth reaching out to her, enfolding her in its tender embrace.

"Going to get the closet light too?" he asked.

She was glad it wasn't light enough that he could see her embarrassed flush.

"No," she said quietly. "I leave it on. I don't like to sleep in total darkness. Does it bother you?"

"Anything that brings you comfort doesn't bother me," he said, further baffling her with his statement.

The man was twisting her in knots. For weeks he'd baited her, annoyed her, pissed her off, and now he was treating her so very gently. As if she was something precious and fragile. She was in way over her head and despite what he'd said about giving her complete control tonight, she felt anything *but* in control. Her mind—and heart—were in utter chaos. Her head was spinning so fast it was a wonder she could even breathe. No, she definitely was not in control.

Because even handcuffed to her bed, there was little doubt that Jensen was controlling the situation.

It should by all rights terrify her. She should be running as fast and as hard as possible in the opposite direction. But something stopped her. And she didn't know what. There was a promise of something in his eyes that made her want to find out *what*. And whether she had any hope of ever moving beyond her past and into the present.

JENSEN woke with a start and cursed viciously under his breath. Kylie was curled into a protective ball on the far edge of the bed. Out of his reach. A low whimper tore out of her throat followed by more sounds of terror.

She sounded like a frightened child. And in many ways she *was* still that frightened, vulnerable child she'd been while she suffered abuse at her father's hands.

This was why he'd insisted on staying with her. After her panic attack at the restaurant he'd been certain she'd suffer nightmares, that her past would be hovering on the fringes of her consciousness, just waiting for when she was asleep and vulnerable to attack.

And he couldn't *get* to her, helpless to watch as she struggled against invisible monsters. Damn him for insisting on the hand-cuffs, even if he'd have done anything to make her feel safe. Because now he couldn't hold her, couldn't soothe her when she was in the throes of terror.

"Kylie. Baby, wake up. You're safe. You're with me. Wake up, baby."

For a moment she was too firmly entrenched in the grasp of her nightmare to respond to his gentle crooning. Then she came awake with a gasp, sitting upright in bed, eyes wild and enormous in her small face. She looked straight ahead, pulling her knees protectively to her chest, and rocked back and forth.

Then she buried her face in her knees, and he could hear the muffled sounds of her sobs.

It broke his heart. Ripped him right in two. His heart was as shattered as hers, her agony his. Her heartbreak his own. Never had he felt so helpless, so full of despair that this beautiful, fragile woman was still a prisoner of her past.

"Come here, baby," he said gently, praying she wouldn't refuse his overture.

To his surprise, she didn't argue. She turned, nearly diving into his one-armed embrace. Then she reached back to her nightstand for the key to the cuffs, fumbling to unlock them, yanking desperately until he was free.

He instantly wrapped both arms around her, pulling her against his body. She clung to him like a burr, her heart pounding against his. Her face was wet with tears and her breaths were coming in ragged puffs as she struggled to gain control.

"Shhh, baby. I've got you," he soothed. "Nothing can hurt you now. I swear it. Let it go. Don't let it control you any longer."

He stroked her hair, kissing the top of her head, waiting for her to calm. To realize she was safe and that he had her. That nothing would hurt her when he was near.

"I'm sorry. Sorry, sorry," she chanted, the words muffled against his chest.

"*No*, baby. Don't apologize. Never apologize for this."

He rubbed his hand down her back, stroking and caressing until he could feel some of the knotted tension leave her body. She wilted, sagging against him, her face buried in his chest.

Her shoulders still shook and he knew she was still crying. Every tear gutted him. Made his heart ache for all the hurt she'd endured. For the hurt she *still* experienced each and every night.

"Just let me hold you," he said softly, allowing all the tenderness he felt for her into those simple words. "Go back to sleep now. I've got you. Nothing can hurt you here."

She gave a little sigh and settled against him, her body sheltered by his own. Their legs tangled and she wiggled as if trying to get as close as possible to him.

He thought for a moment that she'd followed his directive and had drifted back into sleep. But then she went still. He could feel her pulse, a rapid staccato against his chest. She tensed as if gathering her courage to say something.

Instinctively, he tightened his arms around her, offering her silent encouragement.

"I hate this," she said in a broken voice. A statement she'd made multiple times when it came to her weaknesses, as she deemed them.

He rubbed one hand up and down her arm, from shoulder to wrist, before tangling their fingers together, squeezing so she felt the support he offered.

"I hate *him*," she whispered. "For what he did to me. To us. Me and Carson. I hate my mother for leaving us with him. I get why she would want out. But why would she leave us, knowing what a monster he was? Sometimes I think I hate her more than even him. How screwed up is that?"

Jensen knew that he was seeing a side of Kylie she hid from the rest of the world. That she was opening up to him when she firmly held back that part of herself from everyone else.

He was humbled and grateful that she'd chosen him. He realized it was due to proximity and the fact he'd forced himself into her bed, but he'd take whatever he could however he could get it. In time, she'd come to him willingly. Would open up to him without reservation or hesitation. Until then he'd satisfy himself with whatever tidbits she allowed to slip through her carefully guarded barriers.

"It's not screwed up at all, baby. She abandoned you. And not just simply abandoned you but left you with a man she knew would harm you. You have every reason to hate her. I hope to hell you don't spend even a minute feeling guilt over your feelings about your mother. You should have no guilt for hating the two people who should have loved and protected you. Two people you should have been able to turn to when you could turn to no one else. They betrayed you, Kylie. You don't betray them now by hating them and what they did to you."

"Thank you," she said so quietly he almost didn't hear the aching softness of her voice.

He squeezed her, holding on to her, never wanting to let her go.

"You're more than welcome, baby. But I want you to promise me something, okay?"

She shifted in his arms and pulled her head away to look at him, though her lips trembled and he could tell it was difficult for her to meet his gaze. She was mortified that he was witnessing her at her most vulnerable. It made him want to kiss her all the more, but he refused to take advantage of her when she was so achingly fragile. It would make him a complete asshole.

When he was certain he had her full attention, he let one finger drift down the line of her cheekbone and then to her chin.

"In the morning, when this night is but a memory, and you think back on all that's happened, promise me you won't have a single moment of regret. Promise me that you won't be embarrassed or uncomfortable with what has occurred between us. Promise me that you won't start avoiding me even more than you do already. Some things are inevitable, Kylie. You and I are inevitable. No matter how much you fight it. No matter how much you deny it. *We* are inevitable.

"What you've given me tonight is very precious and I'll forever be humbled and grateful that you put your trust in me. That you allowed me inside those carefully constructed barriers that you erect to keep the rest of the world at bay. But I've seen inside. I've seen the real you, baby. And that's the person I want."

Her brow furrowed in concentration and her lips pursed and then fell open as if she couldn't quite form a response.

He put his fingers over those lush lips, not wanting to hear anything but her assent.

"Promise me," he whispered in a husky tone.

She closed her eyes but finally nodded.

"Give me the words, your promise. I need to hear them. We both do. Because one thing about you, baby, is that you're loyal. And you're honest. And once you give your word, you won't go back on it. So give me your promise. Let me hear it. Do this much for me."

"I promise," she whispered, her voice cracking under the strain of having to capitulate.

He leaned forward and brushed his lips over hers. Just a light kiss. Nothing like what he truly wanted. Just something warm and comforting, meant to soothe and not overwhelm.

"Now go to sleep, baby. Here in my arms where nothing can hurt you. I'll be right here. This time when you dream, dream of me."

She snuggled back into his arms to his immense satisfaction and then gave a soft sigh, closing her eyes as she pillowed her head on his shoulder.

He lay there awake, long after she finally drifted into a dreamless sleep. Staring up at the ceiling as he pondered the puzzle that was Kylie Breckenridge. What was he going to do with her?

He knew he couldn't walk away from her. He didn't fool himself into thinking things would miraculously change after one night. If anything she'd be more determined than ever that he'd never see her at her most vulnerable again.

Somehow, some way, he had to break past those barriers. Bust them down for good and insert himself in her heart and soul. He'd already decided that she was well worth the fight, and he knew it would be a fight indeed.

But he wouldn't give up. Kylie was stubborn. Proud. Defiant. But he was every bit as stubborn and determined as she was. For the first time in her life, she'd met her match in him. Because he sure as hell wasn't giving up. This was one battle he would win, no matter the cost.

SIX

KYLIE awoke to a completely alien sensation. She laid there, trying to process just what was different. She felt . . . rested. No lingering darkness from nightmares. She felt . . . safe.

It was then she registered the fact that she was not alone in her bed. Not only was she not alone, but a very male, very hard body was wrapped protectively around her and her head was pillowed on a muscled shoulder.

Jensen.

Oh God.

Memories from the night before—humiliating memories—crashed through her mind like a landslide. She'd made an utter ass of herself. Completely fallen apart on him. For God's sake, she'd handcuffed him to her *bed*.

"Remember your promise, Kylie."

His soft voice rumbled from his chest, bringing with it another reminder of the hastily given promise not to regret. Not to be ashamed or embarrassed. Not to freak out. She didn't have a prayer of keeping the promise because everything about this situation completely freaked her out.

"What time is it?" she croaked out. A perfectly neutral question, one that would remind them both that they had important matters this morning that had nothing to do with the fact they were in bed. Together.

"It's only six," he said in that infuriatingly calm voice of his. He sounded completely unruffled by the fact they were wrapped up like two lovebugs.

"You want coffee?" she asked even as she pushed herself up and away, putting distance between them.

He smiled, almost as if he knew her utter panic. "Coffee would be nice. I'll have a cup and then head over to my place to shower and change. Then I'll run back by and pick you up."

"There's no need," she said hastily. "I can just meet you there."

"You forget you're without a vehicle," he pointed out. "Besides, I thought we'd have lunch after and discuss the results of the meeting. Then I'll run you by the restaurant to get your car."

He made it sound like business, all business, but she knew differently. There was a tone to his voice that had been absent until now. Somehow more intimate and . . . tender. He looked at her so tenderly it made her heart ache. And made her even more desperate to increase the distance between them.

She slid to the edge of the bed and got up, going to her closet to get her robe. Her pajamas more than adequately covered her but she still felt vulnerable and she wanted—needed—that extra barrier of clothing.

"I'll have the coffee ready in a few minutes," she muttered. "Take your time. Feel free to make use of the bathroom."

She turned before she could see his expression, that knowing smile. Her world felt tilted on its axis. She had no idea what to make of this abrupt shift in their relationship. What relationship? He was her *boss*. Well, one of them. She was his employee.

Certainly not his bed partner even if he'd spent the night, part of the night, handcuffed to her bed.

Heat rushed like fire through her cheeks. God, how humiliating. What kind of freak did it make her that she'd handcuffed a man to her bed? How weak did it make her that she'd actually needed it to feel safe? And weaker still, because in the throes of a nightmare, she'd wrenched his arm free so he could hold her.

Jensen Tucker had held her, had wrapped himself completely around her the entire night, and God help her, she'd loved every minute of it. She couldn't remember the last time she'd slept so peacefully. That she'd felt absolutely safe. After that first nightmare, when he'd pulled her into his arms, she'd fallen into a deep, dreamless sleep, completely unbothered by the demons that taunted her on a regular basis. Who needed therapy? Apparently all she needed was Jensen Tucker's strong embrace. Not that she'd ever admit that to him. It would only give him that much more power over her, and she'd vowed never to give anyone that kind of power over her. Never again.

She busied herself making the coffee, her thoughts chaotic and unbalanced. He made her that way. What the hell did he want from her? He'd all but staked his claim. Some of the things he'd said she was still grappling with. Had no idea of their meaning. Or perhaps she knew only too well and was too chickenshit to deal with them with her big girl pants on.

But why did he seem to want her? Why would he even care? She was one hot mess. A head case. And worse, he knew it. Calmly accepted it like it was the most normal thing in the world. He'd inserted himself as her . . . protector? He certainly seemed to accept the role. Even embraced it. He'd made no bones about the fact that they were, what had he said? Inevitable?

He was as crazy as she was apparently. Two hot-mess head cases? Surely a recipe for disaster. He was strong. She was weak. Not the ingredients for a successful relationship for sure. And he was a control freak. She knew that much about him. His world was meticulously well-ordered. No chaos. No messes. He was every bit as dominant as Tate and Dash were, no matter that he said he was nothing like them. He hadn't seemed to like the comparison, but then she could understand why. He was definitely a law unto himself. There were certainly no two Jensen Tuckers. God help her. One was enough. More than enough.

He came in a few moments later and her gaze flitted to him, taking in his rumpled appearance. The fact that he was still wearing the same clothes from the night before. But even wrinkled and unkempt the man was just damn sexy.

She could admit that to herself now. Hell, she'd spent the night with him. No, they hadn't had sex, but in many ways, what they'd experienced was far more intimate than sex. He'd simply offered her comfort. What she'd needed the most. She would not be an ungrateful bitch even if that was her instinctual, self-protective reaction. Her reaction to anything that could possibly hurt her.

She could see that about herself. She could see herself as others likely did and what she saw made her cringe. It was a miracle she had any friends left because God knew she hadn't been a very good friend herself. But she could change that. Starting now. She could bend without breaking. It was time to start returning the unconditional love and support her friends had offered her since Carson died.

She'd been so wrapped up in her own grief and misery that she'd become a selfish bitch. She didn't like herself very much, and if she didn't like herself, how could she expect others to like her? Why the hell did Jensen seem to like her? She certainly hadn't been remotely receptive to any of his overtures. She'd returned every kindness he'd offered her with blatant rudeness. And yet he'd stayed with her last night, offering unconditional, unquestioning support. *Why?*

Was he a masochist?

He sat down at the bar and she pushed a cup of coffee in his direction. For a moment there was an awkward silence between them but then she gathered her courage and took the bull by the horns.

"Thank you for last night," she said in a low voice. "It meant . . . a lot. You didn't have to do it, but I'm grateful you did. That you . . . stayed. Thank you."

His eyes were warm as he stared at her, his gaze stroking her face as surely as if he'd reached out and touched her with his hand. She almost wished he would. Touch her. Her skin came alive at the mere thought and her thoughts drifted to the night before. Of how wonderful it had felt to be in his arms, surrounded by his strength and the unspoken promise that nothing would hurt her while he was with her.

"You're welcome, Kylie. I'm glad I was here so you didn't have to suffer alone as you do many other nights, I'm sure."

She flushed, not even bothering to deny it. He'd know she was lying.

"You going to have a cup?" he asked, his gaze taking in the fact she hadn't poured herself any coffee.

She shook her head. "No. I'm jittery enough. Caffeine would only make it worse."

"Do I make you that nervous?" he asked mildly. "Surely after last night you realize I'm not a monster."

She felt the betraying heat creep up her neck again. "No, I

don't think that at all," she said softly. "This is just . . . uncomfortable for me. You have to understand. I don't allow others to see me as you saw me last night. It bothers me. I feel . . . vulnerable, and I hate that feeling."

He set his mug down and reached across the bar to take her hand. "I don't want to make you feel that way, baby. I want you to feel just the opposite. You can be yourself with me. I understand you. Far better than you realize. We all have our demons to battle. You aren't alone."

She cocked her head, curious at the odd note in his voice. "And what are your demons, Jensen?"

His face tightened and his eyes became shuttered. She instantly regretted the innocent question, but then he'd seen her at her worst. Wasn't she entitled to know something about him? Something that made him vulnerable?

He checked his watch, effectively dodging her question. "I need to get going if I'm going to get back in time for us to make our meeting. Will half an hour be enough time for you to get ready?"

She nodded.

He got up and to her surprise walked around to where she stood and pulled her into his arms. He kissed her. Softly. Just a brush of his lips against hers, but she felt the warmth all the way to her toes. Her entire body tingled. Her breasts became heavy and aching, her nipples straining outward. She was grateful that the robe disguised her reaction to such a simple kiss.

"I'll be back soon," he murmured.

And then he turned and strode out of her kitchen, the front door opening and closing as he walked out.

She stood there a long time, her fingers fluttering to her still-tingling mouth. What the hell had just happened here? Last night? The entire episode? How in the hell had their relationship taken such a dramatic turn?

She shook herself out of her stupor and headed for the bathroom to shower and ready herself for the meeting with S&G. This was important. Her chance to prove herself. Jensen believed in her. She believed in herself. Perhaps for the first time in her life. And she wasn't going to let either him or herself down.

SEVEN

"YOU did very well today, Kylie. I'm very proud of you," Jensen said as they took their seats at the Lux Café. "The CFO was very impressed with your recommendations. I'd say we're a shoo-in for the contract."

Kylie flushed with pleasure and ducked her head, but she knew her eyes glowed with happiness. Her stomach had been tied in knots for the entire meeting, especially when Jensen had let her take the lead and make the presentation. He'd sat back, a bystander, as Kylie had outlined their suggestions for minimizing costs to the corporation.

It had shocked the hell out of her that he'd given her control over such an important meeting. This was a huge contract for him and Dash. Dash would likely have a heart attack if he knew just how much leeway Jensen had given her in this meeting.

But after a shaky start, and with Jensen's confidence in her evident in his gaze, she'd taken control and had crisply and efficiently delivered their recommendations to the CFO.

"Thank you," she said honestly. "For giving me this chance, I mean. It means a lot to me. I had no idea I could do it. I was scared to death."

"It didn't show, though," he said. "You oozed confidence.

You had the CFO in the palm of your hand. Hell, he'd have probably eaten out of it. He was hanging on your every word. I was
tempted to knee him in the balls if he didn't keep his damn
tongue in his mouth."

She frowned. "So you think he was so attentive because I'm
a woman?"

Jensen laughed. "No, I think he was attentive because you
are an extremely intelligent, well put together, beautiful woman.
Make no mistake, Kylie. Your looks certainly don't hurt, but no
businessman worth his salt is going to make such a huge decision based on sexual attraction. He may have enjoyed the view,
but you damn well got his attention because of your intelligence
and attention to detail."

Feeling somewhat mollified, she relaxed in her seat as the
waiter approached to take their order.

"You have nothing to prove, Kylie," he said in a soft voice
once the waiter drifted away. "The only person who doesn't
believe in you is you."

She dropped her gaze because he was right. She didn't have
the confidence she should. But damn it, she wanted it. Wanted it
so badly she could taste it. She wanted to take on the world and
grab on with both hands. Wanted to be someone unafraid to
walk into a room like she owned it. But she'd learned from a
very young age to be as unassuming as possible and to draw as
little attention to herself as possible. It was a matter of survival.
Of self-preservation.

As if reading her thoughts, he reached across the table and
twined their fingers together. What did it say about her that it
no longer startled her when he touched her? That she'd come to
like it. Crave it even.

"You'll get there, baby. It won't happen overnight, but you'll get there. I see inside you to the real you. I know she's there just waiting to break free. And she will. One day."

"How is it you know so much about me?" she whispered. "Things I don't even know myself? You haven't worked with Dash that long."

He smiled. "I watch people. I study them. It's helpful in my line of work and, well, in life, for that matter. I'm good at reading people. Knowing when they're sincere and when they're just bullshitting me. And my instincts tell me that you're a fierce, brave woman who's faced a hell of a lot of adversity in her life but who's come out stronger for it."

She laughed, the sound brittle and not at all joyful. "Stronger? I disagree there. I'm scared of my own shadow. Or did you forget that I handcuffed you to the bed last night?"

His expression grew tender. She'd grown to love the way his eyes warmed when he looked at her just so.

"And yet you took them off," he pointed out. "You trusted me enough to take them off when you were at your most vulnerable. I'd say that was very brave of you."

She flushed because he had a way of turning around every argument she posed. Made what she deemed as weaknesses, strengths. If only she had as much confidence in herself as he apparently did.

"I'd like to take you to dinner tomorrow night," he said casually. "And not a business dinner. A date. You, me, no office talk. Just us and we see where this takes us."

"There is no us," she blurted, stunned by his invitation.

He arched an eyebrow. "I spent last night in your bed, baby. I'd say that makes us something."

"You didn't give me a choice!" she sputtered. "That's hardly the basis of a date!"

He smiled. "So forget last night then if it bothers you so much. But you know and I know that I'll be back there. It's only a matter of time."

Her throat threatened to close off. She could barely breathe around the knot growing larger by the second. This man thoroughly intimidated her. She found it telling that he didn't scare her. Not physically. She knew in her bones that he'd never lift a finger to her. It seemed to enrage him, the thought of anyone or anything hurting her. But there were other kinds of hurts. Some more painful than even the physical kind.

"I won't play games with you," she whispered.

His eyes lost the playful, flirty glimmer and his expression grew suddenly fierce and very serious.

"This is no goddamn game, Kylie. Not to me. Never to me. You are not a game. You aren't a challenge, a notch on my bedpost. I don't fuck around. I haven't fucked my way through countless women and I'm not some bored bastard who sees getting with you as a victory."

She was speechless. Utterly speechless. Her hands shook so hard that she had to put her water glass down because liquid sloshed over the rim, spilling onto the table.

"What do you want from me?" she croaked.

His gaze was direct and unflinching. Grim and unrelenting.

"You. Just you, Kylie. And everything you have to give."

She was light-headed from holding her breath for so long and she forced herself to breathe as spots appeared in her vision. She had to hold it together and not melt down right in the middle of the restaurant.

"I don't have anything to give you," she said softly.

For some reason the starkness of her statement made her want to cry. Tears burned her eyelids but she refused to let them fall. She had nothing to offer this man. Any man. But certainly not someone like Jensen who could have any woman he wanted. Who would never have to look far for female companionship. There was probably a line outside his bedroom door.

"You're wrong," he said just as softly.

He didn't expound. Just kept staring at her with that intense gaze, his eyes never leaving her face, taking in every thought, every reaction. She was certain he could see the tears glittering in her eyes, burning, begging to fall free. She swallowed hard, her head aching with the effort not to allow him to see how affected she was by . . . him.

But he knew. Damn the man, he knew. At least he wasn't smug. He didn't look triumphant. He just stared tenderly at her, like he always did, as if he knew exactly the battle she waged with herself. Saw every fear. Heard every doubt. And yet he still wanted her.

It baffled and awed her all at the same time.

"It's just a date," he said mildly. "Dinner. Maybe a movie. We could rent something and relax on the couch. I won't try and get into your pants. Yet," he added with a sly grin.

His teasing should infuriate her, but she was grateful because his levity took the burn from her eyes and lessened her need to weep.

It was just dinner. What was the harm? Even as she asked that stupid question she knew the answer. Giving in to him would be like opening the gates to an invading army. Give him an inch and he'd take the whole bloody mile.

"You're starting to bruise my ego," he said dryly. "Surely I'm not so terrible."

"No," she said quietly, not willing to let him think so. He'd done too much for her. Been too kind, understanding. He'd seen her at her worst. How could she ever think he was horrible?

"Well, that's something," he said, breathing out with exaggerated relief. "Now, about dinner. I promise not to take you back to the place that caters to rich old farts. Is it a date?"

She laughed, unable to prevent her reaction to him. He could be quite charming when he wasn't all broody and intense—which was most of the time. Why was it she thought that she was the only person who saw this side of him? It was awfully egotistical of her to assume and yet the thought took hold and wouldn't go away. She'd seen the way he was with others. Polite, but distant. Observant. Ever watchful.

"All right," she finally conceded.

She'd vowed she was through being a coward, and to turn him down would be the height of cowardice. Especially after last night. She refused to tuck tail and run even if that's what her instincts were screaming at her to do. But it was time to start refashioning her outlook on life and stop cowering at the least bit of conflict. She couldn't avoid the rest of the world forever. Perhaps going out with Jensen would give her back a little of herself in the process.

Or maybe she'd end up losing every part of herself to him.

"Oh crap," she murmured, her eyes closing.

"What?"

She reopened them, hoping he could see how earnest she was. "I can't go to dinner with you Friday night."

He frowned. "Why not?"

She sighed. "I promised to have dinner with Chessy. Tate is entertaining an important client and with Joss gone, she's been lonely. I can't ditch her, Jensen. Tate's been so busy with work and I worry about her."

Jensen smiled at her. "You're a very loyal friend. She's lucky to have you. I'll let you off the hook if you'll give me Saturday night."

Relief rushed through her veins. "Deal."

"Perfect then. I'll pick you up at six thirty. Dress casual. You want to watch movies at your place or mine?"

It was stupid that panic frayed her nerves at the idea of being in Jensen's space. Of being alone with him in his home. He'd been alone with her in hers! Hell, he'd slept in her bed, wrapped solidly around her.

"My place," she said quickly, hoping he didn't pick up on that sudden surge of panic and take it personally.

But he only smiled that same damn smile that told her he knew exactly what she was thinking *and* feeling.

"Your place it is. If you'd prefer not to go out, I could cook you dinner at your house and then we can watch movies," he said in a casual tone.

She frowned. "That hardly seems fair. Shouldn't I be cooking for you?"

He lifted an eyebrow. "I invited you on a date and if you're giving me your hospitality, the least I can do is cook a meal for you. Besides, I'm an excellent cook, if I do say so myself."

She held up her hands. "Okay, okay. You win. Give me a list of everything you need and I'll run by the store Saturday morning."

He shook his head. "I'll take care of it. All I ask is for you to sit and keep me company while I work my magic in your kitchen."

"It certainly appears I'm getting the better end of this deal," she said dryly.

"On the contrary," he said softly. "I get your company. I find that's worth a hell of a lot more than one cooked meal."

She was speechless again, an affliction she seemed to suffer on a regular basis around him. And the hell of it was he sounded absolutely sincere.

"I swear I don't know what I'm going to do with you, Jensen Tucker," she said in a bewildered voice.

He smiled. "If you don't know, I'll be happy to show you."

EIGHT

IF Kylie expected hers and Jensen's relationship to be strained in the office, she was wrong. She'd expected awkwardness. Even outright discomfort. She wasn't a fool and even she wasn't so ensconced in denial that she could ignore the current of attraction between her and Jensen.

What was the old saying? Opposites attract?

And in their case, could they possibly be more opposite? She and Jensen were *polar* opposites. He was strong, invulnerable, courageous, confident. Nothing would ever get him down. He oozed authority and self-assurance and she envied him that. She was weak, a coward, and confidence could never be listed as one of her better qualities.

She sat in her office, staring down at one of the many reports she was supposed to proof and get back to Jensen within the hour. But she was numb, her mind blank. And if she was going to be honest, and she certainly hadn't held back with herself yet, she was terrified to face him.

They had a date tomorrow night. He'd spent the night in her bed. They'd gone to lunch where he'd asked her on a real date. And he'd made it clear that it would have nothing to do with business.

How was she supposed to act around him? She nearly laughed

at the idea that somehow she was living one of those cracka-licious category romances she read about CEOs and their secre-taries. Bosses and their personal assistants. In real life, most people were well aware of the difficulties in mixing business and pleasure and most companies had strict rules about their employ-ees becoming personally involved.

But Dash and Jensen answered to no one save themselves. They weren't a typical corporation and Kylie pitied the person who ever tried to tell them how to run their business.

They didn't have an employee handbook and there certainly wasn't a rule against employee fraternization. But that didn't mean that Kylie wasn't a complete idiot for becoming involved with Jensen Tucker.

"Let's separate the fact that he's your boss," Kylie muttered grimly to herself. "That's the most obvious one under the 'no' category."

There was also the fact that he was the antithesis of what she wanted or needed from a man. She couldn't really say what she wanted, though. Because the truth was she hadn't sought out relationships with men. Sure, she'd had a few casual dates here and there, but it had quickly become evident that Kylie's issues weren't endearing her to the men who asked her out.

She couldn't blame them. She could reflect on herself objec-tively and realize that she was difficult. Bitchy, prickly, defen-sive and timid. Not the hallmarks of a desirable, kickass woman who made men drool at a hundred paces.

Still, it was nice to think about having that effect on men just once. That Kylie could actually summon the courage to be ballsy and confident. Walk into a room like she owned it in a pair of killer heels and a dress to die for and have every man there wanting her.

"Yeah, and then what would you do with them?" she said in disgust.

Absolutely nothing. That was what. She'd run like the chicken she was and she'd stick her head in the sand like an ostrich and pray that life passed her by and didn't use her as a whipping post anymore.

At what point was she going to say *enough*? She was in her midtwenties. Still young by all accounts, and yet there were days she felt so much older. The weight of a lifetime bearing down on her, suffocating and miserable. Her childhood had seemed to last an eternity, her imprisonment stretching to infinity.

At her worst times, when she and Carson were just children, she'd had the secret hope that she could end it all. It shamed her now to even think of just how close she'd come to taking her own life. She'd been just a child, and what child had such dark, horrific thoughts?

The only thing that had stopped her was the fact that Carson would be by himself. He and he alone would bear the brunt of her father's rage. And she wouldn't allow that.

Carson had put himself in between her and her father many times, but just as many times, Kylie had done the same for him.

When her father was in a drunken rage, he seemed to target Carson. It was the other times, when he was absolutely sober, that his hatred for Kylie shone through and nothing she did was right. Everything was a punishable offense. Carson had tried to protect her just as Kylie protected him when their father drank too much and vented his rage on his son.

She'd never admitted to Carson that she'd considered suicide. It would have destroyed him. Kylie had never told anyone at all. It had remained her darkest secret, buried under layers of hurt and despair but still there. A memory that burned brightly in Kylie's mind. A reminder of how close she'd come to her breaking point.

And yet she seemed to be drifting further in the direction of that dark, murky past. Seemed to be reaching that breaking point that she'd never quite come to before. Why now?

She was safe from her father. No one could hurt her. She had a home, her fortress, where she could lock herself behind the walls and have a safe haven, no intrusion from the outside world.

Carson's death had been a strain on her. Was still a strain. Maybe she'd never properly dealt with her grief. She'd performed robotically during the entire ordeal, unable to comprehend that the only person who'd ever loved and protected her was gone. That she was alone in the world, the one thing she'd always feared the most.

She'd known that Carson and Joss would be her only family. That she had no desire for one of her own. She'd also known that Carson didn't want children, though Joss did. She understood his fear. That somehow their tainted genes would be passed down to his children. It was a fear she shared.

Her own mother had abandoned them to a monster she knew was capable of horrific atrocities. She had no example. No one to look up to. An absent mother and a father who was alcoholic and abusive and a misogynist to boot.

She shook her head, her lips tight. No, she didn't want to risk having children either. What if she was a horrible mother? What if her children turned into monsters like her own parents? God only knew all the things that could go wrong if she or Carson ever had children.

She was perfectly content for her father's name and blood to die with her, his only remaining blood relative in this world. If only she could take him to hell with her. Because God knew, she lived that hell every single day and had since she was just a baby.

"Do you have those reports ready?"

Jensen's crisp voice came over the intercom, startling Kylie from her dark thoughts.

She ruffled the papers frantically, glancing to see that she had indeed finished proofing the stack.

"Yes," she replied, hating the catch in her voice. "Would you like me to bring them to you?"

"Yes, please."

She rose and gathered the papers, tidying them into a neat stack. Then she sucked in a deep breath and strode down the hall to Jensen's office. His door was open and he wasn't paying attention. His attention was focused on his computer and he wore a slight frown.

His shirt was unbuttoned at the top and his tie had long been shed. His sleeves were rolled up to his elbows and his jacket tossed over a nearby chair.

He was a creature of comfort, and while Dash and Carson both seemed comfortable in finer clothes and embraced the world they'd created for themselves, Jensen seemed less at ease. He was quiet, reserved. And he seemed content to allow Dash to do most of the talking.

But Kylie would bet her entire paycheck that Jensen didn't miss a single beat. That he knew every single client and the ins and outs of the contracts and the job that needed to be done.

She approached his desk hesitantly, not wanting to disturb his obvious concentration. She slid the stack of papers onto the edge and turned hastily, intending to get out quickly.

"Kylie, wait," Jensen commanded.

It shouldn't have surprised her that he'd known the moment

she'd come through the door. Even though he hadn't acknowl-edged her in any way and had kept his focus on whatever he was studying on his computer screen.

She glanced up to see him staring at her, his gaze stroking over her skin like a tangible touch. She loved the way he looked at her. She loved the way it made her feel. Safe. Protected. Like he cared about what happened to her.

Those looks were addicting. She soaked up every single one of them with unabashed greed.

His look changed to one of displeasure, and apprehension gripped Kylie's chest. She hated conflict of any kind. It was her nature to avoid it at all costs and if she couldn't avoid it, then soothe, soothe, soothe.

"Is something wrong?" she asked anxiously. "Is there some-thing I can help you with?"

Jensen reached for her hand, shocking her, because he'd always maintained a semblance of casualness between them at work. He gently squeezed and pulled her closer until she stood right by his chair, her back to his desk. He pushed back his chair so he was looking squarely at her.

"I have to go out of town Monday. I fly back in Wednesday night so I'll be in the office early Thursday."

She nodded, wondering why that had set him off. It certainly wasn't unusual for him and Dash both to be out of town.

"It's the S&G contract," he continued. "The CFO was very impressed and wants to move forward with our proposal. He wants me to attend a meeting with the CEO and the board of directors in Dallas. The contract is ours. We're just going through the motions of getting approval up the chain. And of course they want to meet me—us."

It was then that he grimaced and ran a hand through his hair.

"This is your contract, Kylie. It's you who should be going. Not me. At the very least, you should be attending with me. But with Dash gone, we can't leave the office unattended for three days."

"Of course not," Kylie said, shocked that he'd even considered it. "My job is to run the office, Jensen."

"But you deserve this," he said, his lips still turned down into a frown. "Most of the suggestions were yours, even if they were in agreement with mine. You handled yourself very well in the meeting with the CFO. I have absolute faith you'd have their entire corporation eating out of your hand if you gave the presentation."

She shook her head, pleased beyond measure with his praise, but at the same time, panic-stricken over the idea of presenting their proposal alone. Without Jensen there to back her up. She might like the idea of breaking out of her shell and taking on the world one day, but it wouldn't be today. Or tomorrow for that matter.

Baby steps, she reminded herself.

"So you'll be gone Monday, Tuesday and Wednesday," she said lightly. "I believe I can hold the fort down while you're gone."

"Oh, I know that much," Jensen said, his tone serious. "But damn it, I wanted you with me."

Kylie's eyes widened as finally the reason for his irritation became clear. He hadn't wanted to leave her behind and yet they had no choice. They didn't employ a full staff, though Kylie had been after them to hire one or two more office assistants. For that matter, both men needed personal assistants. Employees who would travel with them, work side by side with them and take care of personal as well as professional matters.

Kylie's job was to manage the office. Ensure that everything ran smoothly, that things got done on time and accounts receivable were kept up to date. But she acted as a personal assistant to both men instead of just an office manager, and they definitely kept her on her toes. There was enough work for two more employees but neither man seemed to have any interest in taking on anyone else. They claimed to like the job Kylie did for them and seemed content with the services she provided.

She made a mental note to ask for a raise if one wasn't automatically given in her annual performance review, which was coming up in just a few weeks. She deserved it. The old Kylie would have never rocked the boat. Continued to take the same pay and not complain when she took on more of a workload. Anything to keep peace and to keep away from conflict.

The new Kylie? Knew she was worth more than what her paycheck reflected. Not that either man ever took her for granted. She felt appreciated. Both men went out of their way to tell her she was doing a good job and that they couldn't manage without her.

The new Kylie was going to be crisp and efficient and ballsy. She was going to ask for a raise. And not a small one.

She had goals just like everyone else did. She wanted a new house, one not in the same neighborhood as Dash, Joss, Tate and Chessy. Jensen lived just a mile away in another upscale gated community. It was time for her to break free. To not be so dependent on the people around her and for them to constantly have to baby her.

Kylie felt like a fraud living where she did. Carson had insisted that she live near him. Where he could look in on her, protect her. Just like he'd always done. And she'd failed him when he'd needed her most. It should have been her. Not him.

He had Joss. Someone who loved him and whom he had adored beyond reason. Kylie had no one. Just Carson, and by extension Joss.

It should have been her.

It had nothing to do with a death wish. Not since she'd been a little girl and had that awful moment when she'd considered that she'd be alone, protected, away from the violence and turmoil of her everyday life if only she gave in and took the easy way out, had she given any serious consideration to giving up and ending her life.

"What the hell is going through your mind?" Jensen muttered.

She glanced guiltily in his direction, knowing she wasn't giving him the attention he deserved as her employer. Heat scorched her cheeks. Shame. That she'd even dwelled on those awful moments in the past.

"Nothing worth repeating," she said honestly.

Jensen shook his head. "One of these days, you're going to trust me enough to share those dark thoughts you seem to have on a regular basis. You may think you hide them from the world, and maybe you do, but not from me. I see past the practiced façade, Kylie. And I don't want that to alarm you. I want you to trust in the fact that I will never hurt you. I'll never do anything to cause you pain."

She swallowed and nodded, not knowing what else to do. How could she explain that some things just weren't meant to be shared? Even if he thought he knew about her past, there was no way for him to know it all. Because no one did. Not even Carson.

"Everything will be fine," she said calmly. "You'll go seal the deal with S&G and I'll keep things running here at the office.

Dash will be back in a week. He and I used to run the office ourselves, so I'm certainly capable of running things alone while you're away."

"That's not the point," he said patiently. "You deserve this, Kylie. It should be you going. Not me."

She paled, shaking her head in instant denial. "I appreciate the opportunity. I appreciate your confidence in me, Jensen. But you did enough. You let me help with the proposal. That's enough. I wouldn't feel comfortable presenting to the higher-ups. That's your specialty. Not mine. No way I want the responsibility of us losing a contract like this because I'm not experienced enough to pull it off."

His eyes warmed with understanding and gave her that peculiar shiver she experienced every time he looked at her like that.

"We'll get you there, baby. Maybe not right now, but in time definitely. I plan to have a long talk with Dash when he returns about your position in this company."

Her eyes widened. A protest was already forming on her lips but Jensen shushed her with a look.

"You aren't changing my mind on this."

Her lips curved into a rueful smile. "All I was going to ask for was a raise—a big one—at my next performance review. I'm afraid that would have used up all my assertiveness for at least a year."

Jensen chuckled. "You'll get your raise, and if I have any say, a promotion will come with it. Which means we'll be in the market for another office manager, because if you're going to be working more closely with me and Dash, you won't have time to juggle everything else."

She frowned at that. She was territorial when it came to the office. It was her domain. She ran it. Organized it. Knew the ins and outs even better than Dash and Jensen. It was she who kept things going smoothly. She liked that she was indispensable. That she had worth.

"You're better than being an office manager, Kylie. You have a degree. You certainly have the intelligence. All you need is the confidence. Once you gain that, you'll be an unstoppable force. I guarantee it."

She flushed again, a warm glow enveloping her. He seemed utterly confident in her abilities, and if he was that confident, shouldn't she be as well?

"Thank you," she said softly.

He gave her a smile and she shifted, knowing she'd spent too long in his office when she had other work to be doing.

She turned to go and Jensen's call stopped her.

"Have a good time with Chessy tonight. I'll see you tomorrow. Your place. Six thirty."

It was a reminder of their date. And the way he dropped the casual reminder told her that he likely thought she'd cry off or come up with some excuse.

But she did neither. She turned, making sure her turmoil wasn't evident in her expression. She answered him as calmly as she could.

"See you at six thirty then."

NINE

"SO what's new with you?" Chessy asked as they were seated in their favorite booth at the Lux Café.

For as many times as they ate here and requested the same booth, it ought to have their names engraved on it. The waitstaff was certainly on a first-name basis with all three women and didn't even ask where they wanted to be seated. They just escorted them to their booth in the corner as soon as they walked through the door.

Kylie took her seat, wondering if Chessy could see her every thought. Because typically Kylie never had anything "new" to share. She always just listened to whatever was going on with Joss and Chessy and responded to whatever they wanted to talk about.

Now that Chessy had forced the focus on her, Kylie was at a loss as to what to do. They were girlfriends, which meant that they were supposed to share intimate details. Secrets. Gossip. Things they wouldn't share with anyone else. Only Kylie had never really held up her end of the deal.

"Not much," Kylie said lightly. "Same ole same ole. Work is keeping me busy."

Chessy studied her, her green eyes gleaming with mischief. "There's something different about you. I can't quite put my finger on it, but my first guess would be a man."

Kylie flushed to the roots of her hair. Good God. Save her from all-knowing and interfering friends. Without Joss, the peacemaker, as a buffer, Chessy would latch onto Kylie's ass and wouldn't be able to be pried loose with a crowbar.

"Oh my God, I'm right, aren't I?" Chessy crowed.

She leaned forward, her eyes alight with mischief and curiosity.

"Spill," Chessy demanded. "And don't leave a word out."

Kylie sighed but at the same time, warmth invaded her veins. This was what having girlfriends was about. She'd never really felt she'd taken advantage of her close friendship with Joss and Chessy because she'd never had anything to share. But now?

The question was whether she wanted to confide in Chessy when she herself had no clue what the hell was going on between her and Jensen.

"I don't know," Kylie said honestly.

Concern entered her friend's eyes. "What's going on, hon?"

"It's Jensen," Kylie blurted.

Chessy's eyes widened. "Jensen Tucker? As in works-with-Dash Jensen?"

Kylie nodded. "One and the same."

"Oh my," Chessy murmured. "Talk about biting off more than you can chew! That guy intimidates me."

"Join the crowd," Kylie said ruefully. "I have no idea what the hell he wants from me. But he's different with me. I mean different than he is with everyone else."

Chessy grinned. "Well a woman—the right woman—can do that to a man. But explain this *different*. What do you mean?"

Kylie sighed again, knowing Chessy wouldn't rest until she dragged every detail out of her.

"We're going on a date. Tomorrow night. He was specific in saying this was a date. No business talk. Nothing to do with the office. A real date. Oh my God, just saying that makes me freak out."

"Do you *want* to go out with him or did he pressure you into something you don't want?"

Chessy frowned fiercely, clearly going into protective mode. Kylie smiled.

"I agreed. I may need my head examined, but yes, I do want to go out, although we're not exactly going anywhere. He's cooking dinner for me at my place. And then we're going to watch movies. Not exactly an exciting date, huh."

"It sounds perfect to me," Chessy said wistfully. "I'm tired of eating out all the time. It seems like Tate is always entertaining a client and he likes for me to be with him when possible. A nice evening at home, alone, him cooking dinner for me and afterward spending the evening on the couch? Heaven."

Kylie frowned and leaned forward. She'd been worried about her friend for months. She and Joss both had been worried about Chessy and her marriage to Tate. Chessy was perpetually cheerful. She could warm even the hardest heart. Good as gold. Naturally sunny and generous. But lately? The light had been extinguished in her eyes. She seemed . . . unhappy. And that bothered Kylie a lot.

Kylie had even worried that Tate was somehow abusing her, though Joss had been adamant that it wasn't even a possibility. But then Joss hadn't seen the darker side of men like Kylie had. She knew that behind a perfectly polished exterior sometimes lay a monster.

"Is everything okay between you and Tate?" Kylie asked bluntly, finally putting to question what she and Joss had both privately wondered over the last few months.

Chessy looked startled, but it was the hesitation that sold Kylie on the idea that she wasn't far off the mark. Chessy didn't immediately deny it, nor did she act horrified over the idea. In fact, she didn't say anything at all. Just sat there with those sad eyes.

"Everything is fine," Chessy finally said lightly, though her lips weren't smiling. "I guess I'm just feeling lonely. I see so little of Tate and— I guess that isn't true. I do see him, but never in private. We're always entertaining clients or in a public setting. What we haven't had is time together, if you know what I mean."

"But are you happy?" Kylie persisted.

Chessy glanced down, not meeting Kylie's gaze. "No," she said softly. "Not now anyway. It's silly. I'm being selfish. Tate takes very good care of me. He's busting his ass because he wants to provide for me. For us. For me to never want for anything. But all I want is him, Kylie. Not money. Not things. I just want him and for things to be the way they were before."

"That's not selfish," Kylie said. "Have you talked to him? Have you told him how you feel?"

Chessy shook her head. "I can't. It would destroy him if he thought he was making me unhappy by doing the one thing he thinks will make me happy. I just have to ride it out. Things will get better. Marriage isn't easy. If it was, there wouldn't be so many divorces, and the last thing I want is to plant a seed of doubt in Tate's mind. I don't want out. I just want him. I love him so much."

Kylie reached across the table and squeezed her friend's hand. "I know you do. And I know he loves you. It'll work out, Chessy.

You have to believe that. Have you given any more thought to whether he's cheating? I know that was a concern, however brief, and you didn't want to ask him because of what it would do to your relationship if he thought you ever doubted him."

Though Joss had been the first person Chessy had confided in, Chessy had later brought up the issue with both Joss and Kylie, but only after Chessy had made Kylie swear she wouldn't confront Tate over it. Kylie was more of a take-the-bull-by-the-horns kind of girl, not as sweet and understanding as Joss. And well, maybe Kylie *would* have confronted Tate if Chessy hadn't exacted the promise from her. She hated the idea of her friend hurting in any way. And she knew, whatever the reasons why, that Chessy wasn't happy and she hated that she couldn't fix this for her friend.

Kylie had never admitted to Chessy that she'd been concerned that Tate abused her. She'd only shared that fear with Joss. She was glad now she hadn't because it might have caused an unmendable rift in their relationship. And Kylie was trained to believe the worst of people. She'd very likely overreacted. She didn't really believe Tate was capable of abusing Chessy, but then such was the case of many abusive men.

Chessy shook her head. "I was being silly and emotional. I don't really believe he'd ever cheat. I can't allow myself to even think that way or the seed of doubt will be planted and it will just drive me crazy. Besides, when would he have time to see another woman? I know he loves me. I really do. It's just hard right now. I wanted to start trying to have a baby. It's what we both want, or did want. Now I'm not so sure. Tate hasn't talked about it lately. The one time I mentioned it, he said he'd rather wait until his business was more secure. So I haven't brought it back up again. And maybe I'm just looking for something to fill the void so I'm not so lonely all the time. Which is a pretty lame reason for having a child."

Kylie grimaced in sympathy. But she agreed that Chessy should wait. Kylie wasn't altogether certain things were that good even though Chessy made the best of it. Bringing a child into an uncertain situation would only make it worse. If Tate was gone so much, how would Chessy cope with being a new mother without her husband as a support system?

But she kept those thoughts to herself because she didn't want to upset Chessy any more than she already was. Her heart ached for her friend. Loneliness was an emotion Kylie was intimately acquainted with.

She made a mental note to spend more time with Chessy, especially while Joss was gone on her honeymoon.

"But let's get back to you and Jensen," Chessy said, the teasing light back in her eyes. "How on earth did the two of you hook up? Is it one of those office romance things we read about in novels?"

Kylie snorted. "At first I thought he was an overbearing ass whose sole ambition was to make my life miserable. He told me I looked like hell. What a great prelude to asking me out on a date, right?"

Chessy seemed to choose her words carefully. "He wasn't wrong, exactly, hon. You do look . . . tired. Have you been having nightmares again?"

Kylie shrugged indifferently. "When don't I have nightmares? It's not something you can just get over, you know."

She hated when they spoke of things personal to her. She was much more comfortable talking about Chessy or Joss and what was going on with them. She rarely ever volunteered personal information because she didn't want her friends to worry.

They knew of her childhood. Joss knew because of Carson and Chessy had learned after they'd become friends. But them knowing didn't mean it was a subject open to speculation.

"Yes, I know and I'm sorry," Chessy said. "I wish there was something we could do to help you. Have you considered talking to a therapist? Getting medication?"

"Now you sound like Jensen," Kylie muttered.

"Honey, it doesn't make you weak to ask for help," Chessy said softly.

Chessy well knew Kylie's hatred of appearing weak. It was the one thing Kylie had confided in her best friends. She hated feeling powerless, like she wasn't solidly in control of her life and her surroundings. Hell, maybe she did need a shrink, but the very idea of sharing deep dark secrets she'd never confided in anyone with a complete stranger freaked her out.

Kylie shook her head. "I can't, Chessy. I don't expect you to understand. Hell, I barely understand it myself. But the idea of allowing a complete stranger inside my head scares me to death. I think it would only make things worse, not better."

"You can talk to me, you know," Chessy said quietly. "You know I'd never betray your confidence. I wouldn't even tell Joss if you didn't want me to. And I certainly wouldn't share anything you told me with Tate."

"I love you," Kylie said sincerely. "I don't know what I'd do without you and Joss. I don't know why y'all put up with me. I know I'm bitchy and prickly. It baffles me why either of you want to be my friend. I've said some horrible things. Just look at how I ripped into Joss when she and Dash got together. It still embarrasses me when I think about it. Joss didn't deserve my vitriol. I acted like such a hateful shrew."

Chessy smiled, her eyes softening with love. Unconditional,

unwavering love. Something Kylie had never experienced except with Carson. It still unbalanced her. At times it even made her uncomfortable, which was pretty messed up when she thought about it. But the simple truth was she didn't know how to handle such devotion and loyalty because she'd never had it.

"You're a wonderful person, Kylie. And a very loyal, loving friend. Joss and I are lucky to have you. And hell, no one is perfect. We've all been bitchy with each other at some point. That's how friendship works. You hurt the people you love the most but then you apologize and you forgive and you move on, even better friends than before. Joss certainly doesn't hold any animosity for the things you said. She knew you were upset and out of sorts. Heck, I didn't even see that one coming. Her and Dash? Or that Dash had a thing for her for so long? I mean, like I told you both in the beginning, there was a time I suspected, but then so much time went by and Dash never acted so I thought I'd imagined the way he looked at her. I think it took us all by surprise. Even Tate."

"You'd tell me if things got bad between you and Tate, wouldn't you, Chessy?" Kylie asked. "You know I'd do anything at all to help you."

Sadness entered Chessy's eyes again and Kylie cursed the fact she'd ruined the mood. Again. Her and her big mouth. She was going to have to seriously work on the bitchy, prickly part of her personality. Her friends didn't deserve that from her. They deserved better. They deserved the person Kylie hoped to become.

"Thanks for the offer, hon, but I'm not going anywhere and Tate sure as hell isn't either. I'll tie him to the bed if it becomes necessary, never mind it's usually him tying me to the bed."

Chessy's eyes sparkled with humor and Kylie breathed a sigh of relief that the mood had lightened.

Kylie grinned mischievously. "Okay, here's one for you then. You can never accuse me of holding out on you after I tell you this. And if you ever tell anyone, I'll kill you!"

"What?" Chessy demanded. "This has to be good if you're getting all serious on me."

Kylie laughed. "You'll laugh. I couldn't laugh at the time. I was pretty freaked-out. But now? I have to admit, it's pretty damn funny, especially in light of the kind of guy Jensen is."

"Don't make me drag it out of you!" Chessy growled. "Spill!"

"Okay, so Jensen wanted me to work with him on this latest contract. Completely shocked me. I mean I'm their office manager. I don't get involved in the actual dealings with their clients. Only, he wanted my input. And he took my suggestions seriously. Then insisted I go with him to the meeting. But we met at Capitol Grill the night before to go over the final proposal."

"And?" Chessy said, leaning forward eagerly.

Kylie grimaced. "I freaked. I mean completely freaked out. I saw someone who reminded me of my father. I'm so embarrassed over it now, but to me it was real. It was like looking at him. He was just a few tables away and I lost it. Complete meltdown and panic attack."

"Oh honey, I'm so sorry," Chessy said, her face drawn in sympathy.

"So Jensen gets all worried and goes into alpha protective mode."

"Okay, stop a moment and let me savor that image," Chessy said, shivering in exaggerated delight. "Because that is just too good not to imagine."

Kylie laughed. "At the time I didn't even really notice, but yeah, he's pretty impressive in alpha protective mode. Not the kind of guy I'd usually even give a second glance but I have to admit, he made me feel . . . safe."

Chessy smiled. "I know that feeling well. Tate does the same for me. I just feel . . . safe. Like nothing can ever hurt me. That he'd go to the wall for me and never allow anything to happen to me. So? Go on. What happened next?"

"He took me home and I was all prepared to thank him, say good night, retreat to my bedroom and die of embarrassment. Only he insisted on staying. And not only staying, but he was going to sleep in my bed."

Chessy's eyes went wide. "Holy shit. Did y'all have sex?"

Kylie shook her head. "No, here's where it gets funny. At the time? Not so much. But now, yeah, I can laugh about it."

"I'm all ears."

"He was so gentle and understanding. The way he looks at me. I can't explain it. It just makes me warm inside, you know?"

"Yeah, I know."

"He told me to handcuff him to the bed so I'd feel safe with him. So I'd know he couldn't hurt me."

Chessy nearly choked on the tea she'd just taken a sip of. She put the glass down, her mouth gaping open. "And did you?"

Kylie nodded.

"Holy shit," Chessy breathed. "Now that is a guy I can never imagine giving up control. Especially to a woman. I mean he seems like the ultimate dominant guy. Like Tate and Dash, you know?"

Kylie nodded. "Yeah, I do know. I was shocked. But I was also so freaked-out that I didn't really know what to do. Part of me wanted him gone so I could huddle in my bed and put the covers over my head and die of shame by myself. The other part of me really didn't want him to leave but at the same time him being in my bed freaked me out."

Chessy's eyes softened with understanding. "I think that's pretty amazing that he offered that. I mean, he put himself in a vulnerable situation for you. So you'd feel safe. That's pretty awesome."

"Yeah," Kylie said softly. "So he goes to bed, fully dressed, and I'm in my granny pajamas. I handcuffed one of his hands because it looked really uncomfortable and I was humiliated that the only way I could let a man sleep in my bed was with him handcuffed and helpless."

"Don't ever feel shame for your need to feel safe, honey."

Kylie huffed out a breath. "So we both go to sleep, only I had a nightmare about my father. Seeing someone who resembled him so closely in the restaurant just brought it all back, and then Jensen was calling my name. Telling me to wake up, that I was safe with him. And I don't know. I just kind of freaked. I dove into his arms, only one of his hands was still handcuffed to the bed and all I could think about was wanting both of his arms around me. So I tore off the handcuffs and he held me. Just held me and told me to go back to sleep, that nothing could hurt me, that he'd never allow it. So we slept that way the rest of the night and I've never had a better night's sleep once I was in his arms."

Chessy smiled. "That's wonderful, Kylie. He sounds delicious. And so tender and caring. I mean, what more can you ask for? The guy is drop-dead gorgeous, extremely alpha and protective. And he made huge concessions for you so you'd feel safe. He put you and your needs before his. Not many guys are willing to do that."

"I know," Kylie said softly. "And the thing is, Chessy, I do feel safe with him. I can't explain it. He's the kind of guy who should terrify me. He's the kind of man I'd usually steer clear of by a mile. And yet the way he looks at me, the way he is around me. I just melt into a puddle. It's ridiculous."

"Not ridiculous," Chessy refuted. "Sounds to me like you've got yourself a solid winner. So you're going on a date tomorrow night?"

"Well, he wanted to do it tonight but I told him I had dinner plans with you so he changed it to Saturday. And then he's going out of town for the first three days of next week. I guess that'll give me plenty of time to think about our date and figure out what the hell I'm doing and if I'm in way over my head," she said ruefully.

"You should have called me!" Chessy exclaimed. "We could have rescheduled."

Kylie shook her head adamantly. "No. Friends come first and I've been worried about you, Chessy. I know you've been lonely and I know what that feels like. I don't want you to feel like that ever. You come first."

"You're not the bitch you call yourself," Chessy said firmly. "You have the biggest heart of anyone I know, honey. If I ever hear you disparage yourself again I'll kick your ass. And I love you for it, but in the future? If you have an opportunity to go out with a delicious specimen of an alpha male like Jensen? We *will* reschedule. You and I can get together anytime. I think it's wonderful that you're venturing into the dating world. It's time, Kylie. You're ready. You need to do this for yourself. Prove to yourself that not all men are assholes."

Kylie's heart filled with love for her friend. She missed Joss and couldn't wait for her to return, even though it was selfish since Joss was on her honeymoon and should enjoy every minute of it. But Kylie loved Chessy and Joss. They were solid. Her anchor after Carson died. The only two people who'd kept her sane and had given her a reason to keep living.

They didn't know that. Maybe they'd never know how much Kylie depended on them. But she couldn't fathom her life without them.

"I'm going to try," Kylie said truthfully. "I'm tired of being a coward. Of hiding from the world. Maybe Jensen is the one. Maybe he's not. But at the very least he's my opportunity to work on my courage."

"That's my girl," Chessy said. "And you know I'm going to want to hear all the juicy details Sunday. If you don't call me, I'm so coming over. But in the afternoon. You know, in case Jensen sleeps over again."

She winked as she said the last and Kylie rolled her eyes.

"Don't get ahead of yourself," Kylie said dryly. "Remember the fact that I had to handcuff him to the bed in order for him to be able to sleep in the same space. I'm such a head case that I wouldn't count on me having sex with anyone for a long time."

Chessy's eyes sparkled. "At the risk of sounding disloyal, my money's on Jensen. I bet you two do the deed much sooner than you think."

"Gee, thanks," Kylie muttered.

But at the same time, hope unfurled in her heart like a flower budding in the spring. Could she be intimate with Jensen? Was it possible that he was the man who could get past her barriers? The fact that she wasn't melting down over the mere thought said a whole lot. The fact that she was actually anticipating the act itself said far more.

TEN

KYLIE wiped her hands down her jeans, removing the dampness from her palms. She stared at her reflection in the mirror, critically surveying her appearance. This was stupid. Utterly ridiculous for her to be so worked up over a date.

Women dated. People dated. And now, apparently, *she* dated. It was an absolutely ordinary occurrence in the world. Except that her world and the rest of the world were two entirely different things. In her world, she didn't date. Didn't pursue relationships or encourage men's attention.

Only now it would seem she did indeed date and she was in fact trying to gain the attention of Jensen.

She couldn't figure out if it annoyed her or pleased her, this tilting of her universe. On one hand she was actually looking forward to the evening with Jensen. Craved his company and how safe and comforted she felt around him. Was she simply using him because he was a security blanket of sorts? And would she chicken out the minute things became more intimate?

Because she sincerely doubted Jensen was just signing up to be a source of comfort. He was a man. An attractive, mouthwateringly gorgeous man. Of course he'd expect sex at some point.

He'd pretty much said as much. The question was how patient he'd be.

She wasn't opposed, in theory, to the idea of having sex with him. The *idea* appealed. But what appealed more to her was her being *capable* of having a physical relationship with him. Of being able to overcome the panic that such an idea instilled within her.

So, in fact, it did mean that she was using him. For all the wrong reasons.

She closed her eyes, willing herself to stop being so analytical. Did it matter *why* she wanted to be around him? Did it matter the reasons why if they ended up having sex? To most men reasons would be very far down their list. They wanted sex. Most red-blooded men did. It was the women who got all touchy-feely and analytical over the reasons behind sex.

Jensen wanted her. He'd made that clear enough. But *what* exactly did he want? How much? Would he be satisfied with physical release? Hot sex? Or did he want more? Something she couldn't give him?

Her head was spinning and she was making herself crazy over a simple date. She'd changed clothes four times, each time deeming herself too obvious. Too blatant, like she was seeking his approval. But what normal woman wouldn't want to look good for her date? Especially a man like Jensen who oozed sensuality just by breathing.

She'd finally opted for jeans and a comfortable top. Casual. Not too desperate. She wanted to appear as though she were comfortable with him. And that wouldn't be a stretch because she did feel at ease with him even if she hadn't in the beginning. All of that had changed during the night he'd spent with her.

Trust, something she didn't readily give to anyone, had been formed the night he'd held her through her nightmares and offered her comfort. A part of her recognized that this man wouldn't hurt her. Her mind protested, used to self-preservation. Her heart, on the other hand, had quickly offered its trust, leaving her brain to wonder if she'd lost what little of her sanity she had left.

The doorbell rang, spurring her into action. She nervously gave herself one last glance in the mirror, satisfied that she looked . . . normal. Then she went to answer the door.

Jensen filled her doorway the minute she opened the door. He loomed there, larger than life. Tall, muscular. Strong. To her relief, he too had dressed casually. Faded jeans that conformed to his body and made her want to get an eyeful of how his ass filled them out. And a simple T-shirt that stretched over his muscled arms and chest.

If she thought he looked sexy in his business clothing, seeing him in jeans and a T-shirt was mind-blowing. God, was she actually *lusting* after him? She hadn't thought herself capable of feeling physical attraction to a man—any man. And yet here she stood, drinking her fill and having decidedly naughty thoughts.

Who knew she had it in her?

Instead of inspiring panic, she was filled with the unfamiliar sensation of . . . optimism. She offered him a genuine smile and then gestured for him to come inside. He was carrying two grocery bags and had a bottle of wine tucked under one arm.

"Let me help you," she offered.

"Nope," he said. "I'll dump it all in the kitchen and get started. I'd love for you to join me and keep me company, though."

She followed behind and slid onto one of the barstools as he unloaded the items from the grocery bags.

"What's on the menu?" she asked lightly.

"Aussie chicken," he said. "Ever heard of it?"

She shook her head.

"Then you're in for a treat. It's basically baked chicken breasts in a homemade honey mustard sauce with bacon, mushrooms and cheese. Can't go wrong with that combination."

She took in his warm smile, soaked it up like an addict in need of a fix. He just had a settling effect on her. She worried she'd become too dependent, that she'd need him too much. She'd never considered herself a clingy person. Just the opposite. She avoided relationships, any bonds with people other than her immediate circle of friends. But she could well see how dependent she could become on Jensen and that scared her. She didn't want anyone but herself to have any control over her happiness.

But was she truly happy?

Even she knew the answer to that one. She wasn't unhappy but neither was she happy. She just . . . existed. Went through the motions. Lived day-to-day on autopilot. Wasn't it time for her to wake up and live? *Really* live?

"It sounds delicious," she said, huskiness lacing her voice.

He smiled again and she caught her breath. Good God. She was sitting here *lusting* over him. Her! She breathed in, savoring the newness of such overwhelming emotions. Feelings she'd kept under tight rein her entire life. What was happening to her? Had she merely been waiting for him? Was he the one who'd break through her barriers and make her get over her fears?

"How did your dinner with Chessy go?" he asked as he set to work preparing the dish.

He poured two glasses of wine and slid one across the counter to her. She picked it up and brought it to her lips, inhaling the aroma. She rarely drank and usually only with friends. Alcohol made her uneasy because she was intimately acquainted with the dark side of it. Being around people drinking heavily was something she always avoided.

"It went well," she said, after sipping the drink. "She's lonely. Tate's so busy with his job."

Jensen glanced up, his expression seeking. "She unhappy?"

Kylie grimaced. She shouldn't have said anything. She felt like the worst sort of friend betraying Chessy's confidence. But there was something about Jensen that caught her off guard and made her relax. Her lips loosened around him and she found herself telling him things she'd never share with anyone else.

"I'm not going to betray your confidence, Kylie," Jensen said in a low voice. "We're just having a conversation. Nothing more. You don't have to worry about me involving myself in someone else's relationship. Besides, Tate and I are mere acquaintances, brought together by circumstance more than friendship. I like him and Chessy both. I'd hate to know she was unhappy."

"It's me who's betraying a confidence," Kylie muttered. "For some reason I find myself blurting stuff out to you."

"That's not a bad thing," he observed, staring thoughtfully at her. If there had been any hint of triumph in his eyes, it would have annoyed her, but there was just intent consideration.

"I'd like you to feel as though you can talk to me about anything," he continued.

Kylie sighed. "Tate's just super busy and Chessy is lonely. I understand that feeling but unlike me, she isn't used to it. She's outgoing and bubbly. She needs to be surrounded by people and she needs more of Tate's time than she's currently getting."

"Does he know how she feels?" Jensen asked. "Just from observing them the few times I've been around them, I'd say the man worships the ground she walks on. Most men, upon learning their woman was the least bit unhappy, would move heaven and earth to correct the problem. But if he doesn't know . . ."

"He doesn't," Kylie supplied. "Or at least she hasn't confronted him. It's a difficult position she's in because she feels that if she were to tell Tate she's unhappy, he would feel as though he failed her. There was a time we talked about her fear that he was cheating. But she wouldn't confront him because she knew if she ever expressed that kind of doubt in him that it would be a rift that wouldn't be easily mended. She didn't want to give him any hint that she didn't have faith in him. I just want her to be happy. I hate seeing her so sad. It makes me want to smack Tate upside the head and ask him if he even sees what he's doing to his wife."

Jensen grimaced. "That doesn't sound like a fun place for her to be. Worried but unable to voice her fears. I prefer open communication myself. I'd hate for my woman to ever fear speaking to me about anything."

There was an undertone to his statement that was aimed at her. She knew it. He wasn't talking about Chessy and Tate. He was talking about him and her. He was telling her not to fear ever talking to him about anything.

"For some reason I don't seem to suffer that affliction around you," she said in bewilderment. "In fact I'd say it's just the opposite. I can't seem to quit just blurting stuff out. I'm not usually such a blabbermouth."

"Then I'll take that as a compliment," he said, his expression sincere. "I like the idea that you're comfortable enough around me to speak your mind. I hope that it's the beginnings of trust between us."

"I do trust you," she whispered. "I have no idea why. God knows I don't trust *anyone*. But for some reason I feel safe with you and that kind of freaks me out."

He stopped what he was doing and walked around the counter to where she sat. He spun the stool until she faced him and he framed her face in his hands. His eyes glittered with intensity as he stared down at her. She thought he was going to kiss her and he did, just not where she expected.

He pressed his lips tenderly to her forehead and she closed her eyes in pleasure over the simple gesture.

"You *are* safe with me, Kylie," he said as he drew back, his hands still framing her face.

He stroked his thumb over her lips, lips she thought he would kiss.

"If you believe nothing else, you can believe that. You are absolutely safe with me and I don't just mean physically. You are safe in all ways because I will absolutely protect you from anything that could hurt you."

"Why me?" she blurted. "I don't get it. I'm not fishing for compliments, Jensen. It's a sincere question. You can't have to look far for female companionship. You could likely have any woman you wanted. So why are you interested in me? Do you have any idea what you're getting yourself into?"

His smile was so tender that it made her heart leap and speed up.

"I know exactly what I'm getting myself into," he murmured. "As for why you? I can't answer that. Some things just are. And for me that's you. I see beyond the image you present to the world to the woman underneath and that's who I want."

"We're too different," she said in a fretful tone. "And you're a control freak and I'm a control freak. It's not like I have some

OCD thing, but I like things a certain way. I *need* them a certain way. Two control freaks in a relationship? Surely that's a recipe for disaster."

He continued to smile at her, his eyes warm. He didn't seem at all put off by her fretting.

"I understand you far more than you realize," he said softly. "I'm no threat to you, Kylie. For the right woman, I have no issue with relinquishing control. What I'm after has nothing to do with physical submission."

His words puzzled her. He was speaking as though he were dominant. Like Dash and Tate. And he probably was. Which made his interest in her all the more mystifying.

"Are you dominant?" she whispered. "You never really answered me before when I asked if you were like Tate and Dash. I know you said you were you and not them. But that wasn't what I meant. Do you like submissive women? Do you like to dominate them?"

"I prefer submissive women, yes," he said calmly. "Until you I would have said that it was the only kind of relationship I would entertain."

Her heart sped up, thundering in her chest. "You said what you were after had nothing to do with *physical* submission. What does that mean?"

He ran his fingers through her hair, his hands returning to her face as he caressed and stroked over her skin.

"What it means is that I would never act out any of the more physical aspects of dominance and submission with you," he said gently. "Have I ever? Yes. I've been involved in dominant/submissive relationships with other women where I employed the physical components that sometimes accompany such a lifestyle. But I would never ever demand of you what you can't give.

So when I say that what I'm after has nothing to do with physical submission, in effect what I want is your *emotional* surrender."

"I don't know what that means," she said in a low voice. "But it sounds scary. Perhaps even scarier than physical surrender."

He nodded solemnly. "It's certainly more powerful. A woman can give of her body and never share her heart or her soul. A very hollow victory indeed. But a woman who surrenders emotionally to the man who has her care in his hands is a very precious thing. And that's what I want from you, Kylie. Your emotional surrender. Your trust. Your heart. Your soul."

"Wow," she whispered. "You don't ask for much."

He chuckled, the sound low and rumbling from his chest. Then he kissed her forehead again. "You'll get there, baby. Just breathe. Don't overanalyze it. Just breathe and go with it and know I've got you."

She nearly toppled off the stool when he released her to walk back around and resume dinner preparations. Her pulse was racing and she was light-headed. A heady, euphoric feeling took hold, replacing her earlier panic and worry.

She took a steadying sip of the wine and tried not to let how rattled she was show.

Several minutes later, Jensen opened her oven and slipped in the casserole dish. He set the timer and then turned back to her.

"Let's have another glass of wine in the living room while we wait for dinner to finish cooking."

She slid from the stool, hoping she didn't face-plant. She felt giddy and a little silly around him, like a teenager crushing on the quarterback. But then what did she know about such feelings? She'd never experienced them before because she'd never allowed herself to.

He waited for her at the end of the bar and held out his hand for her to take. She slid her fingers through his, enjoying the firm imprint of his hand against hers. They walked into the living room and then simply stood there, hands still entwined.

After a moment, he lifted her hand and pressed a kiss to the inside of her wrist then lowered their clasped hands between them once more.

"Dinner will be ready in half an hour. Would you like to start the movie now or wait and watch it from start to finish after we eat?"

"We can wait," she said breathlessly. "No reason we can't sit and wait, right?"

"None at all," he said in smooth tones.

He led her to the couch and sat, tugging her down beside him.

She was out of her element and she well knew it. She had no idea how to hold cutesy, flirty conversations. What was she supposed to say? Or do? Did they just sit here and stare at each other?

She glanced sideways at Jensen, looking for some clue, but he seemed perfectly content to sit next to her in silence. Several long, painful minutes ensued, the awkwardness growing more pronounced with each passing second.

"Maybe we should wait in the kitchen," she hedged, uncomfortable with the quiet that had descended.

He glanced at her, his gaze indecipherable. It wasn't warm like she'd become accustomed to. Just seeking. Had she committed some dating faux pas she was unaware of? God, she hated this. Surely there were rules or something.

"Look, uhm, you should know I really suck at this," she said lamely.

Amusement glimmered in his eyes. "Breathe, Kylie. Like I told you before. It's all right. We can go back into the kitchen if that makes you more comfortable. Why don't you set the table and I'll check on the progress of the chicken."

Relieved to have something to break the awkwardness, she eagerly rose and headed back to the kitchen. Jensen's hand on her shoulder stopped her just as she reached the bar.

"Relax, okay?"

His voice was soothing and as gentle as his touch. Her shoulder sagged beneath his hand and she turned.

"Sorry," she muttered. "I told you I suck at this. I don't know what I'm supposed to do. I don't date. I don't know how this is supposed to work."

He put his other hand to her shoulder and pulled her carefully into his embrace. He tucked her head beneath his chin and simply hugged her. It baffled her that such a mundane thing as a hug from this man instantly calmed her.

"It's supposed to work however we make it work," he said matter-of-factly. "I have no expectations for you to fulfill, Kylie. I merely want to spend time with you. Share a meal and enjoy your company. That's all. Nothing more."

She groaned. "I'm an idiot. You can say it."

His body shook with laughter and then he patted her on the behind. "Go set the table and let me finish my pièce de résistance."

She busied herself putting out plates and silverware and then got fresh wineglasses and placed the opened bottle on the table just as Jensen took the casserole dish from the oven.

It smelled heavenly and there was oodles of gooey, melty cheese bubbling over the bacon and the chicken. Her stomach rumbled in appreciation as he set it down on the table.

"It looks fabulous," she said. "Is there anything you can't do?

You're like Superman or something. I bet you don't suck at any-thing."

He pretended to give the matter serious consideration before grinning at her. "I guess it'll be up to you to find all my faults. And believe me, the list is long, as I'm sure you've already sur-mised during our somewhat short acquaintance."

She marveled at just how different he seemed around her. Somehow lighter and not as . . . *broody.* She'd had the thought before but it was reinforced all the more now. He no doubt was good for her, but maybe she was also good for him? It made her feel better to think so.

"I don't suppose we did get off on the right foot," she admit-ted ruefully. "I'm willing to admit that I was mistaken about you. You aren't quite the ogre I thought you to be."

He arched one eyebrow as he dished out portions onto the plates. "Not quite? So there's still room for some ogreness in your dissection of me?"

She grinned at the mock seriousness of his question. "That remains to be seen, but I'm willing to give you the benefit of the doubt."

"So very generous, this woman I'm cooking for."

Her smile broadened, all the early awkwardness dissipating. It was starting to feel like a real date. Like two people flirting and verging on the cusp of something new. Good God, an actual relationship even.

Okay, she had to stop that line of thought or a panic attack would hit her full force. She focused instead on the delicious-smelling plate in front of her and dug in with her knife and fork.

The first bite hit all her taste buds in just the right spots. It was perfectly seasoned, tender, the homemade honey mustard sauce utter perfection, and bacon and cheese? It was a well-known fact that it was pretty damn hard to ruin anything by putting bacon and cheese on it.

"This is wonderful," she breathed as she swallowed her second bite. "A man who looks like you and who can cook. I can't imagine why you're still single."

There was a brief flicker in his eyes, gone almost before she registered it was there. But there had been something. A shadow. A remembrance. A sore spot, evidently, judging by that betraying flash. But it was quickly gone, replaced by that warm smile that she loved so much.

"Perhaps I'm merely waiting on the right woman to settle down," he said sagely. "One can never be too finicky when choosing the person they want to spend their life with."

"Boy, did you say a mouthful," she muttered. "I couldn't agree more. Or in my case, it would be more applicable to say that there is no desire to choose that person."

He studied her a moment, pausing in eating his meal. It was that intent, steady stare that told her he was reaching into the heart of her, like he could read her mind and pull out every secret. His scrutiny made her feel vulnerable and she didn't like that at all. Especially when she'd admitted how very safe she felt around him.

"So you never intend to find the right guy? Settle down, have a family, fall in love. Not necessarily in that order mind you. Usually love comes first and then the rest, but these are modern times after all. I'd say there no longer is a rhyme or reason to relationships."

"God, we sound like an episode of Dr. Phil," she said with a grimace.

He laughed. "And yet you avoided the question. Sorry if I'm

getting too philosophical, but you fascinate me and I've made it my mission to figure you out. What makes you tick, what makes you happy. Or rather what it will take to make you happy."

She blinked in surprise. "Why would you care? This is technically our first date. Surely you can't be thinking of all of those things yet."

He shrugged. "One never knows when the one will walk into his life. It pays to be prepared. Besides, like I've said, you fascinate me. You're a puzzle I haven't quite put together yet."

She sighed. "It doesn't take a rocket scientist to figure out I have more issues than *TIME* magazine. You know my history, or at least the major points. No need for all the sordid details. So I'm sure you can understand why I'm not lining them up in the dating department nor am I freaking out because I haven't found my soul mate at the ripe old age of twenty-five. I figure if it does ever happen, I have plenty of time to figure it all out. For now I just concentrate on living. Surviving. Taking it day-by-day. It's what has gotten me this far. If it ain't broke, then don't fix it."

"Such cynicism and pragmatism from someone so young is astounding," he observed. "You lay it out so casually, as if it doesn't bother you one way or another, and yet there's something there. Maybe others don't see it. But I do. You want those things, Kylie. You just haven't worked up the courage to reach out and take them. Nor have you admitted to yourself that you do have needs just like everyone else."

"Do you have a degree in psychology or something?" she asked with narrowed eyes. "Because I swear you sound like a damn shrink."

He chuckled and held up his hands in mock surrender. "Nope. Just observations on life and my experiences with people."

"With women, you mean," she muttered.

"That too," he said, unruffled by her correction.

"Just how many women have you been with?" she blurted. Gah! There she went again. Just spewing stuff out without reason or thought. It made her sound like some jealous shrew. Quickly trying to cover up her gaffe, she amended her statement.

"I mean submissive women. Or have all of your relationships revolved around the dominant/submissive lifestyle?"

"I don't keep count," he said dryly. "There have hardly been enough to need a catalog. I've already told you I don't fuck around nor have I fucked my way through countless women. I'm not that much of a bastard. I've had casual sex, yes. I've had relationships. More than five, less than a dozen."

She blinked in surprise. "How old are you anyway?"

"Thirty-five. You look surprised. Why?"

She shook her head. "Most single thirty-five-year-old men have been with far more than a dozen women. It just surprised me, that's all. I wasn't judging you. Or condemning. I was genuinely curious about your relationships, and if you enjoy having a submissive woman, why then did those relationships end?"

"They weren't the one," he said simply.

His response puzzled her. "How do you know when you meet the one?"

He smiled then, his eyes warming, giving her that heady pleasurable glow that was ever present when he looked at her that way.

"I'll know."

She let out a snort of aggravation. This was a man who could well drive her crazy. Crazier than she already was. Vague. His words full of hidden meaning. Some innuendo she was supposed to catch on to. And maybe she was able to read between the lines but was too chickenshit to admit that or to venture into the area of understanding.

"So you believe in love and all that accompanies it? Undying loyalty, fidelity and trust?"

"Of course. Don't you?"

He seemed genuinely confused that she spoke so blithely of such an important issue. And she supposed it was important to other people. Just not to her. Love to her was a four-letter word and not the good kind. She'd seen the many manifestations of love in her lifetime and she wasn't sold on the concept, even if her two best friends were disgustingly happy and head over heels in love with their husbands. She saw Chessy's unhappiness and knew that love wasn't a cure-all and that in fact, love was often a complication. It certainly wasn't an inconvenience she wanted to suffer.

Love meant giving up the essential part of herself. Her trust. And that wasn't given lightly to anyone. Loving someone meant making yourself vulnerable. It meant placing your emotional well-being into another's hands. No thanks. She'd seen the turmoil Joss had suffered as she and Dash had struggled in their relationship. She saw the effects of love in Chessy's eyes. Saw the hurt and pain brought to you by the letter *L*. Love.

She finally shook her head when she realized he was waiting for an answer to his question.

"I'm not saying I don't believe in it, I guess. I mean obviously Joss loves Dash and he loves her. She loved Carson and Carson loved her. And while I know Chessy is currently unhappy, I do know that she loves Tate and that Tate loves her. But love is messy and complicated. It seems much simpler and safer to just avoid that kind of emotional entanglement."

"You're a hard-core cynic," he murmured. "I hadn't realized just how much of one you were. You're going to be a tough nut to crack, baby, but I'm up for the task. I've never backed down from a challenge and I don't plan to start now."

She stared incredulously at him. The things she'd said to him had sent every other man she'd ever attempted to date running for the door like the hounds of hell were after them. And yet Jensen wasn't remotely put off by her "issues." If anything they seemed to make him more determined to break through those walls she'd erected. Walls that had been solidly in place her entire adult life and most of her childhood.

She'd learned at a very young age how to protect her mind, her sanity. To shut out the world around her and stay in self-preservation mode. It had served her well, but had made personal relationships impossible. Because who wanted to deal with such a head case, much less make a commitment to one?

She glanced down at her plate, surprised to see it was empty, then she looked over at Jensen's to find he too was finished. What now? Once again, she felt the awkwardness of not knowing what came next.

The movie. He had a movie. The plan was to eat dinner and watch a movie. Simple enough. She could handle that.

"You ready for the movie?" she asked, proud of the initiative she took. "I'll just put the plates in the sink and wash them later. Why don't you go start up the movie and I'll bring us both a glass of wine, unless you'd prefer something else?"

"Wine is fine. Your company is what I want most. Anything else is just bonus material."

Damn it. What to even say to that? He was seducing her with mere words and that heart-melting, warm, fuzzy smile he sent

her way every so often. He hadn't even tried to get into her pants
and they were already halfway down.

Disgusted with her raging hormones—why had they picked
now to rear their ugly head?—she took the plates and did a
quick rinse before leaving them in the sink to take care of later.

She took a moment to compose herself and calm her racing
pulse down. It was just a movie. *For God's sake, get it together.*

She poured two glasses of wine, though she had no intention
of drinking hers. She'd already had her limit and the last thing
she wanted was a fuzzy head. Jensen did that to her all on his
own. No alcohol needed, though the liquid courage aspect
might be appealing.

When she entered the living room, Jensen was leaning back
on the couch looking very much at home. The remote was in his
hand and he had the movie paused at the beginning. She didn't
even know what they were watching. Did it matter? She doubted
she'd remember much of it anyway.

He held out his hand to her, not for the wine, but to take her
hand once she placed the glasses on the coffee table. She allowed
him to slide his fingers through hers and pull her gently to the
couch beside him.

"There, that's better," he murmured. "Now the evening can
begin."

"What are we watching?" she asked.

"Some zombie apocalypse movie," he said with a twist of his
lips. "It seemed like a good idea at the time. I had to be careful
with my selection so you didn't read anything into my choice or
my intentions."

"So should I worry that you'll bite me and infect me with
some virulent strain of some super virus?" she said dryly.

He chuckled. "I like your sense of humor, Kylie. It fits mine well. Though some would likely argue that neither of us has one. But I think we fit just fine."

Her cheeks warmed because no, no one had ever accused her of having a sense of humor, twisted or not.

He laid his arm over the top of the couch, a silent invitation for her to move closer. She hesitated at first, not wanting to be obvious, but she found herself gravitating to the warmth and strength of his body.

Soon she was cuddled up next to him, his arm hung loosely over her shoulders. His fingers danced idly over her upper arm, eliciting a trail of chill bumps. His touch was like fire, even through her shirt. She tried to focus on the movie but found herself increasingly distracted by her proximity to his body.

At one point she turned to look at him only to find him staring intently at her, his eyes glowing. So very warm. Comforting. Unconsciously she leaned in, not even realizing what she was doing. He met her advance and brushed his lips softly across hers.

It was an electrical shock to her system. She shivered uncontrollably and then he deepened the kiss, his tongue swiping over her lips, licking and then sliding inside to brush over hers.

He tasted of the wine they'd drunk. That and something altogether different. Heady. Masculine. The taste was undefinable. But she liked it. A lot.

She breathed out a soft sigh as his arms wrapped around her, turning her more solidly so the angle was better. His lips never left hers, his mouth devouring hers hungrily.

She was lost in a cascade of sensation, dizzying, intensely pleasurable and also warm and soothing. Her breasts ached, pressed flat against his chest. Her nipples beaded, pushing outward as if begging for his attention. His mouth.

Shocked that she'd have such a thought, she went still, the strong beat of his heart thudding against her chest. His respirations were fast, rushing into her mouth and over her face.

And then he lowered her to the couch, angling his body over hers, pressing hard and heavy down on her. Panic snaked up her spine as dark memories surfaced, clawing their way to the present.

She lost her sense of awareness. Of where she was and who she was with. All she knew was that she was in immediate danger. His strength overwhelmed her. She felt helpless. Weak. Unable to prevent whatever he wanted to do to her.

Blackness gushed through her mind, wiping away all sense of euphoria and safety. Her chest caught on fire as she desperately tried to breathe but found no air. Her throat constricted as she tried to scream. To beg him to stop. To have mercy. Not to hurt her.

And then self-preservation kicked in and she began to fight. She went wild beneath this predator, wanting only to escape the harm he intended. She scratched, kicked, and finally was able to gather enough breath to scream.

Hysteria rose sharp, quickly overwhelming her. She was unaware of the firm hands around her wrists, holding them so she couldn't hurt him or herself. Of the soothing voice calling her name. Telling her it was all right.

She dimly registered those things, but they were so distant. All she was cognizant of was her will to survive. Not to ever again endure what she'd endured before.

Tears bathed her face and she became aware of a high keening sound. It was coming from her. God, it was her making that god-awful sound. Why wouldn't it stop?

"Kylie! Kylie! Listen to me. It's me, Jensen. You're safe, baby.

God, please come back to me. I won't hurt you. I'd never hurt you."

The entire room was spinning like some crazy Tilt-A-Whirl at the fair. Nausea rose, swift and violent, and she bolted upward, the bands around her wrists suddenly gone.

She hunched over in a protective position, shielding her most vulnerable parts. Her ribs, her belly, places that could easily be injured. Wetness soaked into her shirt sleeves and she realized she was sobbing. Giant, silent sobs welling from the deepest recesses of her chest.

A strong hand hesitantly touched her shoulder and she flinched, turning, determined to ward off an attack.

"Kylie, God, baby. It's me. Please, baby. Look at me. *See* me."

Jensen's worried plea broke through the haze. Some of the panic dissipated, leaving her with only humiliation and abject despair. She was broken. Broken. Unfixable. Nothing would ever be right. Not for her. Never again.

She buried her face in her arms and rocked back and forth, too mortified to even look at him. How crazy he must think she was. Not think. Knew.

"Please, just go away," she begged, her voice muffled by her arms. "Please. I can't bear it. I'm so sorry. Just go. Please. I'm sorry."

"Goddamn it, you *won't* apologize for this," he seethed.

The fury in his voice made her wary again and she risked a quick peek at him to gauge his temper, readying herself for the violence that would surely follow.

But he was sitting a distance from her, almost as if he were careful to maintain a barrier between them. A barrier *she'd* erected. Damn it, but when would she stop freaking out? Could she ever expect to have a normal life? Was it too much to ask?

Another sob welled low in her throat and tears ran like rivers down her cheeks.

"Tell me what to do to help you, baby."

Jensen's voice was pleading. He sounded desperate and as out of sorts as she was.

"It's not your fault," she choked out. "It's me. I'm sorry. It's me. You didn't do anything wrong."

"The hell I didn't," he bit out. "It was a stupid, boneheaded thing of me to have done. I got carried away. That's on me. Not you. Goddamn it, Kylie. I'm so sorry."

She lifted her head, shaking it almost violently, tears still running in rivulets down her face.

"No," she said, her voice cracking. "Not your fault. Please, just go. I just want to be alone."

He looked uncertain. It was obvious he didn't want to leave her in her present state but neither did he want to further upset her.

"I'll be okay," she said, attempting to reassure him. "I'll be fine. Just go. I've ruined everything."

"I don't want to leave you like this," he said, fury lacing his voice. "I did this to you. I reminded you of him and I'd goddamn die before ever making you feel that way with me. I can't stomach the thought."

She lowered her head miserably to her arms, grief overwhelming her. Jensen had been nothing but kind and gentle with her. So very understanding. And she'd repaid him by making him feel like some abusive asshole. Her father. Oh God, why couldn't she control her reactions? Why did she have to freak out the minute things got heavy?

"Kylie?"

His voice was tentative and seeking. But she couldn't look at him. Not knowing how she'd made him feel. She shook her head, the words sad and defeated as they slipped from her lips.

"Please just go, Jensen. That's what you can do for me. And please, don't bear the burden for what happened. It isn't your fault. You were nothing but gentle and patient with me. I'm mortified and just want to be alone right now."

"That's the very last thing you need," he huffed out in frustration.

She looked up to see him run an agitated hand through his cropped hair. He looked utterly indecisive, something she'd normally never associate with him. He was a man who was self-assured, if nothing else.

"Please," she whispered. "Just go. I'll be fine. It's nothing I haven't dealt with before."

Her statement only seemed to enrage him more. "There's no reason for you to deal with this alone. But if I'm making things worse, I'll go. It's not what I want, but for you, I'll do it. But I don't have to fucking like it or agree with it."

She managed a shaky smile through watery eyes.

He hesitated, as if deciding whether to touch her or do anything other than say good-bye. Then finally he rose from the couch, defeat burning in his eyes. She hated that she'd done that to him. That she'd taken him down with her in her never-ending mire of despair.

This was a lesson to her. A hard one, but a lesson nonetheless. She wasn't capable of a normal, healthy relationship with anyone. She was an idiot to have dreamed, even for a moment, that it was possible.

ELEVEN

JENSEN got behind the wheel of his car and pounded the steering wheel in frustration. Goddamn it! It went against every instinct to leave Kylie in the state she was. Only the knowledge that his presence was making it worse, that she was utterly humiliated and he was only adding to her distress, had convinced him to go.

What he wanted to do was barge back in, take her in his arms and hold her the entire night. Even if it meant spending another night handcuffed to her bed.

The idea that he'd brought back even a moment of her past gutted him. That going forward she would associate her abuse at the hands of a monster with him was more than he could stomach.

Seeing her pale and shaken, utterly broken and in despair, had reopened old wounds of his own. Memories long suppressed crowded to the surface making him feel as helpless as he had as a kid, watching his mother being abused, powerless to make it stop and then feeling the brunt of his father's rage when he tried to intervene.

No, Kylie wasn't the only one who had demons to fight. But it was evident that she'd never found a way to cope. She, unlike

Jensen, was still rooted solidly in the past. It was as alive and vivid in her mind as if it had happened yesterday.

How the hell was he supposed to break through? How could he ever gain her trust? And why was it so important to him that he did?

Kylie was a woman who was all wrong for him and yet so very right at the same time. She was nothing like the other women he'd involved himself with. She was fragile and so very breakable and being around her meant suppressing everything of himself that made him who he was.

Was she worth it?

As soon as the question fluttered through his mind he already knew the answer. Knew he'd already committed himself to the fact that she was very much worth the effort. But for the first time, failure seemed a possibility and he was not accustomed to failing in anything. Not since he was a child.

While he sat in the driveway of Kylie's home, he picked up his cell phone and scrolled through his contacts for Chessy Morgan's number. He hit Send and then put the phone to his ear, waiting for her to pick up, praying that she would pick up.

"Chessy?" he said when a female voice answered. "This is Jensen Tucker, Dash's partner," he added hastily so she wouldn't assume it was a telemarketer and hang up.

"Hi, Jensen."

Her voice was friendly and wary at the same time, as if she was puzzled over him calling her. Hell, he couldn't blame her. They'd only met once, though Dash had given Jensen Tate's and Chessy's numbers in case there were problems while Dash and Joss were away.

"You know Kylie and I had a date tonight," he said bluntly. "It didn't go well. At all."

"Oh no," Chessy said in a stricken voice. "What happened? Is she okay?"

"No, she's not," he said grimly. "She was hysterical and then humiliated and embarrassed. She insisted I leave and she doesn't need to be alone right now. I thought maybe you could check in on her. I don't like leaving her this way but neither will I stay and add to her stress."

"Of course. Thank you so much for calling, Jensen. It was very thoughtful of you to do. I'll come right over. She won't like it, but I'm pushy that way and she loves me, even if I piss her off."

Jensen smiled, some of the tension easing from his shoulders. Kylie would be in good hands. Caring hands. She'd be with someone who loved her and wouldn't allow herself to be pushed away. Not like Jensen had.

"Thank you," Jensen said sincerely. "I'm very concerned about her. I . . . care . . . about her," he said carefully.

"I think that much is obvious," Chessy said softly. "Try not to worry, Jensen. I'll call you if things don't get better or they worsen."

Jensen thanked her again and then hung up, backing out from Kylie's driveway before he gave in to his impulse to burst back through her door and take care of her himself.

IT was a long time before Jensen drifted into an uneasy sleep. And when sleep did finally come, so too did the nightmares he'd thought he'd left behind.

Kylie's panic and stress had opened a door he'd firmly shut on his past. It brought back so much of what he'd tried to forget. To shove firmly to the back of his mind never to haunt him again.

He'd told Kylie they shared far more in common than she

realized, but he'd never intended for her to know just how much. He wouldn't burden her with that. Ever.

He woke in the firm grasp of a nightmare. He came awake with a gasp, sweat soaking his skin. His fingers curled into fists, lashing out at an unseen attacker. Someone trying to hurt not him, but Kylie. Kylie had replaced himself, his mother, in his nightmares and helplessness gripped him, just as it had so many years ago when he'd been forced to stand by, unable to prevent his father from hurting either of them.

Only now it was Kylie. Hurting. Crying. And he was as helpless now as he had been then. A vulnerability he'd sworn never to suffer again.

He rolled to his side, his breaths coming short and ragged, the images still too bright in his mind for him to settle. What was Kylie doing right now? Was she being tortured in her sleep just as he was? And was there hope for either of them?

Or were they too fucked-up to ever be able to build a solid foundation?

Being with her was a hell in itself. Being without her was worse. But if he hurt her . . . He closed his eyes, warding off the invading darkness, the violent spiral spinning round and round his head.

He cursed the fact he was leaving the next day and welcomed it in turns. He hated the thought of being away from Kylie that long, of not knowing how she was doing. If she was eating and sleeping. Taking proper care of herself. But he also welcomed the break. Perhaps it was what they both needed. It wasn't what he wanted, but it could well be what he needed.

A break. Like they were some longstanding couple in a relationship where one or both needed to take a step back and gain perspective. They weren't a couple. They'd only had one official date.

The question was whether she'd ever give them—him—another chance or if he'd fucked up any possibility at something special with her. They were kindred spirits. Both wounded souls in need of solace. She was a much-needed balm to his senses, to those dark memories that lurked just beneath the surface. But what was he for her?

A nauseated feeling entered his gut once again at the thought that his touch had made her think even momentarily of the sick fuck who'd abused her. It honest-to-God made him want to vomit.

"I can't give you up, Kylie," he whispered. "Even if I never had you to begin with. I can't just walk away even if that's what you beg me to do."

He closed his eyes on the fervent vow, holding it close, like a talisman.

The next four days would be the longest of his life. But when he returned? He was coming back to Kylie and whatever it took, they'd face down her demons together.

TWELVE

KYLIE closed her eyes, mentally getting it back together before she refocused on the stack of memos in front of her. Chessy's admonishment still rang in her ears. Her friend hadn't wanted her to go into work Monday. Or Tuesday for that matter. Now it was Wednesday and perhaps Chessy had seen the inevitability of her trying to make her friend stay home because she hadn't gotten her usual morning phone call, nor had Chessy come over to try and persuade her not to go into work.

It should have comforted Kylie that Jensen had cared enough to ask Chessy to come over, that he hadn't wanted her to be alone, but somehow Chessy seeing her at her worst just made the edge of humiliation worse. Chessy had insisted on staying the night, and she'd been there when Kylie had woken, screaming, in the throes of a nightmare. God. The idea of anyone seeing her like that made her sick.

It was bad enough Jensen had witnessed two meltdowns already.

She opened her eyes, though the papers still swam in her vision. Her head ached vilely, the product of sleepless nights. Instead of seeking rest, she'd made herself stay awake, too afraid to slide into the blackness of her dreams. She was safe as long as she was awake and able to control her thoughts, her memories. Only when she slid into sleep did her past torment her.

Eventually she'd *have* to sleep and hopefully by then she'd be so exhausted that her body would shut down and she would sleep dreamlessly.

If she were completely honest with herself, she'd admit that she missed Jensen's presence in the office. With it just being her for the few days Jensen was gone, the office seemed bigger, so quiet. Intimidating. She hadn't realized until now just how safe she felt when he was just down the hall. Or in her office bugging her.

She imagined whatever had been between her and Jensen, or whatever it was he wanted, was impossible now. He'd likely keep his distance from her, and who could blame him? Who wanted a stark raving lunatic to deal with?

She glanced at the clock, willing the hours to pass. Not so she could go home and exist in solitude, avoiding Chessy and her concerns. But she was counting the hours until Jensen returned.

Tomorrow. Which meant one more night where she'd do whatever it took to stay awake. Exhaustion was heavy in her veins, bearing down on her shoulders and making her mind muggy and fuzzy.

She lay her head briefly on her desk, resting it on the piles of paperwork to sort through. Just a moment to close her eyes. It was all she needed.

She gave a soft sigh and let her eyelashes flutter closed only to fly open when she heard a noise at her office door. She whipped her head up, instantly regretting that action. The room spun dizzyingly around her as she drank in the sight of Jensen standing in her office door, a grim expression on his face.

Her heart sped up and it shamed her, the surge of utter relief she felt that he was *back*. A whole day early. She was positively *weak* with relief.

"What the hell have you done to yourself?" he asked, his voice hoarse with concern. "Jesus Christ, Kylie, have you even slept at all while I've been gone?"

She rose defensively, standing straight up, her fingers clenched into tight balls on her desk.

She started to say she was just fine and that it was none of his business, but the room seemed to blacken around her, and she had the sudden urge to sit back down.

She heard Jensen's biting curse from across the room, seemingly a mile away. And then strangely, she found herself on the floor with no recollection of how she got there.

Her last conscious thought was Jensen's worried calling of her name. But blackness surrounded her, lulling her with its soft embrace, and she reached for it, because within it she found peace. Finally. Jensen was here. She was safe. She could let go now.

JENSEN quickly gathered Kylie into his arms, pulling her close, checking to make sure she was breathing. He suspected she'd merely worked herself into exhaustion and probably hadn't slept the entire time he'd been gone, but he couldn't be too certain.

The soft puffs of her exhalations, the slow rise and fall of her chest, soothed the raw edge of his temper—and his worry.

She looked like hell, and yet she was still the most beautiful woman he'd ever seen. Dark smudges seemed permanently imprinted below her eyes. Her face looked thinner, drawn. If he thought she looked fragile before, she looked even more so now.

She'd reached that breaking point. The one he'd feared so much. And now it was up to him to go in, take over, and make damn sure she got the care she needed.

He stood, bearing her slight weight with him. Uncaring of leaving the offices unlocked, he carried her into the parking garage and gently laid her in the backseat of his car. When he was sure she was comfortable, he stalked around to the driver's seat and roared the engine to life. He peeled out of the garage going as fast as safety allowed him.

He had only one direction in mind. *His* home. Not hers. Not this time. He'd take her where he knew he could keep her safe, where he could be certain she got the rest she needed as well as the care. And she damn well wasn't going back into work for the rest of the week.

He could work from home and put out any fires that arose. If he knew Kylie, ever efficient Kylie, she'd made certain that everything else that had cropped up had been taken care of. The rest could rot. Dash would be home this weekend and he could take over Monday morning. Kylie wasn't doing a damn thing for a long time if Jensen had any say. And he would.

Kylie had reached her breaking point and *goddamn it* but he'd pushed her solidly over the edge. It horrified him, was still an ache in his gut, that he'd reminded her of past hurts. It set his teeth on edge. He only wanted to make it right, however that had to be done. And he only knew one way to do that.

It meant pushing her, but in a different way. He only wanted to take care of her. To allow her to lean on someone else, something he was certain she'd never done. She was a solitary figure, a reflection of himself in many ways. Two lonely, scarred souls. Maybe together they could heal.

Somehow he had to break past her barriers, follow the path

to the very heart and soul of her and prove that she could trust him. That she could rely on him, that he'd never willingly hurt her. Nothing in his current thoughts even alluded to sex. That could wait. Forever if necessary.

This wasn't about sex or making love. He couldn't very well lie and say that he didn't want her, that he didn't lie awake at night aching with need to make love to her. But she wasn't ready. And when the time did come, he knew he was going to have to do something he'd never done with any other woman.

Relinquish control.

It wasn't an entirely comfortable thought. It made him feel . . . vulnerable. But however vulnerable he felt, the emotion was tenfold for Kylie. For her he could and would make the ultimate sacrifice. She was worth it. He knew it to his bones.

Some things were just meant to be and he and Kylie were one of those things. He'd recognized it the moment they'd met. She'd been unable to meet his gaze. She was understandably skittish around him. But something about her fragility and the iron core he saw, the resolve and strength in her even as fragile as she'd seemed, just struck a chord with him.

Here was a woman who was meant for him and he hoped to hell he was meant for her.

He'd never been a big believer in fate or destiny, but the moment he'd laid eyes on Kylie he'd realized that she *was* his destiny. The hell of it was whether he would be hers.

He pulled into his drive and quickly got out, opening the door to the backseat where Kylie still lay unconscious. He wondered if she'd slept at all during his absence. He needed to call Chessy. He'd touched base with her only once, the morning after when Chessy had told him she'd spent the night and Kylie had awakened screaming from nightmares.

He closed his eyes briefly as the pain of that phone conversation hit him all over again. The knowledge that he'd done that to her. Had pushed her too far too fast too soon. He'd been remiss in not checking in more frequently with Chessy, but guilt had kept him from making another call. He'd been a fool. It wasn't a mistake he'd make again. Ever.

Not again. This time it would all be up to her. She was in the driver's seat except when it came to matters of her health. That he would solidly take over and he felt zero remorse for what he was embarking on. Kylie needed someone. And that someone was going to be him.

He gathered her gently in his arms and carried his precious bundle inside, kicking the door shut behind him. Bypassing the living room, he walked into his bedroom and eased her down on the bed.

She never even stirred when he pulled the covers from beneath her and then repositioned her so her head was resting on a pillow. He slipped off her shoes but left her clothed. He was in no way taking advantage of her weakened state and she'd be freaked-out enough when she woke in a strange bed. He wanted no question in her mind that he'd not so much as touched her.

He slid the covers up over her body and then tenderly pushed the strands of hair from her face, tucking them behind one ear.

For a long moment he simply stood there staring down at her, filled with the sense of rightness. She belonged here. In his bed. In his home. She didn't know it yet, but this was where she was the safest. Where he could protect her from whatever threatened her. He'd move heaven and earth to ensure she felt protected.

Had she ever truly felt safe with anyone except her brother? He knew she had good friends, a tight circle of people, only a handful. But he wondered if any one of them ever truly saw to the heart of her. If she ever confided her darkest fears and secrets.

Everything he'd learned about her had been from a third party. But he wanted her to trust him enough to share her past with him herself. Not because he had any morbid curiosity. What he did know sickened him. He simply wanted her trust and knew it wouldn't be given easily.

But she'd already said that she trusted him on some level. Had said somewhat in bewilderment that she seemed to just blurt out things to him she wouldn't ordinarily confide. That had to mean something, didn't it?

Only time would tell. He was a patient man when the reward was worth it. He hadn't become the success he was by being impulsive or impatient. And he knew that Kylie would present the biggest challenge of his life. Be the ultimate test of his patience and endurance.

He'd have to be strong enough for the both of them because she needed that above all else. And perhaps she would chase his own demons away. She'd certainly challenge his entire lifestyle, his dominance, things he'd ordinarily never surrender to any woman.

She required special handling. He knew this, acknowledged it. It was new territory for him and he didn't try to delude himself into thinking it would be easy. He *needed* control. He didn't just desire it. It wasn't some kink he enjoyed. It was a necessary component of his existence and yet he'd give it up without a moment's thought for this fragile woman lying in his bed.

It was unnerving. He could admit that. Tendrils of fear clutched at him, because for the first time in his life he was contemplating giving up the one thing he held dear above all else.

Control. It wasn't something he'd ever do lightly. It wasn't something he'd even ever considered until now.

Love was sacrifice. It was making the ultimate compromise.

Love? Was that what he felt for Kylie?

He shook his head in confusion. He wasn't at all sure *what* his feelings for this woman were. It was certainly too soon to be in love with her. Their relationship was tenuous at best. They had only a fledgling trust that had begun to build and that may have all been ruined on their last night together.

He certainly felt more for her than he'd ever felt for another woman. That much he could acknowledge. But he'd never considered himself in love with a woman before. To be so would have meant relinquishing control over his tightly held emotions. And he'd never entertained such a thing. Until now. Until Kylie.

"Fuck me," he muttered.

He was in deep. Way deep. And this was by far not a slam dunk. The path before him was long, winding and uncertain at best. It would be the biggest risk of his life. And it all came down to his earlier question. Was she worth it?

Even as he posed the question again, his answer was still the same.

Yeah, she was worth it. God only knew why but there it was. He couldn't simply walk away from her, no matter that it was the path of least resistance.

He was stuck, for lack of a better word. In between a rock and a hard place no doubt. His fate, his future, was in the hands of this delicate woman and the hell of it was she had no idea. No inkling that she had him so tied in knots.

He massaged his nape, weariness assailing him. He'd wrapped things up in Dallas a day early, eager to be back, to see for himself how Kylie was faring. Now he realized he never should have left, no matter that this contract was huge for his company. She'd needed him and he'd failed her. Just as he'd failed her their last night together.

That would all end now because going forward she was his primary concern.

THIRTEEN

KYLIE climbed through the heavy veil of sleep, realizing at once that something was very different. Oddly, no panic registered. Just a sense of . . . well-being. She felt warm and safe.

She emitted a contented sigh and snuggled deeper into the strong embrace that surrounded her like the thickest blanket.

"Hey, you with me?"

She blinked in surprise, her eyelashes slowly fluttering open. Only to collide with a very familiar, very warm gaze.

Jensen?

She struggled to remember all that had happened. For that matter, where the heck was she?

"Don't panic, baby. You're safe. I've got you."

His murmur of reassurance calmed her but her brow furrowed in silent question.

"You collapsed at the office. Do you remember?"

More came into focus, and she blinked, realizing they were in bed. Together. And not *her* bed.

She pushed herself upward, surprised at the strength it took to perform such a simple function.

"Easy. Don't move too fast," he cautioned. "Take it nice and slow. Breathe for me, okay?"

"I'm okay," she whispered. "Just confused. Where are we?"

"My house. I brought you here. You worried the hell out of me, Kylie. When was the last time you slept? You were obviously running on fumes. Thank God I got there when I did."

She glanced around, taking in the masculine feel of the room. The furnishings. The colors and the huge bed they currently occupied. She was nestled up close to him, their legs entwined.

Immediately her gaze shot downward, and she was relieved to see she was fully clothed. Surely she'd remember if they'd had sex!

He nudged her chin upward with a gentle finger, his gaze sincere.

"Nothing happened, baby. I wouldn't take advantage of you that way. You passed out at the office and I brought you here and put you to bed. You've slept sixteen hours straight."

Her eyes widened in shock and then horror. "Oh my God. I should be at work! What time is it?"

His eyes narrowed and his lips turned down into a frown. "Don't get any ideas. You aren't going near the office any time soon. What you're going to do is stay here and catch up on much-needed rest. You aren't going to so much as lift a finger for the next several days and that's not negotiable."

She had absolutely nothing to say about that. What could she? She stared at him in bewilderment. Why was she here? Why hadn't he washed his hands of her?

"What are you thinking?" he murmured, his brow furrowing in concentration.

"I'm wondering why you're here, or rather why I'm here," she blurted. "I can't imagine why you didn't run as fast and as far away from me as possible after what happened."

His expression softened and he stroked a hand down her arm to rest on her hip.

"I'm not going anywhere, baby. And neither are you for the time being."

"You can't possibly want me after what happened," she whispered.

"I can and I do," he said simply. "You're going to have to work a hell of a lot harder than that to scare me away. You and I are inevitable, Kylie. I've accepted that. Now you have to as well."

Warmth rushed through her veins and with it, relief. Overwhelming, mind-boggling relief. She sagged against the pillow, her strength leaving her. Why was she so relieved? Shouldn't she be pissed? Shouldn't she be arguing the point? Convincing him that *they* weren't possible and that he should leave her alone?

What did it say that the only reaction she could conjure to his autocratic demand was . . . relief?

"I seem to do nothing around you except freak out," she muttered. "You have to be some kind of a masochist to sign up for more."

Humor glinted in those dark eyes. "We'll get through it, baby. Together."

Longing like she'd never experienced flooded her heart. And hope. Genuine and unfettered hope. He wasn't giving up on her. He was sticking it out, and he'd seen her at her absolute worst. If he could get past that, he could get past anything, couldn't he?

She hadn't realized just how much she'd hoped for such a thing until now. She'd braced herself for the inevitability of his rejection. She'd known with absolute certainty that he'd drop her like a bad habit after the ass she'd made of herself on their date. And yet here he was, resolve shining in those beautiful eyes.

"Together," she whispered.

Hope flared in his own eyes. Had he been as convinced that she'd reject him as she had been that he'd reject her?

"Are you hungry?" he asked. "It's obvious you haven't slept since I left, but have you not eaten either?"

She struggled to remember, to get through the fog of the last few days.

"I'll take that as a no," he muttered. "Okay, you stay put. Don't even think about getting out of bed. I have a T-shirt you can change into and some sweat pants too. But that's it. Get up long enough to change if you like but then you get your ass back in bed and wait until I bring you something to eat."

"Yes, sir," she said crisply.

He grinned and tousled her hair affectionately. "I like that attitude, baby."

Then he pushed off the bed and she saw that he too was fully dressed. She was touched by the knowledge that he'd taken such care to make sure she had no doubts as to what went on when he'd brought her here.

The man had to have the patience of Job because God knew he was dealing with a complete head case.

She watched as he walked away and then glanced down to the end of the bed where the clothing he'd set out for her was. She felt grubby and wanted a shower, but that might get her into trouble since he'd been adamant that she stay in bed. And, well, the idea of going through the motions of taking a shower exhausted her. She was still tired and the idea of staying in bed certainly appealed. Breakfast in bed? Even better.

She hurriedly changed, not wanting to chance him returning and seeing her naked. She tossed aside her work clothes and slid into the much more comfortable shirt and sweat pants.

They smelled of him. It was almost as good as having him wrapped around her. Almost but not quite.

She slid back underneath the covers and inhaled deeply, savoring his scent on the pillow next to her.

It was a ridiculous thing to do but she quickly exchanged her pillow for his, glancing guiltily at the doorway to make sure he hadn't seen. But she wanted his pillow. Wanted his scent surrounding her.

She settled back down, closing her eyes, savoring the warmth and comfort of his bed, his pillow and his clothing. Him.

A few moments later, he came back into the bedroom carrying a tray. She hastily sat up, plumping her pillow behind her back as he set the tray in front of her.

Waffles and bacon. Perfect.

"This looks wonderful," she said huskily. "Thank you."

He scooted onto the bed beside her so they were shoulder to shoulder.

"Eat up," he encouraged. "I don't want a single bite left over."

She grinned as she swallowed a scrumptious bite. "Admit it. You love getting to boss me around. It's that whole dominant thing you have going on."

He looked surprised at the ease with which she spoke of the matter. It surprised her as well. It should freak her out. Certainly everything else had. And yet she knew to her soul that this man would never willfully hurt her. She might not know much else, but she did know that. Maybe it made her a trusting fool, but she felt safe with him. He'd seen her at her most vulnerable and he didn't lord it over her. He didn't try to press his obvious advantage. He treated her like she was precious. Breakable. With tenderness she didn't fully comprehend but that she savored wholly.

"You'll learn in time that you have all the power where I'm concerned," he said in a serious tone. "And that I have none."

She swallowed hard, the food stuck in her throat as she processed his declaration. Everything about him radiated authority and yet he was saying *she* had all the power? How was that even possible?

"What does that mean?" she asked in a low voice.

His gaze was intent, unfaltering, stroking over her face like sunshine. "What it means is that you're in the driver's seat, baby. Whatever happens from here on out is up to you. It means that when or if we make love, you'll be in complete control and I will be at your mercy. It means that when it comes to you, I'm not dominant, nor do I have any desire to be. I am, in effect, at your feet."

Whoa. How the hell was she even supposed to respond to that? Emotion knotted and welled in her throat and suddenly she felt like crying. Not because she was sad but because she was utterly overwhelmed by the magnitude of what he was offering her. This was not a man who made concessions like this lightly. Everything about him screamed dominant, alpha male. And yet he was willing to suppress what made him who he was for her.

She didn't deserve this kind of gift. She wasn't worthy of it. And the fact that he was offering it to her destroyed any wall she would have erected between them. She was defenseless against such unselfishness.

"I don't know what to say," she choked out.

"The first thing I want you to say is that you'll stay here with me for the next several days. Let me take care of you. Let me work on building trust between us."

"And the second?"

"I want you to give us a chance."

"Is there an us?" she whispered.

"I want there to be," he said sincerely. "But you have to want it too. If you only want it half as much as I do it's a starting point."

She held her breath until she was light-headed and then, before she could chicken out and tuck tail and run, just like she did in every other aspect of her life, she took the plunge.

"Yes and okay," she said, the words tumbling out.

He blinked. "Be a little more specific, baby. I need to know what you're saying here. This is too important for me to make assumptions or to think you're saying something you aren't."

She sucked in a breath and blew it out, steadying herself before inevitable meltdown occurred. "Yes I'll stay with you, and okay, I'll give us a chance."

The relief was so stark in his eyes that it was like a punch in the stomach. She hadn't realized how much he wanted this—her. It was mind-boggling that they'd gone from antagonists to potential lovers, or something more than just acquaintances. She couldn't quite make the leap to lovers in her mind because that night was still too bright in her mind.

He gently framed her face in his hands, turning her to face him. He stroked her cheekbones with his thumbs and then lowered his head, tenderly touching his lips to hers. He licked syrup from her lips in a light brush that sent a spark shooting through her veins.

Her body wanted him. Now her mind just had to follow suit.

Her heart was in accord with her body. Now she just had to get her damn brain to stop freaking the fuck out every time things got heavy.

God, maybe she did need to see a shrink. She'd never even entertained the thought. She'd never had a solid reason to want to try and deal with her issues. But Jensen gave her that reason. He gave her hope. He gave her many things she'd never thought she'd have or even *want* to have.

"What did you mean when you said, uhm, that if we made love that I would be in control?" she asked hesitantly.

He stroked her face again, pushing her hair back as he stared into her eyes. "It means that if we decide to take that step that I will willingly put myself in a vulnerable position so you feel absolutely safe. Whatever that takes. But baby, it doesn't have to be now. It doesn't have to be soon. It will be whenever you're ready for it to happen. I don't want you to ever be pressured to offer me something you're not ready to give. We have all the time in the world."

"You'd wait that long?"

She tried to keep the doubt from her voice, but knew she failed miserably. Still, he didn't look offended or angry at her skepticism. If anything his look grew even more tender.

"For the right woman, I'd wait forever."

It came out as a solemn vow. There was absolutely no doubt in his voice and his conviction was unwavering.

She shook her head in wonder. "I don't get it. I really don't. I was so bitchy toward you. How could you possibly even *like* me?"

He smiled and placed his hand over her heart. "Because I could see through the prickly, protective barriers to the woman in here, and I liked what I saw. You didn't fool me for a minute, baby. Maybe others are more easily fooled or perhaps they can't be bothered to look beyond the exterior. That's not who I am, though."

"I like you," she admitted. "A lot, actually. And I know you don't think I trust you, but I do. I can't even explain it to myself. But I feel safe with you. I tell you things I don't tell other people."

His smile broadened. "I'm very glad you feel safe with me, baby, because you are. Always. Absolutely. I will do anything and everything in my power to always keep you safe. Not just physically but emotionally as well. And I'm humbled by the fact that you've given me your trust. It's a gift I don't take lightly. I'll do my best to ensure you never regret giving me that very precious gift."

She sighed and leaned back, her gaze still on him. She was absorbed in him. How quickly he'd become her security blanket. How easily she found herself sharing things with him she'd never share with anyone else.

"I missed you while you were gone," she admitted. "I was counting the hours and minutes until you got back. I wouldn't let myself sleep after that first night. I was too afraid because I knew I'd have nightmares and you weren't there. I didn't feel safe."

He picked up the tray and placed it on the floor on his side of the bed. Then he turned back to her and pulled her down into his arms until she was nestled against his side, her head resting on his shoulder.

"I should have never left you," he said in a low voice. "I'm sorry I let you down, baby. It won't happen again because from now on you come first. And I missed you too. I wrapped up things early so I could hurry home to you. I've never had anyone to come home to. It was a nice feeling. And then when I saw you, my heart nearly stopped. You scared me."

"I'm sorry," she whispered. "I know I can be difficult. I don't want to be. I want to be better, Jensen. I *can* be with you. I feel it. For the first time, I feel like it will be okay. That I don't have to continue living like I have for so long. It's kind of scary and yet exciting all at the same time. I don't react to change very well as you've probably noticed."

"We're two peas in a pod, you and I," Jensen said. "We're more alike than you think. I understand you better than you think and in time you'll understand me as well."

"I want to," she said honestly.

She turned her head up so she could see him.

"You said once that you had demons too. Will you tell me about them sometime?"

He picked up her hand and brought her fingertips to his lips. "One day, yes. But not right now. I don't want anything to ruin right here and right now. You in my arms. Us just being. That's a conversation for another day and time."

She let it go because if he shared then she'd have to share as well and she was no more eager to ruin the moment than he was. She nestled back into his arms and let out a sleepy yawn.

He stroked a hand over her hair, further lulling her to sleep.

"Get some rest, baby," he said. "You have a lot of sleep to catch up on. I'll wake you for a late lunch and then you can stay up until bedtime tonight. We'll stay in for dinner. Watch a movie. Whatever you want. But for now rest and know you're safe."

"I could fall in love with you so easily, Jensen," she said in

barely above a whisper. "That scares me. I've never allowed anyone to be in a position to hurt me. I'm not sure I like it at all."

He kissed the top of her head. "That's what establishing trust
is all about. When you learn to trust in me fully, then the idea of
loving me won't scare you so badly because then you'll know
that I'd never do anything to hurt you."

FOURTEEN

KYLIE watched as Jensen dressed for work Monday morning, indecision wracking her. This was a huge step in this trust thing she was working so hard at. The rest of last week and the weekend had been . . . beautiful. The best four days of her life. And she didn't say that lightly, though God knew it wouldn't take much to top her life up until now. Not that she was taking anything away from Jensen by acknowledging that, but she had to admit, she'd lived a pretty sterile existence up to now. Going through the motions but not taking risks and not really . . . living.

There had been no freak outs, no meltdowns, nothing even resembling her epic meltdown on their first date. But then Jensen hadn't pressured her. He hadn't made any kind of move on her. Their interactions had consisted of a few affectionate kisses, hardly the passionate, breath-stealing kind. Lots of snuggling and hugging.

She liked the hugs the best. It sounded silly, but her life had been devoid of true affection. Sure, her girlfriends were touchy-feely with her but that had never extended to a man. Even Tate and Dash always treated her very gingerly, never crossing the boundaries, ever mindful of her "issues."

And most notably, since Jensen had brought her here, to his home, and they slept together each night, her nightmares had eased. Just peaceful, dreamless sleep, safe in his arms. That told her more than anything that she belonged with him. Maybe it made him her security blanket, and while the idea of depending on anyone else in the past may have freaked her out, she found with him it didn't bother her. She'd achieved something far more precious than anything else during the last several days together. She'd achieved what she'd never allowed herself to hope for. Peace.

This morning she'd awakened, fully prepared to accompany Jensen into work, only he'd shut her down cold. And he couldn't be swayed. Dash would be back in the office today. She knew the two men had talked the previous evening and had set up a meeting to discuss several matters. One of which concerned Kylie. She knew that much.

She wasn't sure how she felt about being shut out. Not going to work. Not being there when she was being discussed. But Jensen had asked her to trust him in this. To remain at his home and be there when he returned from work. It was important to him and after all he'd put up with from her, it seemed a reasonable request.

She just wished she weren't so anxious and worried over what the two men would be discussing. But Jensen had promised to fill her in and leave nothing out when he returned from work. He wanted them to venture out tonight. Have dinner out. Go on a real date outside their homes. It was a test, she was sure, one she felt capable of passing without issue. But then who really knew what the hell her brain would do at any given time. She'd learned to trust Jensen perhaps, but she didn't fully trust herself. Not yet.

Jensen finished cinching his tie and then turned to where she was still lying in bed, wearing the pajamas they'd gone to her house to collect, along with her other clothing. At least two weeks' worth by her estimate. He'd told her to pack enough to stay awhile. It would appear he had no intention of allowing her out of his sight anytime soon. A fact that strangely didn't fire panic on all cylinders in her. Maybe she really was getting the hang of this whole trust thing.

He came to the bed and sat down on the edge, taking her hand and pulling her into his embrace. He kissed the top of her head and then framed her face as he'd done so many times before. She'd come to identify this as an affectionate gesture, one he seemed to favor, especially when he was being serious or tender.

"I know I'm asking a lot," he said seriously. "And I know this requires a lot of trust on your part. But trust me to handle things with Dash today. There's a lot I have to fill him in on, and the fact is, you still need to rest. You worked yourself into the ground last week and you still have dark circles under your eyes, though you're certainly starting to look a hell of a lot better than when I found you in your office."

"Gee, thanks," she said dryly. "I'm now a step above death warmed over. I feel so much better now."

"Cheeky wench," he said with no heat. "There's a lot I need to catch Dash up on and I'd rather to do it when we're alone. That's no reflection on you. I've promised to protect you and that's exactly what I'm doing. Trust me in this, baby. Okay? I'll fill you in tonight and I won't leave a word out. I promise. Today I want you to spend resting, being lazy, doing absolutely nothing. Maybe catch up with Chessy and Joss since I'm sure Chessy has filled her ears full of everything that happened while she was away on her honeymoon. I'm sure they'll both be coming at you, so prepare yourself for that. I know I haven't known your girls for a long time, but I know they can be ferocious when it comes to you, just as you're fiercely protective of them. So I imagine while I'm tied up with Dash, they're going to double-team you and interrogate you about me."

He said the last with an arrogant grin as if he had every confidence that everything she would say about him would be good. And hell, it would. He was right about that much. She just wasn't sure how much she wanted to share, even with her closest girlfriends. Some things were meant to be kept private. To savor and hold secret just for a little while.

"Will it make Dash angry, the decisions you made while he was gone?" she asked nervously. "I don't want you to jeopardize your business relationship with him. Especially over me."

He put a finger to her lips to shush her. Then he followed his fingers with his lips, lightly kissing her. "You let me handle Dash. He's a reasonable guy or I wouldn't be in business with him. I'm going to lay it all out to him and he'll agree with my assessment of your capabilities. I have no doubt about that. You'll get that raise, baby. I can guarantee it. And a promotion will be likely as well. And it won't be because I'm *giving* you anything. Our relationship has nothing to do with your abilities. You've earned what you've got coming. Never doubt that. Business is business. What's between you and me is strictly personal and doesn't interfere with work. I don't make emotional decisions when it comes to business."

Feeling oddly comforted by that statement, she nodded her agreement.

"If you do go out, text me and let me know, okay? This isn't me being overbearing or monitoring your comings and goings.

I'd just like to know if you're okay, and if you need me for anything at all, I will not be pleased if you don't call me immediately. Got it?"

She smiled, absurdly pleased over his concern. "Got it."

He kissed her again and then stood, a regretful expression on his face. "I hate to leave you. The last several days have been nice. Unfortunately it's back to the real world. But I'll be home at my usual time today. If I'm running late for any reason I'll call so you know when to expect me. Dress casual for dinner. We'll go someplace comfortable."

"That sounds nice," she said softly. "I'll look forward to it."

He cupped her cheek, giving her one last caress, and then he was gone, leaving her bereft of his presence.

The house was too quiet, silent in fact. She'd grown accustomed to his presence. They'd spent every minute of the last four days together. They'd slept together in his bed, her in her pajamas and him in boxers and a T-shirt. He'd been super careful not to in any way make it seem like he was pressuring her for anything at all. It only endeared him to her all the more.

She'd told him she could see herself falling in love with him, but she was afraid she was already more than halfway there. Or maybe she already was. She struggled with the idea of separating genuine love with dependence. Or perhaps one was simply a by-product of the other. Who the hell knew? She'd never been in love before. Had no idea what it felt like.

But if it meant being utterly content and happy in his presence and preferring his company to anyone else's, then yeah, she was definitely in love. Her fucked-up mind was the only obstacle she still had to overcome. It was simply too used to stepping in and overriding all her decisions. It had been in self-preservation mode for so many years that it knew no other way to be.

Maybe she should reach out to Chessy and Joss and not wait until they tracked her down. It would be a positive step in the right direction. To actually share a part of herself she usually reserved, even around her best friends.

This could be part of the "new her." Being more open. Open up and share as much as Chessy and Joss had shared with her.

Liking the idea, but more than a little nervous about actually going through with it, she got out of bed and went for her phone. Maybe a text to both of them. Set up lunch? It was a sad testament to just how inexperienced she was with taking the initiative that it took her five minutes to compose the text and another five to work up the nerve to actually send it.

Not wanting to sit there glued to her phone, she opted to shower, just in case they did take her up on her offer of getting together for lunch. At least she'd be ready to go. And well, if they were otherwise occupied, she'd get out and maybe do some grocery shopping. She and Jensen were eating out tonight, but he'd made it clear he had no intention of her going back to her house anytime soon.

She hadn't really put a timeline on her staying with him. The last four days had been too comfortable and she was reluctant to pull back and potentially destroy the progress they'd made. The progress *she* had made.

She could cook dinner for them tomorrow night. If he didn't allow her to go into work the next day she could have it ready for him when he got home. And if she did go to work, she could always cook for him when they both got home.

How easily she'd given over so much control to Jensen, she mused as she got into the shower. More surprising was the fact she wasn't freaking out or melting down. Maybe she *was* making progress.

Their relationship, however tenuous, had strengthened over the past days. No, they hadn't even come close to true intimacy. Well, that wasn't exactly true. Just because they hadn't had sex didn't mean there wasn't decided intimacy in their relationship. Perhaps more so than if they *had* made love.

His statement of her being in absolute control intrigued her. It wasn't something that had ever occurred to her and she was curious as to whether it would make her feel less panicky, or perhaps she could prevent the inevitable meltdown if she had complete control of the situation.

She still wasn't sure of how it would work exactly, but she planned to work up the courage to broach the subject with Jensen. Soon. Because she *wanted* to take that next step. She wanted it badly. But she didn't want a repeat of their last experience. One humiliating meltdown was enough. Another wouldn't likely endear her to him. At some point his patience would wear thin. And the last thing she wanted was to be a tease. Get him hopeful and worked up only to yank the rug out from under him. Or herself for that matter.

Maybe Chessy and Joss could give her some advice. That would certainly be something new. Her asking them for advice when it came to men and sex. They might never get over the shock of it!

When she got out of the shower, she had responses from both women. Lux Café. Noon. She smiled at their willingness to drop everything for her. Not that she ever doubted such a thing, but it wasn't usually her sounding the alarm. They'd likely be rabid with curiosity. She was sure Chessy had been on the phone with Joss the minute Joss was back in town.

No better way to set the record straight than to do it herself.

After puttering around Jensen's house, exploring more, learning more about his personality, she dressed in jeans and a T-shirt and then sent Jensen a quick text, remembering his request for her to keep in touch with him about her comings and goings.

Having lunch with the girls. I'll let you know when I get back home.

She faltered a bit as she hit Send, biting her lip in consternation. Perhaps she shouldn't have referred to his house as "home." But it was too late now.

Her phone chimed almost immediately with Jensen's reply.

Have fun and be careful. Call me if you need me.

Her smile was a little—okay, a lot—ridiculous over his expression of concern. The command for her to call him if she needed him. It gave her a measure of reassurance she'd never experienced, the idea that he'd come the minute she needed him.

She climbed into her car, a bite of sadness hitting her, the same as it always did when she got inside the car her brother had given her for her twenty-first birthday. She missed him. He'd been her rock in so many ways. Life without him had been a huge adjustment. He'd always been there for her. Steady. Unwavering. He was the only other person who not only knew, but shared the horror of her childhood.

When she arrived at the Café, predictably Chessy was already there and Joss was late. They teased her mercilessly about always being late. But neither of her friends ever minded waiting on her.

Joss was just a ray of sunshine and she brought warmth with her everywhere she went. There was no gentler and kinder a person to be found anywhere. Dash was very lucky she had such a forgiving nature, because he'd very nearly lost her over his stupidity.

"How are you?" Chessy asked in concern, her eyes crinkled as she studied Kylie. "You look . . . better."

Kylie smiled. "I am. Let's go sit and wait for Joss. Then I'll tell y'all everything."

Chessy's brows rose in surprise. Usually they had to pry any information out of Kylie and she was usually reluctant to offer it. Not this time. Kylie was turning over a new leaf and it was starting now. Perhaps it had started the moment Jensen entered her life.

Five minutes later, Joss breathlessly hurried up to the table, sliding into the booth next to Chessy.

"Sorry, sorry!" Joss said. "I just lost track of time. Honeymoon brain, I'm afraid. I'm too used to doing nothing at all. I've become quite lazy over the last two weeks!"

Both women smiled at their friend. She was flushed with happiness, her eyes sparkling like twin diamonds.

"I guess we don't have to ask how it went," Kylie drawled.

Joss blushed to the roots of her hair and grinned mischievously. "It went . . . well."

Chessy rolled her eyes. "Now why do I believe that's a huge understatement?"

Joss turned her gaze on Kylie, her eyes bright with concern. "How are you, sweetie? Chessy told me what happened. Are you all right?"

Kylie nodded, suffering only a hint of embarrassment over the fact her friends had discussed her.

"I wanted to get y'all's . . . advice," Kylie said uncomfortably.

Joss and Chessy exchanged quick surprised looks but they were also obviously delighted with Kylie's statement.

"It's about Jensen," she blurted before she lost her courage and clammed up.

Joss's eyebrows shot up, but she couldn't have been that surprised if Chessy had told her about Kylie's epic meltdown and the fact that Jensen called her to come over. Or perhaps Chessy had glossed over the facts, waiting for Kylie to confide in Joss in her own time. She sent her a friend a look of gratitude and Chessy smiled warmly back as if to say, "Hey, I got your back."

"We've sort of become . . . involved," Kylie said lamely. "In a good way, I mean."

"That's wonderful, Kylie!" Joss exclaimed. "You have to catch me up on all the details. Are you happy? Do you like him?"

Kylie sighed. "It's complicated. Really complicated. But I figured you two were in a position to give me some guidance here considering the lifestyle you both live."

"Then you know Jensen is a Dominant," Joss murmured.

Kylie nodded. "But here's where it gets complicated. He swears that for me he'll give up complete control. That he'll deny that part of himself. For me. That when and if I'm ready to make love, I'll have complete control because he doesn't want me to ever be afraid of him."

"Whoa," Chessy breathed. "That's pretty heavy. I mean wow. That's huge, Kylie. Huge!"

Joss nodded her fervent agreement. "You have to understand just how big that is, Kylie. Men like him don't just give up control. To anyone. I'd say that speaks volumes about the way he feels about you."

Kylie was delighted to hear it. To have it confirmed. She'd suspected, yes, but she didn't truly understand the enormity of his vow. These two women would. They were both committed to dominant men. Men they were submissive to.

"I freaked out pretty bad on our first official date," Kylie said, though this was not news to Chessy. "All we were doing was kissing on the couch, but I just kind of shut down and then freaked completely out. Jensen was worried. I wanted him to leave and he finally did only because he worried he would do more damage by staying. But he called Chessy to come over because he refused to leave me alone."

"He sounds like the real deal," Joss said softly. "He sounds like he cares a lot about you, sweetie."

"I hope so," Kylie murmured. "I care about him. I may even love him. I'm not sure yet. It's all very confusing. He had to leave on a business trip right after our date and I didn't sleep at all while he was gone. I don't feel safe when he's not there. And I hate that dependency. He came back a day early and I collapsed in the office. He brought me back to his house and has insisted on me staying ever since. I haven't been to work since last Wednesday."

"So it looks like he's only willing to suppress his alpha tendencies in a few areas," Chessy observed, her eyes gleaming in amusement.

"I never thought I'd hear myself say this, but I kind of *like* them. He's arrogant and bossy but he's so gentle with me. He makes me ache. He makes me want things I've never wanted before," she said honestly.

Joss reached for her hand and squeezed. "Then go for it. Give him a chance. And if what he said is true and he's willing to give up control, then, honey, that is huge. It's not something a man like him would ever do lightly and I highly doubt he's ever made that offer to a woman before. Which makes you very special to him."

"I was hoping you'd say that," Kylie said ruefully. "I have zero experience with the whole dominant/submissive thing. And he's admittedly a Dominant. All his relationships have been with submissive women. But he told me he doesn't want my physical surrender, that he'd never bring the physical components of dominance and submission into our relationship. He wants my emotional surrender, and that I think is perhaps even scarier than the physical aspects of that kind of relationship."

"It can certainly make you more vulnerable," Chessy agreed. "But you have to look at the payoff and decide if it's worth it. If he's worth it. Because evidently he's already considered his options and has decided that you're worth the sacrifice he'll make."

"I understand Jensen's sacrifice more than most," Joss said quietly. "I denied that part of myself for Carson because I knew he could never give me dominance. I loved him and I have no regrets, but there was always a part of me that was unfulfilled because submission was something I needed—craved."

Kylie fell silent, pondering her friends' words and reactions. If they were to be believed, what he'd offered her *was* huge. And maybe she'd already recognized the magnitude of what he was offering her, but she'd needed validation from two women who'd know.

"I want to try," she said honestly. "For the first time, I really want to try. I want what other women have. A normal life. Someone who loves and cares for me. Someone who won't run from my past like I have and someone who will protect me. And he fits the bill on all counts."

"Then what are you waiting for?" Chessy said challengingly. "And no, I'm not saying you should rush into a physical relationship with him. But it sounds like the two of you are well on your way to something solid. I'm happy for you, Kylie. I like Jensen a lot. Yes, he's alpha, but it's obvious he's very caring and sensitive to your needs. You can't ask for more than that."

Joss nodded her agreement.

"I'm scared to death," Kylie admitted. "More scared than I've ever been. But it's a different kind of fear. It's not him I'm afraid of. Or having an actual relationship. I'm afraid of screwing this up. Just like I've screwed up everything else in my life."

Both Joss and Chessy frowned fiercely at her. "You are *not* a screwup," Joss chastised her. "Honey, you have legitimate reasons to fear intimacy. And Jensen knows that. Give him a chance, but more importantly, give yourself a chance. Trust yourself and your instincts. You'll never know unless you give it a shot."

Kylie nodded slowly. "I knew all this. I suppose I just needed to hear it from y'all. Thanks. I really needed y'all today."

"Like you haven't been there for us," Chessy snorted. "Between the three of us, we've managed more emotional crises than a psych ward."

Joss and Kylie laughed, the mood relaxing as the three enjoyed their lunch. Kylie sat back, luxuriating in the feel of something new and delicious. The hope of something permanent and real.

All she had to do was reach out and take it. Jensen had put her solidly in the driver's seat. It was up to her to make the next move.

FIFTEEN

JENSEN strode into Dash's office with a sense of purpose. Though the two men had conversed the evening before, Jensen hadn't shown his hand. Not yet. He'd only said he needed to discuss important business matters with his partner the following morning.

This would perhaps be the first real test of their partnership. Jensen was prepared to dig in his heels solidly when it came to Kylie and it had nothing to do with his personal feelings for her. He'd told her it was business and he hadn't lied. Kylie was smart, a go-getter, and she deserved to be a major component of the consulting business. Her talents were wasted in the capacity of an office manager only. Not that she didn't do a damn fine job, but she was destined for bigger and better things. If they didn't act to secure her, someone else eventually would. One day Kylie would reach the same conclusion that Jensen already had. That she was worth far more than an office manager. And in no way did he plan to lose Kylie. Professionally or personally.

"Morning," Dash greeted when Jensen came through his door.

"How was the honeymoon?" Jensen asked, obligated to inquire about the obvious before they moved on to business.

"It was great. Wish we were still there," Dash said wistfully. "How were things here? Any problems?"

Jensen shook his head. "None at all. We secured the S&G contract. Thanks in large part to Kylie."

Dash's eyebrows rose as Jensen took a seat in front of Dash's desk.

"She's good," Jensen said bluntly. "I gave her the lead on this project. Gave her all the info I had and told her to come up with a plan. We met the night before to discuss and I agreed with every single one of her recommendations."

Dash sat in silence, absorbing his partner's words.

"Is there something I'm missing here?" Dash asked. "Because I feel like I'm missing a huge piece of a puzzle. When I left, Kylie could hardly stand to be in the same room as you. And while I'm gone you two partner and she takes the lead on a very important contract to this firm? And you *let* her?"

"Kylie is mine," Jensen said. "I don't care who knows it. But our relationship has nothing to do with her career prospects. I'm perfectly capable of separating business and pleasure, and Kylie has a bright mind. She rose to the challenge beautifully and I intend to see that rewarded. I think we should consider giving her more responsibility and hiring a different office manager to take over Kylie's duties. Eventually she could make a partner. I'm certain of it."

Dash shot him an inscrutable look. He made a V with his fingertips and rested his chin against them in a thoughtful manner.

"And what does Kylie think about all of this? You?" Dash amended.

"Are we talking personally or professionally here?" Jensen asked coolly.

"Personally. We're all very protective of Kylie. I don't want to see her get hurt. You are precisely the kind of man she *doesn't* need."

"I disagree. She's mine," Jensen repeated. "That's all you need to know. She's currently staying with me after working herself into the ground last week while I was gone. She collapsed in the office and I took her home so I could take care of her. God knows someone needed to. But if you think I in any way forced her, you're wrong. She's there willingly. I have every intention of keeping her out of work the remainder of this week as well. She's exhausted and she needs the break. And when she comes back, I want it to be in the capacity of more than our office manager. So that gives you a week to be looking for a new one."

"You're a demanding bastard," Dash mused.

"It's the right decision for our company," Jensen said. "She landed us the S&G contract. I have no doubt she'll be an asset if we turn her loose. I have every confidence in her abilities. She just has to find the same confidence in herself."

"I'll go along with you on this," Dash conceded. "If Kylie proves her mettle then we can certainly make her a partner. But you need to figure out if you can handle that if things don't work out for you . . . personally."

Jensen returned Dash's look unblinkingly. "They *will* work out. However, I'd leave before ever making Kylie feel uncomfortable in her work environment. I will never do anything that hurts her. Period."

Dash let out a long breath. "I hope to hell you know what you're getting into, man. Kylie . . . she's going to be a tough nut to crack. With reason. And she's not going to react well to your . . . dominance."

"For her I'm willing to make special concessions," Jensen said.

It was all he would say on the matter. He owed Dash at least some reassurance because Kylie was important to him and Joss. But this was all he'd give him. What was between him and Kylie was private. Not to be shared. He was as possessive of their relationship as he was of her.

"Then I wish you the best," Dash said sincerely. "Kylie deserves to be happy. I never thought I'd say this but she may well have met her match in you. She needs someone as stubborn as she is. Someone who won't buckle or run at the first sign of adversity. She deserves someone who will stick it out and see her for the treasure she is."

"In that we agree," Jensen said. "Now, what about a new office manager? I vote we start taking applications immediately."

SIXTEEN

KYLIE was waiting anxiously when Jensen pulled into the drive. She'd been anticipating his homecoming ever since she'd returned from her lunch with the girls. She'd been delighted when he'd called and said he'd be home earlier than usual.

She wasn't sure if that was a good thing or a bad thing or if it was in any way indicative of how his talk with Dash had gone.

She met him at the door and all but threw herself into his arms. He seemed delighted by her spontaneous show of affection and caught her up against him. She took the initiative and kissed him. And not one of those gentle pecks he'd been giving her. She devoured his mouth hungrily, licking over his lips and then delving inside when they parted.

"Wow," he said breathlessly when she finally pulled away. "Now that's what I call a welcome home."

"I missed you," she said without any discomfort. She could admit things to him that she'd never admit to anyone else. She didn't feel as vulnerable and as bare with him.

She felt . . . safe.

It was a statement she'd made to herself and to him over and over but it bore repeating because it was such a mind-boggling thing. She, who never felt safe with anyone, felt absolutely secure with Jensen.

"I missed you too, baby."

He kissed her this time, long and leisurely. It sent warm shivers cascading over her body. Now that she'd decided that she wanted to try to have a physical relationship with him, it was all that occupied her mind. She was bursting with hope and anticipation because this would be huge for her. Just as huge as it evidently was that he was offering to relinquish absolute control to her.

"I got used to having you around the last four days," she whispered.

He let out a groan. "God, baby, if you have any intention of us going out, you have to stop now because I'm one second away from hauling you into the bedroom and tying my own self to the bed."

She laughed, the sound joyous and free. How far had she come that they could actually joke about her hang-ups and she could laugh at herself? If she had any uncertainty about whether she loved this man, it was gone in an instant.

"I'm ready to go if you are," she said with a grin. "You said casual, but I didn't want to go *too* casual."

He pulled her away as if noticing for the first time what she had on. She loved that he hadn't paid any attention to the outer trappings. He'd only been focused on her. The woman. What was on the inside, no matter how twisted up she was there.

"If this is your definition of *casual* then I'm dying to know what you consider *not casual*," he said, male appreciation evident in his tone.

She'd donned a short cocktail dress, one that clipped just

above her knees and bared the expanse of her legs. It was simple and could certainly qualify as casual. It was black and sleeveless with a modest neckline that only hinted at the curves of her breasts.

The pièce de résistance, however, were the heels. She was normally a flip-flop kind of girl and wouldn't be caught dead in a pair of heels. But she was feeling brave and a little sassy and so, on her way home from lunch, she'd stopped and bought a pair of spiked, blingy heels that she had to admit looked damn good on her. She just hoped like hell she didn't make an ass of herself by face-planting when she tried to walk in them.

"I wanted to look good for you," she said hesitantly.

He gathered her close again, careful to keep her from teetering on her heels. "Baby, you look good to me no matter what you're wearing, but let me assure you. You look gorgeous. I'm a lucky bastard to be seen with you. Let me change into something besides my work clothes and then I'll take you out. Think you can slow dance with those killer shoes?"

She smiled, taking in his appreciative stare, it stroking her feminine ego. She hadn't ever considered she had one until now.

"If you hold me close enough I won't fall."

He leaned in close, his breath whispering over her face. "I'll never let you fall, baby."

Her heart clutched at the quiet vow and she knew he wouldn't break it. Literally and figuratively speaking, he'd never let her fall. Not when he was around. She was stronger with him, because of him. She felt ready to take on the world because of this man's confidence in her.

She ached to tell him everything that was in her heart, but she knew they still had a long way to go. And it wouldn't be easy. They still had many obstacles to overcome, but for the first time she was optimistic about her chances of regaining control over her life. And she owed it partly to him. Hell, she owed it all to him.

If he hadn't pushed her, if he hadn't been so determined, she'd still be existing day to day, hiding from the world with her head in the sand.

Now she was going on a date. Another date, only this time she hoped for a better result. She wasn't foolish enough to think she'd get there tonight. But she wanted to try. That was something, wasn't it? She wasn't afraid to try. Her only fear was failure. But she wasn't going to use that fear as an excuse not to go through with it. She'd face her fears head-on and not allow them to rule her life any longer.

It took Jensen only a few minutes to change. He chose jeans and a simple polo that fit snugly over his strong shoulders and broad chest. It hugged him in all the right places, accentuating his lean, muscled physique.

And his smell. She wasn't even sure if he used cologne or perhaps aftershave. It wasn't overpowering but wholeheartedly masculine and rugged. She loved his scent.

They drove to a small jazz bar in the downtown area. A band played nightly and the lighting was low and romantic, only the mellow sounds of the music mixed with hushed tones of the patrons evident.

It screamed intimate and quiet. Cozy and perfect. An ideal prelude to what she hoped would be more. She was nervous and yet edgy with impatience and anticipation to see where the evening would take them. She planned to talk with Jensen, to query him further on the control issue and whether he was truly willing to go through with it. It was a testament to her will that she didn't question whether *she* was willing to go through with it.

Her heart wanted it. Her body wanted it. She just had to pray that her mind went along for the ride.

They ordered drinks and shared lingering glances over the rims of their glasses. After they placed their food order, Jensen rose and extended his hand down to Kylie.

"Time to see how well you dance in those heels and how well I'm able to hold you up," he said teasingly.

She went readily into his arms, absorbing the intense masculine warmth and strength his body offered. He wrapped himself around her so that she barely had room to move. Not that she minded a bit.

They stood, swaying slightly in rhythm to the music, her head tucked securely underneath Jensen's chin. She closed her eyes and leaned further into him, allowing him to hold her.

Her breath caught when she felt the firm imprint of his erection against her belly. Even underneath the denim of his jeans, his cock was rigid and straining outward, bulging and pulsing strongly.

He let his hand drift up and down her back, stroking, caressing, his fingers whispering over her skin like a dream. She made a low contented sound in the back of her throat, a hum of pleasure that vibrated against his chest.

"You're killing me, baby."

The whispered words just against her ear sent shivers of need through her body.

She lifted her head and leaned up so she could return his whisper. He bent his head lower to dip his ear to her lips.

"You're killing me too."

His smile was instantaneous. Predatory. It should have scared the bejebus out of her, but it didn't. It was a smile that told her she was in trouble. The good kind.

He palmed her nape, his fingers curling around the slender column. Every feminine instinct was on high alert. Her body was taut with desire, her breasts heavy and aching.

Then, holding her in place, he leaned down and pressed his lips to hers. He was infinitely tender, so exquisitely gentle that tears burned her eyelids. Nothing was more perfect than right here, right now. In his arms, the soft strains of jazz surrounding them.

Intimacy was a heavy cloak over them, enveloping them in its lulling embrace. She swayed in his arms, completely caught up in the moment. She wanted time to stand still. For the mood to never be broken.

He seemed as reluctant as she when he pulled away and glanced toward their table with a grimace.

"Dinner is here, baby."

"What dinner?" she asked huskily.

He smiled and kissed the corner of her mouth. "Come. Let me feed my baby."

She was gripped by a ridiculous, giddy thrill over the endearment. *His* baby. As if she belonged to him and she was his to take care of.

She was acting like a stupid teenager barely in control of her hormones.

He led her back to the table where their entrées awaited them. But Jensen slid her plate toward him while he edged his chair closer to hers. He cut into her steak before forking a bite to her lips.

At first she was embarrassed by the fact that she was a grown woman being fed by a man. She glanced hastily around, but no one was paying them the slightest attention. They were too wrapped up in their own environments and conversations.

"Relax, Kylie. Let me feed you. I enjoy it very much."

Put that way, she felt shrewish to allow her brief discomfort to interfere in their ever-growing intimacy.

She forced herself to heed his dictate and relax, allowing him to continue the intimate act of feeding her each bite.

"There, that's not so bad," he coaxed, his tone raspy.

She shook her head and then glanced down at his own untouched food. "Do I get to feed you?" she teased.

He looked startled and then pleased. "If you like."

She scooted forward and picked up the fork and knife to cut into his steak. Then she began feeding him bites, his gaze stroking her face the entire time.

What was at first an awkward experience for her was transformed into something decidedly intimate. The sensual haze between them was thick, tangible. Building like a thunderstorm, waiting only to be unleashed.

She wanted it. She wanted him. It was new for her, this desperate need for a man. She'd never wanted to overcome her past as badly as she wanted to now. She'd used it as a protective barrier, not wanting those barriers to ever be breached. But now she wanted to break them down herself. She didn't want him to do it for her. She wanted to own it. Wanted them to come down at her instigation.

"Are you ready to go home?" she whispered.

She realized it could be unclear whose home she meant. But she'd been staying with Jensen and she realized she had no desire to go back to her own house. It was where she'd freaked out before. Maybe in Jensen's home, a place she already felt safe and secure, she would finally be able to overcome her demons.

"Hell yes," he muttered.

He pulled out several bills from his wallet and tossed them on the table next to their plates. Then he rose, holding out his hand to her. She took it, allowing him to pull her up next to him, and the two hurried out to his car.

The ride home was silent, but she found comfort in the thick tension between them. Their need was evident. Neither of them tried to hide it or make it something it wasn't.

When they pulled into his drive, she felt a moment's uncertainty, but quickly tamped it down. She was going ahead with this. She had questions. She wanted a much clearer picture of what he'd promised her.

As soon as they entered the house, Kylie started toward the living room, leaving him to follow her lead. She reclined on the couch and then patted the spot beside her in silent invitation.

When he settled beside her, she turned, swallowing back her fears. With this man she could be herself. And with this man, maybe she could finally be whole again. Not again. For the first time in her *life*.

"I wanted—needed—to ask you some things," she said hesitantly.

His hand immediately went to her cheek, soft and reassuring, his touch like fire against her skin.

"You can ask me anything, darling. There's nothing we can't talk about together."

She smiled, encouraged by his sincerity.

"I want . . ." She sucked in a deep breath and plunged ahead. "I want to try again. I mean with you. But I wanted to know exactly what you meant by giving me control."

Fire blazed in his eyes, heat that she could feel. Desire. Satisfaction. Relief.

"I meant just that," he said. "If you want this—me—then what happens is you tie me to the bed, both hands above me, and I'll be yours to do with as you please. And by that, I mean as much or as little as you want. We take it slow. You see what you can handle. And we go from there. But baby, don't put pressure on yourself and don't get upset if you can't handle a lot right away. I'm in no hurry. We have all the time in the world so I want you to take it slow and only do what you're comfortable doing."

Her shoulders sagged with relief. He sounded utterly sincere.

"Then let's do it," she whispered. "I want to try. I don't want to make you promises I can't keep, so for now let's just see what happens."

His smile was achingly gentle and understanding. "I'm yours to command, Kylie. And I don't make that offer lightly. Only for you. Always for you."

"So what do I do next then?"

He rose, extending his hand to hers, a gesture of support and solidarity.

"What we do is take this to the bedroom and I'll get the necessary rope for you to tie me to the bed. The rest is entirely up to you, baby."

SEVENTEEN

KYLIE watched in abject fascination as Jensen calmly stripped himself of his clothing and then reached into one of his drawers for a length of rope.

He was beautiful. Raw masculinity emanated from him in waves. He was utterly perfect and he didn't seem at all abashed by his nudity. Or his huge erection straining upward to his abdomen.

No matter how hard she tried to look somewhere—anywhere—else, she couldn't force her gaze away from his jutting erection. And oddly it didn't terrify her. She was fascinated by it. It—*he*—was a thing of beauty.

She blushed over the idiocy of considering a penis beautiful, but it belonged to a beautiful man so how could it be anything else? This man was without fault. He was physical perfection.

He turned to her, extending the rope. She took it nervously, unsure of what the hell she was supposed to do with it. But he took the lead, thank God. She may have supposed she was in control, but she was anything but. She was following his lead gratefully.

He crawled onto the bed and turned on his back, stretching

as gracefully as a cat, his entire length exposed and vulnerable. Then he brought his arms over his head, placing his hands close to the spindles of his headboard.

"Tie me, baby," he said in a husky voice that sent shivers dancing down her spine. "And then I'm yours to do with as you wish."

Oh my. This delicious alpha male was hers for the taking. To do with whatever she wanted, and God did she want. She wanted so badly that it was a physical ache.

She crawled onto the bed and began coiling the rope around one wrist. Then she pulled it toward his other hand and secured that one as well. She tested the tautness of the rope even though she had no fears of him hurting her. But her mind needed reassurance. Her brain needed to know she was safe.

When she was finished, she sat back and let her gaze wander hungrily down his body. There was so much to look at. To touch. And taste. And suddenly she wanted it all. At the same time. He was a veritable feast laid out in front of a starving woman.

She touched his chest first. It seemed the safest place to start, and she let her hands roam over the wall of muscle, exploring the hair-roughened hollow and his taut abdomen.

His breath hissed out in a long exhalation the moment she touched him. He jerked and she yanked her hands away, worried she'd done something wrong.

"Don't stop, baby. God, you feel so damn good. If you only knew how long I've waited for you to touch me like this. Don't stop. I'm yours to touch and explore however you want. It's all in your hands. I can guarantee there isn't a thing I won't love."

Encouraged by the raw intensity—and honesty—in his voice, she returned to his body, this time roaming over his shoulders and then back down his sides, growing closer to the place she most wanted to touch.

His erection was straining upward, resting against his belly. All she had to do was slide her fingers an inch closer and she'd be touching him.

She shifted her weight so she could face him, wanting to see his reaction when she finally circled his huge cock with her hands.

She trailed one finger up the underside where the plump vein was distended. He let out a moan and arched his hips upward to meet her caress. Growing bolder, she wrapped one hand around the base and gently tugged upward. When she got to the head, moisture beaded and slipped from the tip, coating her hand.

"You're so beautiful," she whispered. "I love touching you."

"I love you touching me," he said huskily. "You're beautiful touching me. I keep wondering what the hell I did to deserve this. A goddess pleasuring me when I should be pleasuring you."

She smiled. "We'll get there. I hope."

His gaze was serious. "We will, baby. We will. There's no hurry and I don't want you to ever feel pressured to give me something you can't. I'll wait because the end result is worth it. You're worth it."

Her chest swelled, knotting with emotion. He made it sound so easy, and she supposed it was. Time. They had all they needed. He'd been very clear about wanting her and waiting for as long as it took. Did he realize the enormity of such a gift?

She leaned down and pressed her lips to his belly, just an inch above where his cock rested. He flinched and let out a gasp, giving her courage to touch him intimately with her mouth.

Carefully, she kissed the tip, just as she had his belly, but then grew bolder, flicking out her tongue to lick the head.

"Jesus," he choked out. "You're killing me."

Feeling powerful, she took more control, sucking the tip into her mouth, holding him there for a long moment while she lapped at the precum seeping from the slit. Then she sucked him deep, enjoying his instant reaction.

She had no experience whatsoever, but her instincts took over and she let her hands roam as she continued her sensual assault with her mouth and tongue.

His chest heaved, his hips arching upward again, guiding his cock deeper into her mouth. His arms strained against the ropes securing his wrists and his face was twisted in beautiful agony.

"Put your hands around me, baby. I'm about to come," he said raggedly.

She wrapped both hands around him, feeling the thick, rigid strength of his cock. Velvet over steel. She stroked up and down, tightening her grip. Then she leaned down to lap at his balls, liking the rugged feel of his sac on her tongue.

His cry split the silence. He erupted, his release spurting onto his belly, marking the tan skin with creamy ropes of liquid. She watched in fascination as the jets of semen spilled onto his flesh and she gently continued stroking him until at last he began to soften in her grasp.

Watching him come had been heady, unlike anything she'd ever experienced before. It left her restless, edgy and unfulfilled. She ached. Her breasts tingled and her clit pulsed between her thighs. But she had no idea how to gain her own release. Now that she'd taken the leap, she was uncertain of what to do next. Or if she should do anything at all to assuage the edge of unfulfillment.

"Take off your clothes, baby."

She yanked up her gaze in surprise.

"You're still in control," he reassured gently. "But you need relief. And I want to see your beautiful body. Remember, I'm still tied. Now take off your clothes and get back on the bed with me. I want to see you come."

Shakily she got off the bed and did as he directed. Keeping her gaze averted, she slowly slipped out of her clothing, hesitating when she got to her bra and panties. It was almost as if she thought the bruises from decades ago would still show on her skin. She felt intensely vulnerable, but at the same time she was driven to follow his dictate.

She snuck a peek in Jensen's direction only to find warm understanding burning in his dark eyes. If he'd looked at her any other way she likely would have chickened out. But it was that understanding that enabled her to go the rest of the way.

He saw to the heart of her. Knew how hard it was for her to bare herself in front of him. It made her all the more determined not to let her fears win.

Before she could back down, she yanked off her bra and pulled off her panties. Then she crawled back on the bed, kneeling beside him before finally meeting his gaze again.

"Touch yourself," he murmured. "Pleasure yourself. Let me watch you make yourself come."

Her eyes widened. For a moment she was at a complete loss.

"Cup your breasts. Hold them up for me and then touch your nipples. Figure out what feels good to you and then do more of that," he encouraged.

Seduced by his husky tone and his eagerness for her to be pleased, she slowly slid her hands up her belly to cup her breasts, plumping them outward. She brushed her thumbs across the sensitive peaks, gasping at the electrical shock that seemed to jolt through her body.

"Now imagine me sucking them," he said in a low voice. "My mouth around them, my tongue licking them."

She closed her eyes and moaned, getting into the spirit of his seduction.

"Now put your hand between your legs," he directed. "Spread your folds, show me that pretty pussy. But keep your other hand on your breast and play with your nipple."

Keeping her eyes closed, not wanting to break the spell, she slipped one hand down her belly and in between her thighs. She shivered as her fingers slipped over her clit, and then, as he'd directed, she spread herself, pulling upward so he could see.

"Beautiful," he murmured. "Touch yourself, baby. Make yourself come. Come for me."

She let out a soft moan as she began to touch herself, finding the perfect rhythm. She arched upward, unable to sit still. She undulated her hips as she continued to exert pressure on her clit, rolling it beneath her middle finger.

"That's it," he encouraged. "Make yourself feel good, Kylie. God, you're beautiful. So beautiful."

His voice was smooth and sensual, heightening her pleasure, taking her higher and higher, closer to the edge of bliss.

She could feel the stirrings of something truly wonderful. Her body tightened. Her breasts grew even more sensitive. Every touch. Every breath. Her womb clenched, her pussy clenched. And still she climbed even higher, getting closer and closer with every touch, with every word that came out of Jensen's mouth.

She threw back her head with abandon, feeling wild and exotic. This wasn't her. She'd become someone else entirely. Someone sexy, a seductress. Someone in control of her sexuality.

Never had she felt so . . . free. Unburdened. Here, nothing could touch her. Nothing could hurt or frighten her. There was only her and Jensen. And her deepest, most intoxicating fantasies.

"So fucking beautiful," Jensen murmured.

She opened her eyes and locked gazes with him, suddenly unafraid and uninhibited. She wanted to share this with him.

"Come for me, baby. Show me your pleasure. Let me taste it."

She slid her fingers inside her, capturing some of her moisture, and then she held out her fingers to his mouth. He sucked her finger inside, tugging at it with the suction. He licked her finger clean and let out a growl of satisfaction.

She quickly returned her fingers to her clit because she was close. So very close. And she didn't want to lose the edge.

Faster, harder. She exerted firmer pressure and then threw back her head again, finally reaching for it. Embracing it. Letting go.

She cried out, shivering violently as her orgasm rose and broke like a huge wave. She fell forward, panting, her palms bracing her on the bed.

And suddenly she wanted Jensen's arms around her. Wanted him touching her. Wanted his strength. Wanted to feel safe.

She tugged at his bonds, nearly too weak to untie the knots. As soon as one hand was free, he turned and worked the other hand loose, seemingly as desperate as she was to get his arms around her.

She dove into his embrace, uncaring that they were both

naked. He wouldn't hurt her. He'd made the ultimate sacrifice. For her. He'd never hurt her. She knew that.

"Just hold me," she whispered. "Please. I need you."

"I won't let you go," he vowed. "I'll hold you as long as you want, Kylie. As long as you need. I'm not going anywhere."

EIGHTEEN

JENSEN lay awake, Kylie snuggled tightly against his body, content and as relaxed as he'd ever been. He knew the enormity of what had happened tonight and he couldn't contain the thrill coursing through his veins. Kylie was his. He didn't fool himself into thinking this was a cure-all and that they didn't have plenty of obstacles still to overcome. But for the first time, he was at peace, and hope was alive in his heart and mind.

He stroked a hand down the length of Kylie's body, simply enjoying the feel of her in his arms. Naked, beautiful, warm and sated.

"Thank you," she whispered. "For what you gave me tonight. I know it couldn't have been easy for you, for a man like you, I mean. But I'll never forget this, Jensen. I can't even put into words what this meant to me."

His chest tightened and he struggled to find the words around the knot in his throat.

"It was the easiest thing I've ever done," he said. And it was the absolute truth. Giving up control to this woman had been a no-brainer. She was worth every sacrifice. "Giving control to you was worth every bit, Kylie. I don't want you to ever worry that I'll regret it or grow to resent you for it. I'm willing to give you control for as long as you need. Forever, if that's what it takes for us to be together. If the end result is having you in my arms just like now, then I'll do whatever it takes to achieve that."

"I love you," she whispered, shocking him to the core with her declaration. "I know it's too soon. I've battled with myself over whether what I was feeling was love. I've made myself crazy worrying, but I don't *want* to worry anymore. I just want to *feel*, and my life has been a study in not feeling anything at all. Not risking being hurt by allowing myself to feel. But what I feel when I'm with you is *love*. I'm certain of it. It can't be anything else. Nothing else could feel this wonderful. I've never loved anyone else. Not like this, I mean. Just Carson and Chessy and Joss, of course, but what I feel for you in no way compares to how I feel about them. It scares me but at the same time it just feels . . . *right*."

He gathered her more tightly in his arms, closing his eyes at the sudden swell of emotion that punched a hole in his chest. The courage it must have taken for her to say those words, especially after taking such a huge leap by trusting him to be intimate with her, was mind-boggling.

He was awed by the precious gift lying in his arms. Overcome by the fact that this brave, courageous woman loved him. He didn't feel worthy of her love or her trust, but God, he wanted both. He wanted her with every breath in his body. He needed her like he needed air to breathe. She *was* the air he breathed. She'd so quickly become his reason to be. And he knew he'd never feel complete again without her. That he loved her unreservedly. That what he felt for her in no way came close to what he'd felt for anyone else in his life.

He stroked her hair, trying to compose himself. He didn't

want to mess this up. It was too important. She'd placed her trust, her faith and her well-being solidly in his hands and he wouldn't fail her.

"I love you too, baby. So much. If you believe nothing else, believe that. I think I've loved you from the very first moment I laid eyes on you."

She turned her face up from where it was buried in his chest and met his gaze, tears shimmering in those beautiful eyes.

"What are we going to do, Jensen? I know tonight was a huge step, but I know we have so many other issues to face. I don't want to ever cause problems between us. I want your love. I *need* it. I never thought I'd want or need this connection to a man and it caught me by surprise. I was blindsided by you. You snuck up on me when I wasn't looking and suddenly you were there— *here*," she amended, placing her hand over her heart. "I don't want to *mess this up*."

He kissed her furrowed brow, trying to ease the strain that was so evident. Her words and expression were so earnest. So heartbreakingly vulnerable. He never wanted her to feel fear when she was with him, but some things were out of his control. He, who was used to absolute control in all aspects of his life, had to accept that when it came to this woman he was in no way in control of anything at all.

"It won't be easy," he said truthfully. "But nothing good or worthwhile is ever easy. We'll work at it together. United, we can conquer anything. I want you to have faith in that. And the other thing you need to know is that I'm not going anywhere. No matter how hard it gets, no matter how difficult things may be, I'm here to stay and I'm never giving up on you or *us*."

Tears glittered more brightly, clinging to her eyelashes, and finally slid soundlessly down her cheeks. He thumbed one away with a gentle touch, his heart aching at the fear and uncertainty in both her eyes and words.

"I won't give up either," she quietly vowed. "Don't let me run, Jensen. Don't let me hide from you—us. It's what I do best. When things get sticky, I retreat, I run, and I stick my head in the sand where I know it's safe. Don't give up on me. I'll try never to hurt you. I need you to believe that I want this. I want you and I want there to *be* an us."

He smiled, contentment ever growing in his soul. "If you run, I'll just come after you and drag you back to me. I won't let you get away, baby. Not unless that's truly what you want. I want you to be mine, but more than that, I want you to be happy and for you to feel safe. Always."

She closed her eyes, visibly collecting herself, and when she reopened them they burned with earnestness. "I love you."

The simple statement with such a wealth of emotion behind it was staggering. He felt humbled by the love and trust burning in her eyes. Never had he felt more unworthy than right here and now but he wasn't going to turn down such a precious gift. Ever.

He squeezed her tight, savoring her softness against his much harder body. "I love you too, Kylie. We'll make it, okay? We'll get there. Just give us time."

Her gaze lowered but not before he saw the flicker of pain in her eyes.

"I feel like such a failure," she admitted. "I *know* I can trust you and yet I couldn't even be intimate with you without tying you up. It sounds so ridiculous. Here I'm saying I love you and I trust you and we didn't even achieve penetration. How does that not make me a huge hypocrite to say one thing and do something altogether different?"

His heart turned over at the consternation in her voice. He nudged her chin up with his fingers, forcing her to meet his gaze.

"Baby, this is a huge leap forward for us—you. There is no hurry and I don't want you beating yourself up over this. I'm happy and you're happy. Nothing else matters. In time you'll trust me enough to let me make love to you. You'll trust *yourself*. Until then, you'll tie me to the bed each time until you feel confident enough to take the ultimate plunge."

Her lips turned down into a grimace. "I wish I were as confident as you."

"I have enough confidence for both of us," he said gently. "We will get there, Kylie. Rome wasn't built in a day. This will and should take time. It's not something we can take too lightly. You have to absolutely feel safe with me, because if we jump the gun, we can do far more damage by trying to rush things. I'm perfectly content to leave things as they are until you're ready to take that final step. You don't have to apologize nor do you have to justify your fears. Not to me. Never to me. I love you and love is about doing whatever it takes to safeguard the one you love."

She leaned up, pressing her soft mouth to his. "I love you so much," she whispered against his lips. "I don't deserve you or your patience but I thank God for both. I never imagined feeling this way about anyone. It's scary and beautiful all at the same time."

He kissed her back, slow and sweet, his tongue tasting her, lapping tenderly at her lips and tongue. Then he leaned back, simply savoring the connection between them. This moment when they both laid themselves bare. He didn't want this moment to end. Didn't want the outside world intruding on something so new and beautiful. Fragile and vulnerable.

"Not to change the subject but we didn't talk about my conversation with Dash and I promised you full disclosure. And I can't think of a better time to talk to you than when you're in my arms all soft and sweet."

She smiled. "What does it say about me that Dash and my job were the absolute furthest things from my mind?"

"I think what it says about you is that you were too focused on me and, while that may make me an egotistical bastard, I like that you aren't thinking of anything else when you're with me."

She kissed him again before settling back so she could see him. Her hair spilled over the pillow like satin. She was nestled on her side, her legs entwined with his. He was already sporting another hard-on, but he didn't try to hide it. He wanted her to know how much he wanted and desired her. How beautiful he found her.

"So what did Dash have to say? And what exactly did you tell him?"

He stroked his hand down her body, unable to keep from touching her as they conversed. There was something decidedly intimate about talking about even mundane topics in bed, wrapped around one another, a barrier to the outside world.

"I told him to start looking for another office manager because your talents were wasted in that area. I told him I wanted you to have the rest of the week off. You need rest, but admittedly that's me being selfish because I like having you all to myself and I'm not ready to let you go just yet or share you with anyone else."

She looked pleased with his statement and not at all angry that he was basically making decisions for her when it came to her job. He had to tread a very fine line because even though he'd given her control when it came to their lovemaking, it was only natural that his dominance asserted itself in other areas.

"I also told him that you'd landed the S&G contract for us and that we needed to allow you to work more closely with us, and that in the future you'd make an excellent partner in the business."

Her brow furrowed even as delight shone in her eyes.

"And how did he take that?" she asked hesitantly.

"He took it well. He agreed to start looking for another office manager now. I told him that you needed to be able to focus more fully on other aspects of the business and wouldn't have time to juggle everything else we throw at you. You'll need someone yourself to help out, so in essence the new office manager will work for the three of us. Not just me and Dash."

"Your confidence in me means the world to me, Jensen," she said sincerely. "In time I hope to be able to see myself as you see me. I'm working on it, but as you said, Rome wasn't built in a day."

He chuckled at having his words thrown back at him. "Very true, baby."

She hedged a bit, obviously struggling with what she asked next.

"And does he know . . . about us?"

Jensen nodded. "I told him the truth. I told him you were mine."

She blinked as if weighing such a blunt declaration. Then a soft smile spread over her beautiful face, her eyes shining.

"I like that," she said quietly. "I like the way it sounds when you say it. I've never truly belonged to anyone. If anyone had told me that I'd be happy with another man being so . . . *possessive*, I would have flatly denied it. I would have never believed that I'd like it or *allow* it."

"You *are* mine," he said just as quietly. "Never doubt that.

And I protect what's mine. I'm going to warn you now. I gave you control in the area of our lovemaking and I was happy to do so. But my . . . dominance, for lack of a better word, will assert itself in other ways. Some of which you may not like or that may frighten or overwhelm you. I don't say that to scare you. I'm just being honest because I don't want it to catch you off guard or freak you out."

She bit her bottom lip and studied him a long moment in silence.

"I know how huge it was, you giving up control to me. I know it goes against everything that makes you who and what you are. I don't want you to ever think I don't know the magnitude of that. I do. Nor do I want you to ever think I don't cherish what you're giving me. And as you said, we'll get there. I have no doubt that we'll be able to work out any kinks in our relationship as long as you understand that there will most certainly be times we butt heads. I can be stubborn and I'm used to doing things my own way. You know that. But I want this to work and I find I don't quite mind the idea of your dominance. At least in theory."

He cupped her cheek in his palm and stroked his fingers over her jaw, pushing away silky strands of her hair. She leaned farther into him so their noses were only inches apart. Her eyes were earnest, burning with sincerity.

"I don't want you to ever change who and what you are for me. I never understood what Joss was talking about when she said she loved Carson too much to ever demand of him something he couldn't give her. But I understand *now*. Because I don't want you to change who you are for me. I love you just the way you are."

His heart melted into a puddle right there on the bed. He

kissed her again, deep, until they were both breathless and their pulses racing.

"The same goes for you, Kylie. I don't want *you* to ever change who or what you are for me because I love you just the way you are."

"Then I guess we'll have to find a way to coexist together, warts and all," she said cheekily.

"Bet your ass," he growled.

She yawned broadly, her eyes looking sleepy and contented.

He pulled her into his arms, nestling her head against his shoulder.

"Sleep now, baby. I'll go into work late in the morning so we can have breakfast together."

"That sounds wonderful," she murmured. "And I'll cook dinner for us tomorrow when you get home from work."

He kissed her forehead, contentment spreading rapidly through his veins to the very heart and soul of him.

He knew they likely had a rough road ahead of them, but optimism was bright in his heart. Kylie was his and he wasn't letting her go. They'd get through whatever issues they had together.

NINETEEN

KYLIE hummed to herself as she brushed out her hair and applied her makeup. The week had flown by and strangely, she wasn't looking forward to going into work on Monday. She'd enjoyed her time with Jensen too much. It had been just the two of them the entire week, settling into a comfortable routine.

Jensen went to work in the mornings after eating breakfast with her and he returned promptly at five. Though Kylie had spoken to both Joss and Chessy on the phone, she hadn't gone into detail about her first time being intimate with Jensen. It just hadn't felt right. It was private. Between her and Jensen, and she didn't want the rest of the world to know what went on in their bedroom or the sacrifices he was making for her.

He was a proud man and while she had confided his offer to her best friends, she wished now she hadn't. At the time she'd needed the sounding board. A way to talk about her fears and perhaps get validation from her friends. But now she regretted confiding Jensen's gift to them. It was beautiful and precious, the most selfless gift she'd ever received.

She immediately brightened when she heard the front door open, and she tossed aside the brush, giving herself a quick once-over before hurrying from Jensen's bedroom into the living room.

He'd called earlier and told her they'd eat out again tonight. Cattleman's was a pub and diner that offered great food in a casual environment. Kylie had eaten there a few times with Joss and Chessy before they'd made the Lux Café their permanent "go-to" spot.

She was looking forward to another night out with him. They hadn't had sex since that first time a few nights earlier. He hadn't pushed and neither had she. Perhaps she feared having another freak-out moment and ruining what progress they'd made. Who really knew?

What she did know was that she was solidly in love and not having sex had in no way impeded their deepening relationship. No need to rock the boat when they were floating along just fine.

Jensen's face lit up when he saw her. She loved that look. The same look he gave her every day when he came home from work. As if he couldn't wait to see her and she was the highlight of his day.

Her earlier thought that she wasn't looking forward to returning to work on Monday fled as she took in the fact that she'd get to spend the entire day with him. They'd ride in together and come home together. What could be better?

"What's that look for?" he asked, his expression perplexed.

She shook herself from her thoughts and dove into his arms, hugging him to her.

"Sorry. I was just rethinking something I thought earlier. Or rather unthinking it."

He chuckled against her, his chest vibrating against her cheek. She closed her eyes and held on to him, savoring their closeness and the comfort he brought her by just . . . being. With her. Coming home to her and being so happy to see her each day.

"That made absolutely no sense," he said in amusement.

She drew away with a smile, absorbing his gaze, drinking in the sight of him. All male, gorgeous and vibrant. She shivered at the intensity of his gaze and wondered if tonight would be the night they'd make love again. But then it was all up to her, wasn't it? She called the shots, so all she had to do was say she wanted him and he would be at her disposal.

"Well, I was thinking earlier that I wasn't really looking forward to going back to work on Monday. I've enjoyed this week so much. But then I realized that when I go back to work, I'll get to spend the entire day with you and not just see you in the mornings and afternoons. So I corrected the idea that I wasn't looking forward to work and decided that I'm very much looking forward to getting to spend the entire day with you."

His eyes glimmered in amusement and a satisfied smile curved his sensual lips. Lips she very much wanted on her. Her heart fluttered as she imagined allowing him to touch her. Would she be able to handle it? Her heart and body recognized the desire and echoed her yearning. Her mind was the only thing holding her back.

"I'm glad you've seen the error of your ways. Although I won't lie. This week has been wonderful with you here, waiting for me to get home. I wasn't ready to share you with the rest of the world. Not yet. And I won't say that I'll be ready on Monday, but I've held you back long enough. It's time to set you loose and let you go kick some ass. That I get to be there with you is just icing on the cake."

"Flattery will get you everywhere," she said with a grin. "Now, are you going to change so you can feed me? It's been a while since I ate at Cattleman's. I'm looking forward to some good bar food and lots of carbs."

"Never let it be said that I denied my woman anything."

He kissed her quickly and then headed into the bedroom, leaving her to stare at his ass and have lustful thoughts.

Did it make her a moron that she got a ridiculous thrill from the words "my woman"?

She shivered because, moron or not, the way he said it just hit all her girly buttons. She was left with a goofy grin, her hormones raging over that ass of his. God, she was turning into a squealing teenager about to go on her first date.

Deciding to be a bit, okay a lot, bold, she followed him into the bedroom, hoping for a peek while he was changing. Apparently she could add voyeurism to her growing list of things she'd never imagined indulging in.

Her breath caught in her throat when she entered to see him stripped down to his underwear. His back muscles rippled as he pulled a shirt over his shoulders and she shamelessly stood there, enjoying the view.

Her gaze drifted downward to the very noticeable bulge in his underwear. It indeed appeared as though he did look forward to coming home to her each day.

Had it been a version of hell the last few days of them not having sex? Had she merely teased him with their first foray into intimacy? She didn't like the idea of being some prick tease. It wasn't in her nature to lead a man on. Not that it was what she was doing exactly. But she didn't like the idea of him being unfulfilled.

He turned, his brow rising as he saw her standing in the doorway. Then he smiled as he reached for his pants.

"Is this where I say 'busted'?" he asked with no remorse.

She shook her head, smiling back at him. "Not at all. I . . . like . . . seeing that you want me. Unless that erection is for someone else?" she asked innocently.

He snorted. "As if. Do you see any other gorgeous, desirable woman here?"

"Nope. Don't even see one," she said, her cheeks growing warm with his compliment.

He scowled at her response and then strode over to where she stood, pulling her into his arms. She landed with a thud against his chest and he tipped her chin upward before crushing his mouth over hers.

He rubbed his groin against her belly so she'd feel just how hard he was. She slid her hands between them, cupping his cock through the denim of his jeans, and caressed him gently.

His moan was guttural, the sound of a male in desperate need. Tonight, come hell or high water, she was going to mount a charge. If she had her way, neither of them would be aching much longer.

TWENTY

KYLIE and Jensen were seated at a table by the window at Cattleman's and Kylie was munching on an appetizer of nachos when an extremely handsome man walked up to their table.

Beside him was a gorgeous woman with brilliant blue eyes and midnight black hair. It was a striking contrast. The couple looked like a million dollars together and it was obvious the man had money.

It wasn't that he looked ostentatious, or he was one of those guys who openly flaunted his wealth. He just had a quiet authority about him and his clothing was designer, very expensive and looked very good on him. Then there was the rock the woman sported on her ring finger. It caught the light and shimmered, nearly blinding Kylie in the process.

Okay, maybe that was a slight exaggeration, but still. She wasn't wrong about this man—and woman—being wealthy. She'd hung out in Carson's circles enough to know the real deal when she saw it. She was also trained to catch on to the wannabes, the ones who tried to make it look like they had more money and status than they had in reality.

"Jensen, it's good to see you," the man said as he approached.

As he stopped at their table, he pulled the woman to his side in a gesture that looked practiced and automatic. It was obvious this man was possessive of her. It was evident in his body language. And the way he looked at her spoke volumes.

Jensen glanced up, his expression easing with recognition. And then he smiled warmly at the couple and stood. Kylie sat there like a deer in the headlights, unsure if she should stand or not. But Jensen reached a hand down to her, collecting hers and squeezing as if to reassure her.

God she loved that about him. That he was always so mindful and protective of her.

"Hello, Damon. Serena," he said to the woman. Then he turned to Kylie, his eyes possessive, positively screaming to the world that she was his. "I'd like you both to meet Kylie. She's very special to me."

A surge of joy flooded her heart at the simple way he declared their relationship.

"Kylie, this is Damon Roche and his wife, Serena."

"It's very nice to meet you, Kylie," Damon said, charm evident in his voice. But so too was there that authority that she'd noticed about him. There was something about him that fascinated Kylie but made her wary at the same time.

Dominance.

The word came silently to her, her instincts telling her unquestionably that this man was dominant. It seemed everyone around her was either dominant or submissive. The world seemed very small, indeed.

"Hello, Kylie," Serena said, a warm smile on her beautiful face.

"Hi," Kylie said shyly. "It's very nice to meet you both."

"We won't keep you," Damon said to Jensen. "But it's been a

while since I saw you last and I wanted to come over and say hello at least."

Jensen shook his hand and then leaned in to kiss Serena on the cheek. Kylie gave them a small wave as they turned and headed in the opposite direction. Then Jensen retook his seat and Kylie looked at him in question.

"Who are they?" she asked.

"Acquaintances," he said. "I haven't known them long and met them through Dash."

A prickle of awareness stirred at her nape. Damon's name rang a sudden bell with her. Joss had mentioned him. If she wasn't mistaken, he was the *owner* of the place Joss had joined and intended to go to in her quest for dominance. And if Jensen knew him . . .

"Are you a member there?" she asked quietly.

He didn't pretend to misunderstand her. He was ever blunt, a fact she appreciated. She never had to wonder where she stood with him or what he was thinking or feeling because he never held anything back with her.

Except his need for dominance.

She flinched at that reminder, still raw over the knowledge that he was denying a huge part of himself. For her.

"I'm a member, yes. But as of yet I haven't participated and now I have no intention of ever doing so."

"Chessy and Tate and Joss and Dash go there," Kylie murmured.

"Yes, I know," he said calmly. "But I've never been there when they were there. In fact, I've only been twice, both times for the application process and to tour the facilities."

She pursed her lips, wondering if she even wanted to know

the answer to her next question. She knew of the lifestyle. She'd heard enough of Chessy and Joss's conversations to have a good idea of just what went on there, but she'd never gotten explicit details. She wasn't even sure why her curiosity was stirred.

"What exactly goes on there?" she finally asked. "I mean Chessy and Joss have talked about it but to be honest most of the time I shut them out because I didn't *want* to know. And I was worried sick about Joss when she first said she was going to start attending."

"Why would you want to know *now*?" he asked softly.

She shrugged. "Just curious, I suppose. I mean it's not that I'm interested in going there. I guess I should drop it. I don't like to remind you of what you're being denied."

"Kylie. Look at me, baby."

She glanced up, meeting his gaze. His stare was intense and utterly focused on her. He *radiated* seriousness.

"I'm not being denied anything. I made a *choice*, one that I do *not* regret. I have no interest in The House any longer. What I want and what I need is right here in front of me."

Even though logically she knew all of this, relief still surged through her veins, leaving a tightness in her chest that was almost painful.

"Do you believe that, baby?"

She nodded slowly. "Yes, I do, Jensen. But I won't lie. At times it worries me that you've given up so much for me."

"Maybe you should focus more on what I've gained," he pointed out. "Because from where I'm standing, I haven't given up a damn thing, and I've gained far more than I ever dreamed of."

Reassured by the sincerity of his words, she plunged ahead.

"So what does go on there?" she asked with more confidence.

Knowing didn't hurt her. It didn't involve her. It did nothing more than assuage her curiosity over the lifestyle her two best friends lived.

"The House is a place for people to indulge themselves in all manner of sexual fantasies. Pretty much everything goes. Within reason, of course. It's not only about dominance and submission. There are plenty of other fantasies that people delight in. It's a place where they can freely—and safely—indulge themselves."

"So is it, like, public? I mean do the people who go there act these fantasies out in front of everyone else there?"

It was a little mind-boggling to imagine Chessy and Joss doing whatever it was they did for everyone to see, and maybe a small part of her didn't *want* to imagine her friends in those kinds of situations. Definitely an occasion for brain bleach.

"Some do. Some don't. The option is there for both," he said with a shrug. "There is a common room where everything is public. But there are also private rooms, monitored by security so no one gets hurt."

"It sounds . . . different," she said lamely, not knowing what else to say about something she had no understanding of. The mere idea of having sex in public gave her hives. She could barely muster the courage to do it in private much less for the world to see.

He chuckled lightly. "It is different. But not so very much for the people who go. To them it's the normal course of their sexuality. Whatever works. As long as it's sane and consensual, to each his own."

Well that certainly put her in her place. And perhaps she needed to not be so judgmental. Who was she to pass judgment on other people anyway? She had so many hang-ups that it would take a psychologist years to sort through, so it wasn't as if she could talk.

"You have nothing to worry about," Jensen soothed. "I would never dream of bringing you there. I have no desire for the place any longer. When I first met Dash and we spoke of it, it intrigued me, yes. I even pursued membership. But then I met you. Or rather I met you and then pursued the membership but then once I got it, I had no desire to go. I wanted . . . *you*."

"I'll never understand why," she said honestly. "But I'm so glad you didn't go and that you do want me, issues and all. You give me hope, Jensen. The first real hope I've had in my entire life to enjoy a normal relationship. Or as normal as we'll ever be, I suppose."

The rueful note in her voice couldn't be disguised.

"Who needs normal?" he asked lightly. "Normal is how *we* define it, not others. So everyone's normal is different. Ours is what we make it. Besides, if not being with you means I'm normal then fuck that. I'd much rather be abnormal with you."

She grinned, her mood lightening. God, but with her plans for later, she was doing her level best to be a huge wet blanket. Or at the very least, sabotaging her own efforts for that normalcy she spoke of.

Their orders were delivered and Kylie found herself eating rapidly. She was occupied with the rest of the evening. Food was the very last thing on her mind. She glanced up to see that Jensen was finished and she spoke before she lost her nerve.

"You ready to go home?" she asked, eager to get on with her plans for the night.

A spark lit in his eyes. Recognition. Was she that obvious? Or perhaps she was merely that desperate. The thought amused her because she would have never described herself as desperate before meeting Jensen. Now all she could think about was getting him naked and them being skin to skin.

An uproar close to the door had Kylie picking her head up to see what the ruckus was about. Her mouth twisted in distaste when she saw an obviously drunk—and loud—man being coaxed from the bar by his harried female companion.

She glanced away, not wanting anything to ruin her night.

Jensen paid the bill and then stood and took her hand, pulling her to her feet. He tucked her against his side and they walked to the door and into the night.

She didn't realize anything was wrong until Jensen went rigid against her. She glanced up in the direction of where he was staring, startled when a low growl rumbled from his chest.

The couple she'd noticed before had evidently taken their altercation into the parking lot. The man had his fist in the woman's hair and was yelling obscenities at her.

Then to her utter horror, the man struck the woman with his fist, knocking her to the ground.

Jensen lunged for the man, knocking him flat with a well-aimed blow. The man went down. Hard. Kylie stood frozen, unable to react or move as Jensen bent over the fallen woman and helped her to her feet.

Kylie's heart was thundering against her chest and sweat beaded on her forehead. Nausea rose, sharp in her stomach, and she had to swallow back the urge to rid her stomach of its contents.

"Are you all right?" Jensen asked the woman in a gentle voice. "Let me help you. I'll call the police and have this bastard locked up."

"No!" the woman all but shrieked. "Please, just leave us alone. You'll only make it worse!"

Her voice turned pleading. She grasped Jensen's hand and shook him, desperation in her eyes and words.

Jensen stared at her in shock and then glanced at where the man lay groaning on the ground.

"You want me to walk away after what he did to you?" Jensen asked hoarsely.

"Please, just go," the woman begged. "I'll get him home. He didn't mean it. He's just drunk. He has no idea what he's doing. He won't even remember in the morning."

"And how the hell will you explain that bruise on your cheek?" Jensen demanded.

The woman glanced in panic at the man who was trying to get to his feet. "It doesn't matter. Okay? Just go, please. I'll deal with him. He didn't mean anything by it. Please just go. It'll be worse for me if you interfere."

Kylie found her feet and her tongue at last. She slid up behind Jensen and tucked her hand into his. He turned as if just realizing she was there. Darkness simmered in his eyes. Rage coiled and burned, his entire body bristling.

"Let's go, Jensen," she whispered. "He'll hurt her more. She doesn't want you to call the police."

"Listen to her," the woman urged. "It's nothing I haven't dealt with before. He'll regret it in the morning, if he even remembers."

"That's *no* excuse," Jensen said flatly. "You should have his ass thrown in jail and swear out a restraining order against him."

Kylie tugged at his hand, desperate to get away before the situation escalated. The man was struggling to his feet and whirling, obviously looking for his companion. The woman he'd just flattened with his fist.

The woman threw them one last desperate look and then

went to the man's side, sliding up against him, supporting his weight.

Jensen swore violently under his breath. His entire body quivered against her. His fingers were squeezing hers so tightly that she realized how tenuous his hold on his control was.

She pulled once more, worried he'd go after the man again. To her relief, this time he came with her. The entire way to his car, he kept glancing over his shoulder, worry evident in his gaze as he searched out the man and woman.

"Goddamn it, that makes me sick," Jensen swore as he guided Kylie into the passenger seat.

Kylie stared out her window as the woman struggled to get the man in the passenger seat of their vehicle. Her heart clenched as she imagined the life this woman must lead. A life where she made excuses for her husband or boyfriend's abuse. She closed her eyes, only wanting to shut out the images bombarding her from all sides.

The evening lay in ruins, her earlier optimism fading rapidly.

The entire way home, silence lay heavy over the inside of the car. Jensen's hands were tightly curled around the steering wheel, his stare fixed ahead as he navigated through traffic. Several times she glanced his way but he never took his eyes from the road.

The tension was thick, a tangible cloak surrounding them, almost suffocating in its intensity. She'd seen the terrible rage in Jensen's eyes and then . . . *bleakness*. So much grief and sorrow that it had overwhelmed her.

What darkness did he have in his past? They'd only spoken briefly about it. He'd hinted that he had his own demons to fight and the one time she'd asked, he'd steered her away from the conversation, saying he'd tell her later.

Now she realized that she had to know. Now, not later.

She'd been so absorbed in her own issues that she hadn't given any thought to his, an oversight she intended to correct immediately.

If he'd open up to her.

She flinched because she hadn't opened up to him but here she was expecting him to bare his soul to her. He knew some of her past, but she knew nothing of his. And if they had any hope of moving forward, they not only had to put her demons to rest, but his as well. Starting now.

TWENTY-ONE

JENSEN unlocked the door to his house and ushered Kylie in. He glanced sideways at her to see her face was drawn and pale. She had her arms hugged around herself and was rubbing her palms up and down her skin in agitation.

He swore under his breath because the night lay in ruins. He knew well what Kylie had planned, what she'd likely been working her nerve up to do all week. And now? Who knew what kind of hell she was enduring after that asshole's behavior in the parking lot.

It went against every grain for him to just walk away when he damn well knew the bastard would hurt the woman again and again. He'd continue to do it until she fought back, until she put a stop to it. But for Jensen to just walk away and pretend he hadn't witnessed what he did?

It made him sick.

His own demons came roaring to life, no longer contained by the barriers he'd erected over the years. They were simmering just below the surface, scratching and clawing their way out of his mind.

"Jensen?"

Kylie's quiet voice shook him from his thoughts. He glanced at her again to see her studying him, her expression troubled.

"Yes, baby?"

"We need to talk," she said in a low voice.

He nodded, unable to say anything in response.

She took his hand, surprising him with the way she seemed to be trying to soothe him. As if she weren't the one who'd just revisited hell by watching in real time everything that had happened to her. Only what she'd endured was far worse. Getting smacked in the face wasn't even scratching the surface of all that had been done to her.

"Come into the bedroom," she said quietly. "Let's get into bed and we'll talk there."

He pulled her into his arms, simply wanting to hold her for a moment. To reassure himself that she was safe. That she was here with him and not a million miles away in another place and time.

He kissed the top of her head, inhaling the scent of her silky hair. She wrapped her arms around him, hugging him fiercely, as if again she was soothing him and not the other way around.

"I'd like that," he said.

She drew away but kept ahold of his hand and then tugged him toward the bedroom. When they entered, she went to the drawer where most of her clothing was and pulled out a pair of pajamas.

She stripped efficiently, not at all bothered by the fact he could see her. He was relieved that for the most part she didn't seem too traumatized over the night's events. Perhaps he was the one reeling the most. Seeing the woman brutalized in the parking lot had brought back painful memories for him. A feeling of helplessness had gripped him when the woman had pleaded with him not to call the police.

God, he never wanted to feel that helplessness again.

His hands were shaking. He hadn't even realized it until Kylie came over to him and slid her hands into his, squeezing in a comforting manner.

"We need to get you undressed and ready for bed," she said.

He stood there while she undressed him piece by piece. She moved slowly and almost reverently, as if she'd taken over the role of caregiver, one usually assigned to him. And yet he allowed it, savoring the sensation of having someone who loved him to care for him when he was vulnerable.

Only with this woman would he ever allow this side of himself to be exposed. With no one else had he ever felt secure enough to allow control out of his grasp.

When he was down to his underwear, she guided him toward the bed, pulling the covers back so they could get in.

As soon as they were both settled in, Kylie snuggled into his arms, pillowing her head on his shoulder.

"What happened tonight, Jensen?" she asked gently. "Aside from the obvious. I saw the look in your eyes. I saw more than anger or rage. I saw grief and . . . despair. You once told me that I wasn't the only one who struggled with the demons of their past. Will you tell me about them now?"

He closed his eyes a moment, wondering just how much he should tell her. It wasn't that he didn't want to tell her or didn't trust her enough to share. He worried that it would bring back unpleasant memories for her if he related his own tormented childhood.

As if reaching into his mind and plucking out his thoughts, she cupped his jaw and smoothed her hand over his cheek.

"Tonight is about you," she said in a soft voice. "I don't want you to worry about me. For once, let me be the strong one for you. I'll listen. To whatever you tell me. And I'll never tell anyone else. You can trust me."

He turned his face in to her hand, kissing her palm. "Ah, Kylie, I trust you absolutely. I trust you more than anyone else. I just don't want to hurt you or bring back painful memories for you."

"You won't," she said solemnly. "Not tonight. Tonight I'm here to listen. To be strong for you like you've been strong for me."

God, but he loved this woman. The idea of not being with her ripped a hole in his heart. He never wanted to contemplate a life without her. Not now that he had her. She belonged to him, and he'd never willingly let her go.

She touched his face again, lightly stroking the curve of his jaw.

"I love you. Remember that. Nothing you say will ever change that."

He closed his eyes, wondering how he'd gotten so damn lucky. Who would have ever thought he'd meet his soul mate in a woman with whom sexual dominance wasn't possible. But then she'd likely never pondered or entertained even for a moment becoming involved with a dominant man, so perhaps they were even.

"I hope to hell that will always be the case," he said.

She nodded, sincerity blazing in her eyes.

He sucked in a breath, taking the plunge. He wanted to get it over with. Like ripping a bandage off quickly.

"Like you I come from an abusive background. My father—"

He choked on the words, hating to give the man who'd been such a monster the reverence of that title.

Sorrow filled her eyes. And understanding. But she remained silent, not interrupting him as he struggled with how to continue.

"Unlike in your case, most of his abuse wasn't directed at me. I wish to hell it *had* been. That I could have dealt with. But he took out his rage on my mother and I was helpless to do anything but watch and then pick up the pieces afterward. I hate that feeling. I *hate* it."

A tear slid down Kylie's cheek, her grief as thick as his own. She understood all too well his feelings on the subject. She knew more than anyone else his pain and the wretchedness of his memories.

Her hand trembled against his cheek but she kept it there, a silent signal of her love and support.

"Did it ever stop?" she asked quietly.

Jensen closed his eyes, pain burning like fire in his chest. It was almost too much, going back to that time in his life. He hadn't opened that door in a very long time and now that it was flung wide, he couldn't keep it under control.

Images flashed in his mind, tumbling faster and faster until he was dizzy from it.

"No," he whispered. "God, no. He was a bastard to the bitter end. The day he was diagnosed with terminal cancer I celebrated. Jesus. I was fucking *thrilled* that the old man was going to endure a painful death. I *wished* it on him. Time and time again, and all I could think when it happened was that God had answered my prayer. How twisted is that?"

"It's not," she defended. "It was justice. It was what he deserved."

"And my mother. God, she sat with him until the bitter end. I never understood that. But when it was over, she cleaned out their bank accounts, gave me the money and told me to go and be happy. Be *happy*. As if it were that easy. She expected me to walk away and leave her, move on with my life and forget the hell he put us both through."

Her brow furrowed. "Did you?"

Jensen shook his head. "I couldn't just leave her. I resented her for sticking by him through his illness, but I couldn't just walk away from her. I didn't understand why *she* didn't walk away at her first opportunity. Maybe I'll never understand it."

"What happened?" she asked softly.

She'd picked up on the fact that there was more.

He lay back, staring at the ceiling, feeling anger and . . . betrayal, a sense of betrayal. One he'd never fully recognized until now. He felt betrayed by his mother, only now he couldn't help but wonder if she'd done the best thing she could have.

"She left," he said, trying to keep the bitterness from his words. "Since I wouldn't just leave her and go on my way, she did."

Kylie's mouth dropped open in shock. Anger flickered in her eyes before she stifled it and blinked it away.

"She left? Just like that?"

Jensen nodded. "I never saw her or heard from her again. There was a time I searched for her. After college, when I landed a job and started making money. I wanted to see how she was doing. I wanted to give her back what she'd given to me, because she was left with nothing. I always wondered how she managed. But she disappeared. I have no idea if she's alive or dead. In my darkest moments, I wonder if she didn't go away so she *could* die. If she perhaps didn't do the job herself. Maybe she was trying to spare me more pain. Who knows? I know that's a horrible thing to imagine, but I can't come up with another explanation."

"Oh, Jensen," she said, her voice aching with emotion. "I'm so sorry. How awful for you not to know. I can't imagine what that's like. To need closure and have no possible way for you to achieve it."

"I just want to know that she's okay," he said in a low voice. "That maybe she's even happy. At times I think I've made peace with it all, and at others, I recognize that I'll never fully be at peace over the entire thing."

"That's understandable."

"And sometimes I wonder if she blamed me," he said baldly. "For not protecting her. For allowing him to hurt her. If she hated me for it. For my weakness."

Kylie rose over him, her eyes stricken. "Jensen, no! You were just a *child*. You were the one who was supposed to be protected. By your father and your mother. It wasn't your job to protect her. You aren't to blame for what he did."

"I wish I could believe that," he said wearily. "I just wish I could tell her I was sorry. She was a good woman. But she'd been beaten down too many times. Her spirit was just broken. She was utterly defeated and in the end I just don't think she had anything left. Maybe she didn't want me to see her that way. Maybe that's why she tried to get me to leave and when I didn't, she did. I guess I'll never know."

She wrapped her arms around him and hugged him to her. He could feel dampness on her cheek. Her tears for him shining on her skin.

The very last thing he wanted was to cause her pain. To make her remember. He wrapped his arms around her, thrusting his fingers into her hair, just holding her close.

"Two wounded souls finding the light," she whispered

against his neck. "We need each other, Jensen. We understand all too well."

"I do need you," he said, the words a benediction. "So much, baby. I can't even explain it to myself, how you mean so much to me in such a short time. I never believed in destiny before but you're clearly mine. Made for me."

"And you were made for me," she said, rising above him again.

Her hair streamed over her shoulders, falling over his face, silken strands caressing his skin. Then she lowered her lips to his, breathing him in as she kissed him.

Warm and so very sweet. Soft and soothing. She sipped at him, tasting and then drinking deeply from him.

She hesitated for a brief moment, sorrow entering her gaze.

"Let me get the rope."

Her words were more of an apology than a statement or declaration. She was apologizing for needing the goddamn rope. Didn't she know that he'd tie himself to the bed for the rest of his life if that was the only way he could have her?

"In the drawer," he said, latching onto her gaze, telling her without words not to apologize. Not for this. Never for this.

She slid off the bed and returned a moment later with the rope and then very gently secured his wrists to the headboard. She wouldn't meet his gaze and it gutted him that she would feel shame for the way they made love.

"Kylie, baby, look at me, please."

She finished securing the last knot and then sat back on her heels, her gaze slowly drifting upward until it locked with his.

"I'm okay with this. I need you to be okay with it too. And we don't have to do this right now. It's been a heavy night. I'm just as happy to hold you."

She shook her head, her eyes going soft with love. Then she leaned down and kissed him, tugging at his bottom lip with a playful nip.

"I want to make love to you right now," she whispered against his mouth. "I need to show you my love. Not just say it. You've been so strong for me. It's my turn to be strong for you. To let you lean on me for once. Let me do this. For you. For us."

He groaned, his dick threatening to tear a hole in his underwear. He was desperate for her. He needed her. Wanted her touch. Her sweetness and her light. Tonight more than ever.

She brushed her mouth over his chin and down his neck, sliding over his chest and further, over his taut abdomen. He flinched, his muscles tightening as her tongue swept a path across his flesh.

She made love to him as sweetly with her mouth as he'd ever been made love to. He was on fire for her, his need a desperate, tangible thing.

She hooked her fingers in the band of his underwear and gently tugged downward. His dick surged upward, bursting free of constraint. Already, moisture beaded and seeped from the tip. He had no control around her, given freely or not.

She licked a path upward on the underside of his erection and then back down again, swirling and lavishing sweetness over his balls. He pulled against his restraints, reaching for her even as he knew the impossibility of such an action. One day. One day he'd touch her as she was touching him. He'd caress and stroke the fire inside her to fever pitch.

She circled the head with her tongue and then sucked him deep into her mouth. His eyes rolled back into his head as pleasure exploded in his groin. Then she slid up, letting the tip fall free from her lips.

Her eyes glowing with resolve, she pulled her pajama top up and over her head, baring her breasts to his avid gaze. He sucked in his breath, afraid to hope when she went for her bottoms.

It took her a moment to get free of the bottoms and then her panties followed suit, baring her completely.

He soaked in every inch of her skin, her curves and swells, a feast of feminine flesh that had him salivating with the need to taste and touch her.

"Baby, you don't have to do this."

There was fire and determination in her eyes. "Yes, I do. I want to. I need to."

"Take your time then," he gently urged. "We have all night."

"You'll have to help me," she said hesitantly. "Tell me what to do."

His heart softened. She was trying so very hard and he never loved her more than at this moment.

"Straddle me," he said huskily. "Put my dick right in the V of your thighs. Let it rest against your belly. We'll take it nice and slow."

And then another thought occurred to him, one that had him swearing. They needed a goddamn condom. He was nearly blinded with the need to have her skin to skin, no barrier between them, but he'd never force an unwanted pregnancy on her. Not when they had so much else to resolve in their relationship.

"Kylie, baby, are you protected? I have condoms in the drawer with the rope."

Slowly she nodded. "I'm okay," she whispered. "I don't want to use one. Unless you want to, I mean. Is it okay?"

Relief surged through his veins, leaving him weak and dizzy with it. "Yes, baby. I'm okay. It's been a while for me."

She grinned crookedly. "It's been never for me."

Though he knew she wasn't physically a virgin, in all other ways she was in fact that very thing. The only thing she lacked was the fragile barrier but in every other aspect she was completely innocent.

How he wished things were different. That he could tenderly make love to her for her first experience. He wanted to show her how beautiful it could be with someone who loved her as much as he did. His only regret over her having control was that he couldn't give back to her all that she was giving to him.

"Touch yourself," he said, keeping his voice pitched low and soothing. "I want to make sure you're ready for me, baby. I don't want to hurt you."

She hesitated a moment, self-consciousness flickering across her face before she finally lowered one hand and slid it between her legs.

The backs of her knuckles brushed over his groin, her touch feather-light. She emitted a soft sigh as she began stroking herself. He ached to be the one touching her so intimately. His skin was on fire. It felt as though a thousand ants were racing just underneath the surface. He was restless and edgy, the thought of being inside her nearly catapulting him over the edge.

He sucked in his breath, determined to get a lock on his control. This had to be perfect for her. He'd withhold his release until she found hers. He was determined.

"Let me see," he murmured.

Her eyelids fluttered open and her eyes were drowsy and passion-laced. Almost a drugged, intoxicated look he was relieved to see. She was into it as much as he was.

She lifted her hand, her fingers glistening with moisture. It called to him, beckoning him to taste. This time he didn't have to ask. She took the initiative and extended her hand to him, sliding her finger over his lips.

He licked the tip, catching it and then sucking it into his mouth. He nibbled gently at it before letting it go.

"Are you ready for me, baby?"

"Yes," she breathed. "Tell me what to do, Jensen. I want this to be perfect for us."

"It can't be anything else but perfect with you. Lift your hips up and guide me. Take me inside you but take it nice and easy. Go slowly until you get used to having me inside you."

Her bottom lip disappeared between her teeth as she shifted her weight up. She grasped the base of his dick and suddenly he was engulfed by her heat. Her silky softness was surrounding the head. He'd never felt anything so goddamn perfect in his life.

"That's it," he encouraged. "Take more of me. Nice and slow."

She began lowering herself down, inch by exquisite inch, gliding like hot velvet, clutching at him like a fist. When she was halfway there, her eyes widened and she glanced down in consternation.

"I'm not sure this is going to work," she said shakily.

He smiled, willing himself not to arch up into her. He wanted to bury himself as deeply as he could go, but he forced himself to breathe through the urge and remain still until she was able to accommodate him.

"It will work. Touch yourself with your other hand. You need to be a little wetter. You're so tight, baby. God, you feel so good."

She obeyed, kneeling up astride him as she began to stroke her clit. She made a humming sound of pleasure and she closed her eyes. He felt the burst of dampness around his dick, felt her open, sucking him deeper.

She slid down another inch, causing them both to groan. He was almost there. So close.

And then she settled her full weight down on him, taking him completely.

She gasped, her eyes widening at the sudden fullness. It was overwhelming to him too. He clenched his jaw, fighting his release with every ounce of strength he possessed.

"Ride me, baby. Do what feels good to you. I want you to come. Touch yourself if you need to. Whatever you need. You're so beautiful. I've never seen a more gorgeous sight than you astride me."

She moved restlessly, rocking forward and then back. After a few tentative movements, she found a comfortable rhythm and she began moving up and down, lifting herself up and then allowing herself to slide back down his erection.

His dick was coated with her honey. Slick with her arousal and his precum. Each time she took him deep, he was surrounded by the lush warmth of her pussy.

It was a sight to behold, this small, curvy woman perched atop his much larger frame. Her hair streamed over her shoulders, playing an erotic game of peek-a-boo with her nipples.

The idea that he was her first lover, the first man she'd trusted enough to make love with, staggered him. He was humbled by such a precious gift. It was one he'd cherish the rest of his life. One he'd protect with his very life.

"I'm close," she said with a gasp. "I want you with me."

"I'll always be with you, baby. Come for me. I'll catch you. Just let go."

She leaned forward, bracing her palms on his chest, and she began to move faster, taking him deep and hard. Her breaths were ragged, her face flushed with heat and arousal.

His release swelled, growing like an impending thunderstorm. He felt her convulse around him, squeezing him tightly as she cried out in the throes of her orgasm. It spurred his own. He was helpless to do anything but arch into her, over and over, his entrance made easier as his release coated her passageway.

His vision blurred. The room dimmed around him until there was only her. She was all he saw, all he felt, all he knew. His arms strained against the ropes holding him down. He reached for her, desperate to hold her, touch her.

She sagged forward, her chest heaving, her breaths coming in ragged spurts over his chest. He was still wedged firmly inside her, still hard, achingly so. He was hypersensitive, still pulsing, each little wiggle from her eliciting another wave of ecstasy.

He waited, his patience fraying. He waited for her to untie him so he could hold her. So he could touch her and share in the aftermath of something wild and beautiful and innocent.

Finally she lifted herself up, her breasts hovering temptingly in his line of vision. They were, as she was, exquisite perfection, her nipples a delicate pink. His mouth watered at the idea of tasting her. Of sucking the rigid peaks into his mouth.

She reached over his head to pull at the bindings around his wrists. And when he was finally free, he wrapped his arms around her tightly, ignoring the stinging discomfort in his numb hands.

He rolled, bringing them to rest on their sides, him still penetrating her. He didn't pull free. He wanted to stay connected, to keep the intimacy thick around them.

He kissed her hungrily, his hips rocking back and forth against her. And then, realizing what he was doing, he stilled, an apology poised on his lips.

As if knowing what he was thinking, she put a finger to his mouth.

"It's all right," she whispered. "I know you won't hurt me."

He closed his eyes and gathered her close. But he was careful to remain still inside her. He'd vowed to give her absolute control. If and when they made love without him being restrained, it would be at her doing. Not his.

"I love you," he whispered against her ear. "I've never loved anyone more."

She nestled further into his embrace, her mouth pressed against the column of his neck.

"I love you too, Jensen. Thank you for sharing yourself with me tonight. For trusting me with your demons."

Left unsaid was that she had yet to confide her demons to him, but he didn't take it personally nor did it anger or disappoint him. What she'd given him tonight was infinitely more precious. She'd given him the gift of herself. That would always be enough for him.

TWENTY-TWO

JENSEN came awake with a gasp, his heart thudding violently in his chest. Sweat poured down his forehead and he sat straight up, his pulse like a hammer in his ears. He immediately sought out Kylie, relief blowing sweet through his veins when he saw she was sleeping undisturbed beside him.

He eased back against the pillow, nausea sharp in his stomach. He blew his breath out through his nostrils and then sucked steadying air back in as he willed the violent images to go away.

He closed his eyes, as if that would shield him from the memories. Of his mother being beaten while he screamed and cried for his father to stop hurting his mama. Oh God, he just wanted it to go away. He wanted peace. He didn't want to be that little boy any longer, incapable of preventing a monster from abusing his mother.

He wished to hell he hadn't told Kylie of his past. That he'd left it tightly covered, suppressed under years of practiced control. He clenched his hands, curling his fingers into tight fists before relaxing them again, flexing in an effort to relieve some of the horrible tension coiling through his body.

It sickened him, the memories. He wanted nothing more than to banish them from his mind forever. But it wasn't possible. He'd opened the door and there was no going back. There was nothing more for him to do than to deal with it all over again and begin the painful process of suppression once more.

How could he ever be good for Kylie when he hadn't even been able to protect his own mother? How could she possibly trust in him after all he'd told her?

He stared at her in the darkness, watching the soft rise and fall of her chest. He ached to touch her but he held back because violence still simmered in his consciousness and he didn't want that to touch her even peripherally. He wouldn't have her awaken and be frightened, didn't want her climbing from a nightmare and fearing his touch.

He turned his gaze back to the ceiling, giving up all hope of sleeping tonight. Pain burned brightly in his soul, the ache fiercer than it had been in a very long time. If baring one's soul was supposed to be so freeing then why did he feel imprisoned all over again?

TWENTY-THREE

KYLIE felt on top of the world Monday morning when she rode to work with Jensen. Optimism, an alien concept to her until now, simmered in her mind.

So she hadn't been able to make love to Jensen without him being tied to the bed. Yet. But they *had* made love! That was a huge step for her.

She was . . . happy. When was the last time she could say that and really mean it? Her old version of happiness was merely a shell, a code word for simply existing. It wasn't until she got involved with Jensen that she realized just how much of her life was passing her by while she kept her head firmly in the sand.

The weekend had been utter bliss. They hadn't made love again since Friday night, and both seemed reluctant to push too hard and too fast, but the intimacy had grown around them to such an extent that Kylie knew it wouldn't be long before they took the plunge again.

And maybe *this* time she'd pluck up the courage not to tie Jensen up for the act.

She'd been worried about Jensen after he'd confided about his childhood to her, but other than being a little quieter than normal Saturday morning, he didn't seem to be much worse for the wear.

She'd purposely kept the mood and tone light between them, not wanting him to go back to the blackness of his past. She'd told him she loved him countless times and had been openly affectionate with him.

She hadn't chosen to confide in him about her childhood, not because she didn't trust him, but because him confiding his had taken a huge toll on him emotionally and she hadn't wanted to add to it. In time, she'd get around to it. When the moment was right. She wasn't looking forward to it, but neither was she avoiding it at all costs.

Dealing with it. That's what she was doing and would do. With Jensen's help. His love and support. What else could she ask for?

Toward noon, Dash stuck his head in her office.

"Can I come in?" he asked from the doorway.

She motioned him forward. "Of course. What's up?"

He sat in one of the chairs, the same one Jensen had occupied seemingly a lifetime ago when she'd pondered getting rid of them. Now? She didn't mind the intrusion of either him or Dash in her office. Especially Jensen.

"You're looking good, Kylie. You look happy."

She blinked in surprise, discomfort crawling up her spine at the personal note the conversation took. But sincerity was clearly etched on Dash's handsome features so she shoved aside her instinct to clam up. It's what she would have done in the past, no doubt. But she was trying on the new Kylie for size. Someone who could open up more to her friends. To people in general.

She'd never be the bubbly, friendly breath of fresh air that Chessy was. Nor would she ever be as sweet and loving as Joss.

But they were rubbing off on her just as Jensen was, and she found herself more relaxed around her circle of friends. More willing to let her guard down. At the very least, she wanted to lose the bitchy, abrasive aspect of her personality. Things she'd used as a defensive mechanism before.

"I am happy," she said simply.

"Joss wanted me to invite you and Jensen over this Friday. Chessy and Tate will be coming too. Nothing fancy. She's itching to cook a good meal and have our friends over."

Heat surged into Kylie's cheeks and she dropped her gaze, ashamed of how her last trip to Dash's house had gone.

"I'd like that," Kylie said in a low voice. "I'm sure Jensen would too. And Dash, I know I apologized to Joss, but I've never really apologized to *you* for how I reacted when you told me Jensen was becoming your partner."

"Already forgotten," Dash said, his voice warm. "I know you didn't mean to hurt Joss. I was pretty pissed at the time, but I know your heart, Kylie. And I know you love Joss and would never intentionally hurt her."

"I'm trying to be a better friend. A better person," she amended. "I know I'm not always easy to love."

She said the last with a grin, marveling that she could even joke about matters she was normally extremely sensitive about.

Dash chuckled. "Well, neither am I. I think we all know that by now. But I also want to offer you an apology."

She lifted her gaze again, her eyebrows rising in confusion. "Whatever for?"

"For taking advantage of you."

"What?"

"You work hard. Damn hard. And Jensen's right. You're more than capable of contributing more to this company than just your duties as our administrative assistant. I read over the proposal you prepared for the S&G contract. I was very impressed."

She blushed, uncomfortable with the sincere praise. But extremely pleased as well.

"Those were Jensen's ideas as well. I can't take the full credit."

"But that's Jensen's job," Dash said dryly. "I'd expect as much from him. I'm only sorry it took his prodding to wake me up to the fact that you would be an invaluable asset as a partner."

She smiled. "It's okay, Dash. I wouldn't have been ready before. I didn't have enough confidence in myself. But I will. I'm working on it. I certainly won't turn down such an opportunity or challenge. But I don't want anything given to me that I haven't earned. And I want to earn your and Jensen's approval and eventually perhaps a partnership as well."

"You have my approval, Kylie. You always have. You have my confidence as well and certainly Jensen's. He recognized your abilities right away, something I'm ashamed to say I didn't."

"He's good like that," she said with a soft smile, warmth flooding into her mind at the thought of Jensen and how much he believed in her when she wouldn't believe in herself.

"I'm very happy for you," Dash said, his voice going quieter. "I know it hasn't been easy for you since Carson died. I miss him too. He was my best friend. He—and you—are family."

She swallowed the knot in her throat, proud of the way she maintained her composure when her brother was mentioned. She truly was making progress. She'd come so far in just a few weeks. Thanks to Jensen.

She knew she couldn't fully credit him with her progress. She'd done a lot on her own. She had to. No one could make her do so but herself. She had to be willing to move forward, and until recently she hadn't been. But Jensen had definitely kick-started her way down the path. Without him she'd still be hiding from the world, going through the motions of each day and not living. Truly *living*.

"I do miss him," she said, a small ache in her chest. "But just like Joss did, I have to let him go. I can't stop living my life just because he lost his."

"I'm glad to hear you say that, honey. Carson would have wanted you to be happy first and foremost."

"I know," she said quietly. "And I'm trying. I'll get there eventually."

Jensen stuck his head in the door, a slight frown on his face as his gaze swept over Dash.

"Am I missing something? What are you doing in Kylie's office?"

Dash rolled his eyes. "We were talking. You know, having a conversation? Something coworkers frequently *do* on the job."

Jensen looked suspiciously at him and Kylie grinned, thrilled with the possessiveness that shone in Jensen's eyes. It was absurd for him to get touchy over Dash being in her office. The man was very happily married to her best friend. But still, she didn't mind that Jensen had obviously staked his claim.

"I was telling Kylie that Joss wants you both to come over this Friday night," Dash said as Jensen ambled farther into her office.

Jensen leaned against Kylie's desk, slipping his hand over hers. Instant warmth invaded her skin where his fingers rested. She really had come a long way. If Jensen had ever come into her office and breached the professional relationship before as he was doing now, she would have kicked him in the balls.

God, she was turning into a total *girl*. Like she couldn't exist without some man to save her. She inwardly winced at the thought. Just because Jensen was being so supportive didn't mean she wanted to turn into a helpless nitwit who couldn't do things for herself or exist without him.

But she didn't want to exist without him and therein lay the truth. Loving him, leaning on him, didn't mean she was helpless or hopelessly dependent on him. It just meant she was better with him.

Weren't all couples better because of their partner or spouse? If one was good, then two united against the world had to be even better. Or at least that's the way she viewed it, but she was hardly an expert on relationships given the extremes she'd always gone to in order to avoid one.

"Chessy and Tate will be there," Dash continued. "Joss wants to entertain y'all at the house. Good food, good wine and good friends."

Jensen smiled in pleasure over Dash's invitation, but what he did next endeared him to Kylie all the more. He didn't blindly accept Dash's invitation. Instead he turned to her, question in his eyes.

"What do you think? You up for something like that?"

She took the initiative and laced her fingers more tightly around his. She loved him for curbing his dominant tendencies around her. For not jumping in, taking charge and making her decisions for her. And that, more than anything, told her how much he genuinely cared for her. To deny an intrinsic part of himself, a part that made him who he was, for *her*. Wow. She still couldn't fully comprehend the magnitude of loving someone enough to compromise to that degree.

"I think it sounds like a great evening," she said, smiling up at him.

Jensen turned back to Dash. "Then we'll see you there. What time? And does Joss want us to bring anything?"

Dash rose, making it obvious he was returning to his own office and leaving Kylie and Jensen alone.

It should be awkward as hell that one of her bosses was leaving her office so she could be alone with her other boss. Oh well. She guessed any prickliness from her was truly gone. Who knew she could be so easygoing and accepting?

"Just yourselves," Dash said. "If I know Joss she'll go completely overboard in the food department. She's already planning her menu. So I'd come with an appetite if I were you."

With that he left Kylie's office and Jensen turned, leaning his behind against the edge of her desk so he faced her.

"Come here," he said gruffly, pulling her up and out of her seat to stand in between his thighs.

He wrapped his arms around her, hugging her close. Then he pulled away, kissing her long and lingeringly. By the time he drew away, she was breathless, her face flushed and her hormones running amok.

"I've missed you," he murmured.

She laughed at that. "You just saw me half an hour ago when you invited me to go to lunch with you!"

His expression was utterly somber. "It was the longest thirty minutes of my life."

She rolled her eyes but settled into his arms, leaning against his chest. She emitted a contented sigh, marveling at how light she felt. So much freer. The past wasn't weighing down on her, an unbearable pressure that she'd lived with for so long.

Her dreams had been devoid of nightmares. Every night she went to bed with Jensen, a solid barrier to the outside world and to her past.

And he loved her.

Every day that passed, she became more convinced that they were in this for the long haul. She hated the thought of jinxing them with her newfound optimism and confidence, but for the first time she could look ahead and actually see a different future for herself than what she'd always imagined.

A man who loved her, issues and all. Good friends. A challenging promotion.

Her life was *finally* coming together.

TWENTY-FOUR

KYLIE and Jensen got out of his car at Dash's and Joss's house and Jensen met her halfway around the hood, extending his hand out in an automatic gesture she loved. She slid her hand into his, giving it a gentle squeeze.

She wore a ridiculously goofy grin that was not typical of her at all. Good God, one might even say she was *chipper.* She shook her head at that thought. Maybe Chessy was rubbing off on her more than she realized.

Or perhaps she was just that damn happy.

"You look beautiful," Jensen said after he rang the doorbell.

His gaze stroked over her like a painter's brush, not missing a single inch in his perusal.

"Know what else I look like?" she asked with that same goofy grin.

"What?"

"Happy."

There was a smugness to her voice that couldn't be missed. She felt positively cocky, and boy was that a novel feeling. Happy, confident and cocky? The world had to be coming to an end.

Jensen smiled warmly at her and then brushed his lips across hers, just as the door opened.

"Hey you two!" Joss greeted, her face and eyes glowing with the same happiness Kylie was marveling over. "Come in, come in. Now that y'all have arrived we can start dinner!"

Kylie stepped inside and pulled her sister-in-law into a hug. Joss seemed surprised and then delighted at Kylie's spontaneous show of affection. The old Kylie was reserved and rarely sought out physical contact. The new Kylie was going to work harder at letting her friends know what they meant to her.

"You look gorgeous, Joss. Marriage agrees with you so well," Kylie said.

Jensen leaned in to kiss Joss's cheek. "I have to agree with Kylie there. You look positively radiant. There's nothing more beautiful than a happy woman."

Joss flushed but seemed delighted with Jensen's compliment.

"I agree wholeheartedly," Dash said as he walked to where the three stood.

He wrapped his arm around Joss, pulling her into his side. The love the two shared was so obvious, and before, it would have made Kylie uncomfortable. Seeing her friends so happy and in love had only reinforced the fact that she'd never had that. Had thought she never would.

"A happy woman is a beautiful woman indeed. I'm just fortunate that I make her that way," Dash added with a smile.

They entered the living room where Chessy and Tate were sitting. Chessy rose and hurried over to hug Kylie.

"You look amazing!" Chessy exclaimed. "And oh my God, look at your shoes! Someone get a camera and quick! This has to be documented. Kylie is wearing *heels*!"

Laughter broke over the room. Jensen slid his arm around her, rubbing his hand up and down the bare expanse of her arm. She'd worried she'd be overdressed for the occasion. After all, they were merely going to Dash's and Joss's house for dinner. But now she was glad she made the effort.

She looked good. With no false modesty, she knew she looked her best. And now that she'd made friends with her heels, she could actually walk without teetering precariously.

"I do love those shoes," Joss said wistfully. "Where did you get them?"

Dash groaned. "Thanks, Kylie. She'll break me now."

Joss elbowed him with a ferocious scowl and Kylie just laughed.

Joss certainly didn't need Dash's money. She had all that Carson had left her plus her share of the profits from the business. She, like Kylie, had inherited a portion of Dash's—and now Jensen's—consulting firm.

Kylie banked her share, not touching it. She used her paycheck for her bills and the necessities. It was invested and she rarely gave it any thought. But perhaps with her new outlook on life she would consider doing something fun with some of the proceeds. Maybe she and Jensen could take a trip somewhere.

There was suddenly so much she wanted to do and experience. Having a new lease on life made her look at everything so much differently now. She saw the world in color instead of a drab gray.

"Y'all go on in to the dining room," Joss said, motioning with her hands. "I'm going into the kitchen to start serving it up."

"I'll help you, honey," Dash said, following her.

Kylie sat next to Jensen at Joss's dinner table that seated twelve. Chessy and Tate sat across from them while Dash sat at the head of the table with a spot for Joss reserved on his right, next to Kylie.

As the food was placed on the table, several *ooh*s and *ahh*s of appreciation sounded. Joss had outdone herself with tonight's feast. As Kylie glanced around the table, she realized that this was how it should be at holidays. Friends. No, not friends, *family*. She'd spent so long focused on the fact that Carson was her only family and now that he was gone she had no one, she'd lost sight of the fact that family was what you made it. This was her family now. Joss, Dash, Chessy and Tate. And Jensen.

Joss had baked Cornish hens with a delicious-smelling marinade. There were at least three casseroles, potatoes, vegetables and of course, a good bottle of wine.

"Oh yummy! Gimme!" Kylie said when Joss uncovered one of the casseroles to reveal Joss's homemade four-cheese macaroni.

"Watch her, Jensen," Dash warned. "She gets territorial when it comes to Joss's mac and cheese. The rest of us have to fight her for whatever we get."

"I'll send the leftovers home with you, Kylie," Joss soothed.

"There won't be any leftovers after they all get done," Kylie groused.

"I made an extra one for you," Joss whispered.

"Hey, I heard that!" Chessy protested. "What about me? Am I chopped liver over here or what?"

"I made dessert for you," Joss said in a placating tone.

Chessy's eyes lit up in delight. "Ohhh please tell me you made your caramel pie."

Joss nodded. "And an extra for you to take home."

"Only if she agrees to share it with me," Tate said dryly.

Chessy sent him a mock scowl. "Only if you're a *really* good boy."

"Good grief, Joss. Where did you come up with all the time

to fix all this?" Kylie asked. "There's enough to feed an army here plus you made extras for me and Chessy!"

"This is wonderful, Joss," Jensen complimented after several bites. "I think I'm in heaven."

Several other praises were offered and Joss sat down, her face pink from all the compliments.

"This is excellent, honey. Thank you," Dash said, shooting his wife a smile that even made Kylie shiver.

Now that she'd found love herself, she could view her friends and their relationships in a whole new light. No longer was she envious of them. She now shared in the wonder of being involved in an actual relationship. Being in love and all the newness that it brought.

She slipped her hand into Jensen's lap, resting her fingertips on his thigh. He reached down, switching his fork from his left hand to his right, and laced his fingers through hers, squeezing.

Contentment settled deep into Kylie's soul. Love was said to get better with age, and if that was true then Kylie looked forward to the days ahead. Because right now was pretty damn awesome. If it got better? She couldn't even imagine.

They joked and talked through dinner. It was a noisy, happy occasion. The atmosphere was relaxed, and even Chessy seemed to be genuinely happy, her eyes sparkling with laughter and love.

Then Tate's cell phone rang and the light diminished from Chessy's eyes. She glanced away so no one would see, but Kylie had already witnessed the resignation in her friend's expression.

Kylie tried to tune out Tate's conversation, hoping it was nothing that would ruin the evening for Chessy. But it quickly became apparent that whatever the situation was, it required Tate's immediate attention.

She still didn't really get it. Kylie didn't understand the nuances of Tate's job as a financial advisor. One would think his would be a job that was only demanding during normal work hours. When the market and banks were open. Not late into the evening. What on earth could require his immediate attention and drag him away from his wife with such alarming frequency?

Doubt crept into Kylie's mind as she pondered the situation and the expression on her friend's face. No wonder Chessy had worried that he was having an affair. It wasn't out of the realm of possibility. Stage a call from a client demanding his attention and then he slips away for a few hours with another woman.

She really had to put a lid on her overactive imagination. Chessy needed support. Not validation for her suspicions.

With a grimace, Tate rose, glancing down the table at Dash.

"Can you run Chessy home afterward?" he asked. "I don't know how long this will take."

Sorrow swamped Chessy's eyes. How could Tate not see how much he was hurting her? Could he really be that oblivious? Everyone else saw it. Even Jensen studied Tate with a frown, his gaze swinging back and forth between him and Chessy. There was concern in Jensen's eyes for Chessy and irritation for Tate.

"Of course," Dash said, though he was frowning too. "Don't worry. Joss and I will see her home."

"Thanks, man," Tate said. Then he leaned down and brushed his lips over Chessy's forehead. And lightly caressed one cheek with his hand. "Don't wait up for me, darlin'."

Then he strode away leaving Chessy staring down at her plate.

The silence after his departure was pronounced and awkward. When Chessy did look up, there was humiliation in her eyes. And defeat.

Jensen and Dash exchanged quick frowns and Joss stared at Chessy with concern.

Knowing the attention needed to be focused on someone other than Chessy, Kylie quickly scrambled for a conversation topic. Which was new to her, because she usually just sat back and observed or commented on what everyone else was talking about.

"How was y'all's honeymoon?" Kylie directed toward Joss and Dash.

Chessy sent her a look of gratitude and even tried to smile, but the light was thoroughly extinguished in her usually expressive, bubbly demeanor.

"It was wonderful," Joss said, though her gaze kept cutting back to Chessy. Then she looked directly at Kylie, one brow rising as if to say, "What are we going to do about this?"

Kylie grimaced and lifted one shoulder in a shrug. She had no idea what to do or say to make her friend feel better. How could she? The only person at this point who could make Chessy feel better was *Tate*.

"The beach was beautiful," Joss continued. "And the food was delicious. Our room had a balcony that overlooked the ocean and at night we'd lie in bed and listen to the waves. I don't think I've ever slept as well as I did for those two weeks."

"You slept?" Kylie asked in amusement. "I'm shocked."

Dash coughed as he put down his drink. Jensen chuckled and Joss looked shocked by Kylie's remark. Then she blushed madly and joined in Jensen's laughter.

"Okay, well maybe I slept a little," Joss murmured.

Dash grinned and reached over to squeeze her hand. "Was the food good? I can't say I really remember much except you. Was there even a beach? My memory is a little hazy."

"Shhh!" Joss squeaked out.

"A beach sounds awesome right now," Kylie said wistfully.

Ever since she'd had her epiphany about living life and maybe enjoying some of the money she had invested, she'd thought more and more about traveling. A vacation. Maybe more than one. Finally she had the courage to see some of the world beyond her sheltered existence. And she had someone to share it with.

"You should go," Joss said, seizing the opening. "When have you ever taken a vacation?"

"Never," Dash interjected.

Jensen studied her thoughtfully. "Maybe we could both take a vacation soon."

Kylie's cheeks warmed with pleasure. "I'd like that," she said softly.

Chessy looked even sadder. Tears glistened in her eyes but she looked away, hiding them from the rest of the table. Kylie's heart ached for her.

"Chessy, why don't you get Tate to go away on a vacation?" Kylie asked, taking the bull by the horns.

They were in the company of friends. Trusted friends. There was no sense dodging the issue. Everyone knew. Everyone could see Chessy's pain. Hiding it didn't change it.

"He'd never go," Chessy said dully.

"Maybe you should arrange a kidnapping," Dash said thoughtfully.

Chessy grimaced. "He'd kill me. He's working so hard to juggle his client load after his partner quit so unexpectedly. He's determined not to lose anyone. I'm just going to have to ride it out and hope it doesn't stay like this forever."

Jensen cleared his throat and looked as though he were

weighing whether he wanted to say something or not. Then he looked at Chessy, his eyes warm with concern and understanding.

"Have you tried telling him how you feel, sweetheart? I know if the woman I loved came to me and told me she was unhappy, I'd move heaven and earth to make it right."

Chessy's smile was sad and aching. Her eyes watered again but she looked at them all directly, no longer trying to hide her upset.

"Thank you all," she said, dodging the direct question Jensen had asked. "I'm just being a big baby. I don't want to be yet another burden on Tate when things are so crazy with work. I just have to be patient and supportive. Our anniversary is coming up and he's promised me a night out with no work."

Dash and Jensen didn't look convinced. Joss was obviously distressed to see Chessy so unhappy. It was just Joss's nature to want to help others. She was so giving and generous. Her heart was incredibly soft.

Recognizing that Chessy wanted to shift the topic off her and Tate, Kylie stood and picked up her plate.

"Come on, Joss. I'll help you clear the table. We can have dessert in the living room, right?"

Joss also stood and began collecting plates. "Absolutely. I'll get Dash to choose a good dessert wine and then I'll cut everyone a piece of pie."

As Kylie walked by Chessy, she leaned down and pressed a kiss to her cheek.

"It's going to be okay, Chessy," Kylie whispered. "And you know I'm here for you whenever you need me, right?"

Chessy flashed Kylie a look of gratitude. "Thanks, sweetie. I really appreciate it. But I'll be fine. We'll be fine," she amended.

Hoping her friend was right, Kylie continued on into the kitchen to unload her pile of plates. Joss followed behind a few moments later, her brow furrowed in consternation.

"I hate to see her so unhappy," Joss said fiercely. "Isn't there anything we can do?"

"Short of hitting Tate upside the head and asking him what the hell his problem is?" Kylie said dryly.

Joss made a sound of disgust. "You know I love Tate to pieces, but right now he's as thick as a brick. I can't believe he can't see the misery in Chessy's eyes when everyone knows how bubbly and outgoing she always is. But she's only that way when she's *happy*. Chessy can't hide her feelings to save her life. When she's unhappy, it shows in every facet of her personality. And Tate can't see that?"

"He likely doesn't *want* to see it," Kylie said quietly. "Because if he acknowledges that she's unhappy then he has to deal with the fact that he's made her that way. I think he knows. Deep down. But he's in denial. By pretending everything is normal, he doesn't feel guilty."

"That just seems so chickenshit," Joss muttered. "I know he loves her. I know that. But gah! This is so not like him, Kylie! I've never seen him this way. So distant. So willing to place Chessy second or even third in his priorities. In the past he's always been so solidly focused on her. The kind of relationship they have, he has to be."

"I don't pretend to know anything about the kind of relationship they share," Kylie said carefully. "But from what I've gleaned from y'all, I'd say he's falling down on the job as her Dominant. Haven't y'all always said that it's the Dominant's duty to see to his submissive's every need? To put her first and above all else? Isn't he supposed to cherish her gift of submission?"

"Yes," Jensen said from the doorway to the kitchen. "Absolutely. Always. No question."

Kylie glanced up quickly. She hadn't noticed him coming in. She'd been too absorbed in her conversation with Joss.

Jensen unloaded dishes from his arms and then picked Kylie's hand up, bringing it to his lips.

"He's supposed to do all those things," Jensen said. "And it would appear, at least right now, that he isn't."

"I'm glad Joss and I aren't the only two who see it," Kylie murmured.

"Well, you two know her better. And Tate as well. I'm just an unbiased observer. But from what you've told me and from what I witnessed tonight I would agree that Chessy is very unhappy."

Joss sighed, closing her eyes. "I wish I knew what to do."

Jensen smiled gently at her. "There's nothing you can do except be there for her. Be her sounding board and her friend. Tate has to work this out between them. No one else can."

"You need help with the pie, Joss?" Kylie asked.

Joss shook her head. "You go back to Chessy so she's not by herself. I'll bring in the plates and give her the biggest and first piece."

Kylie smiled at her friend. "You're the best, Joss. I don't think I tell you often enough, but I love you."

Joss's lips quivered and for a moment she was silent, as if composing herself. Stark emotion shone in Joss's eyes. Kylie felt a surge of guilt for not protecting her friendships better. Going forward she would absolutely. Joss and Chessy meant the world to her. It was time Kylie showed that and they knew it too.

"I love you too, Kylie. And I'm so glad you're happy. Both of you," she said, including Jensen in her declaration.

"Thanks, Joss. Kylie makes me happy. I'm a very lucky man."

The sincerity in his simple declaration hit her square in the heart and flooded her with profound happiness. She almost *skipped* to the living room. She was positively bouncing. Then as soon as her gaze landed on Chessy she felt guilt for being so disgustingly happy when her friend was so obviously miserable.

"Don't feel guilt for being happy, baby," Jensen murmured in her ear.

She swung her gaze upward, her mouth gaping. "How the hell do you *do* that?"

He chuckled. "Do what? Read your mind? It didn't take ESP to figure out what you were thinking. One minute you looked like you swallowed sunshine and as soon as you saw Chessy, your mouth drooped, you lost the smile and you looked guilty. Don't be, baby. You deserve to be happy and Chessy would be the first one to say so. She'd never trade your happiness for her own."

Kylie shook her head in amazement. "You're incredible, you know that?"

"I'm glad you think so," he said with a smile.

Still shaking her head, Kylie went over to plop down beside Chessy. She wrapped her arm around her friend's shoulders and hugged her fiercely.

"Chin up, girlfriend. Isn't that what you always tell me? You always have such wonderful advice, so I'm going to give you back some of what you've always given me so freely. Don't let this get you down. You'll kick Tate's ass and then he'll grovel for your forgiveness, and you being you will forgive him and y'all will live happily ever after."

Chessy grinned. Some of the shadows lifted from her eyes and the sparkle was back. Kylie's heart surged with relief. This was Chessy. Not the shell of herself she'd become lately. Chessy just . . . sparkled. But it was as Joss had said. She only sparkled when she was *happy*. Damn Tate's thick skull for not seeing his wife's unhappiness.

"I swear you fall in love and then you become positively arrogant. I like it! It's so . . . *you*."

"It's the new me," Kylie said blithely. "The old me? Not so much. But she's gone now and I like the new me much better."

"I love you *both*," Chessy said. "There was nothing wrong with the old you except you weren't happy. Now you are. That's the only difference."

"It's not, but I love you for saying so," Kylie said.

Joss came sailing in and handed Chessy a plate with a huge piece of caramel pie. Dash appeared with two glasses of wine for Chessy and Kylie, and Chessy clinked her glass to Kylie's.

"Here's to kicking ass. Regardless of whose."

"I'll drink to that," Kylie said.

TWENTY-FIVE

KYLIE'S heart was a little heavier on the way home than when they'd driven to Dash's and Joss's for dinner. But even concern for her friend couldn't dissipate her optimistic outlook on her future.

She slid her hand into Jensen's and rested them on the center console as he drove back to his—their—home. When had she started considering his home her own? She hadn't been back to her house more than a handful of times since Jensen had all but moved her into his house. Only to get clothes and other items she needed.

There had been absolutely no mention of her returning to her house. But neither had they directly addressed the issue of her moving in. Jensen had just hauled her into his house and informed her she was staying.

Wow, she really was mellowing with age and experience. Amusement gripped her as she imagined someone telling her a month ago that she and Jensen would be an item and that he'd hauled her out of her office caveman-style and told her she wasn't going anywhere.

She would have laughed herself silly.

And yet, here she was, in love. Happy. Living with Jensen. Having *sex*.

She winced over the word *sex*. True, it *was* sex but it seemed a crass description of their lovemaking. She'd never fully considered the difference between sex and "making love." She'd never had any reason to. And she certainly hadn't imagined herself having sex. With any man, but especially a man like Jensen.

While her experience might be limited, she did know the difference between mindless sex and actually making love. It was silly of her to be having this argument, or rather, discussion with herself. The old Kylie wasn't into self-reflection or analysis and she certainly had never entertained the idea of making love.

And yet that was absolutely the right description for the intimacy she and Jensen had created. Sex was . . . Well, it was sex. Nothing more, nothing less. Making love involved so much more. Trust. Mutual respect. And well, *love*.

"You're quiet, baby."

She glanced over to see Jensen give her a sideways glance as he turned into their neighborhood.

"Anything wrong?" he asked.

"Not at all," she said with a wry smile. "I was pondering the differences between having sex and making love."

One of his eyebrows went up. "Do tell. This sounds like an interesting conversation you were having with yourself."

She laughed. "I'm being silly and philosophical all at the same time."

"And? Are you going to enlighten me or leave me ignorant of this epiphany you had?"

She squeezed his hand, enjoying just . . . being with him.

Happy. She'd never used the word *happy* so much in her entire life as she had these last weeks with Jensen.

"I was thinking that sex was not the right word for what we do," she said, a little embarrassed to get all "girly" with him.

But he didn't laugh, nor did he indicate she was in any way being silly. He squeezed her hand back and stroked his thumb over the back of her knuckles.

"For the first time in my life I truly recognize the difference between having sex and making love."

Even as she said it, she wished she would have kept her mouth shut. She couldn't imagine him agreeing with her when both times he'd been tied to the bed. Hardly the hallmark of traditional lovemaking. She was embarrassed and suddenly ashamed by the fact that she acknowledged her love for a man when she didn't trust him to make love to her.

"Baby, what is that look for?" Jensen said quietly as he pulled into the drive and turned off the engine.

"I wish I hadn't said anything," she replied honestly.

"Why?"

There was obvious incredulity in his voice. He'd turned sideways in his seat so he could see her more fully.

She closed her eyes. "Because for all my declarations of love and trust, I haven't shown you either. Actions speak far louder than words and I doubt most people would consider you being tied to a bed 'making love.'"

"Now you're just pissing me off," he said in a near growl.

She blinked, returning her gaze to him. He'd never gotten angry with her. Oh, it was inevitable. What couple didn't argue or get pissed off at each other occasionally? But indeed he did look . . . pissed.

"I'm not having this conversation in the fucking car," he said, opening his door. "But we are having it. Inside."

She hesitantly opened her door, instant agitation buzzing through her mind. Her heart fluttered and her pulse jumped up. As she got out, she swallowed back the fear that gripped her by the throat.

She was being an idiot. No matter how angry Jensen became with her, he'd never hurt her. She knew that. And yet at the first sign of his anger, her reaction had been one of wariness. Anger equaled violence in her world. The two had always gone hand in hand during her childhood. She hated arguing. Hated confrontations even though her prickly, bitchy persona would indicate differently.

Jensen waited for her in front of the car and she curled her fingers into her palms, wondering if she should reach for his hand. It's what she would have done anytime they'd gone out and returned home. Only now she wasn't so certain even as she admonished herself for being such nitwit.

Jensen put his hand on her shoulder, his gaze intent as he stared down at her. "Are you *afraid* of me?"

There was such shocked recognition in his eyes that she flinched. She was making matters worse with every passing second.

"No. Yes. No, damn it, I'm not!"

She shook her head for emphasis but he didn't move. Didn't look at all like he believed her. Who could blame him? She'd contradicted herself in just those few words she'd spoken.

She closed her eyes and exhaled in a long rush.

"I'm not afraid of you, Jensen. I'm afraid of *anger*. The repercussions of anger. It took me off guard. I haven't pissed you off yet, certainly not for lack of trying on my part," she said in disgust. "So I wasn't expecting it. Had no time to steel myself or tell myself what an idiot I'm being. Fear was my natural, instinctive reaction. I hate arguing. I hate confrontations. I'd normally do anything at all to avoid them. And I know we'll argue. I don't expect us to be perfect. I don't even know why fear struck me the way it did. Well, I do know," she said, her voice trailing off.

"Come inside with me, Kylie," he said, his voice quiet but also tender.

She glanced back up at him to see the warmth in his eyes. His sincerity. His love for her and his understanding.

He tugged her hand and guided her to the front door. Once inside, he directed her toward the bedroom.

"Get undressed for bed," he said. "We'll talk while I'm holding you."

Relief fluttered through her throat and chest. They were okay. She was okay.

She changed into a pair of pajamas while he stripped down to his boxers. Then he climbed into bed, pulling back the covers and patting the spot beside him.

She went readily, snuggling up against his body. Her self-admonishment from earlier still rang in her mind. It was time to back her words with action. Prove to him that she did trust him. She could start by being more openly affectionate and willing to get close to him without coaxing.

"Now, I want you to listen to me," he said in a firm voice.

He stroked one hand through her hair and then down her arm. His fingertips lightly grazed her skin, sending chill bumps dancing in their wake.

"Just because my hands were tied to the bed during the act of our lovemaking, and yes, it is lovemaking, doesn't mean we had mindless sex. You gave me something very precious both times. Your trust."

"How can you say that when I tied you up both times?" she asked fretfully.

He squeezed her to him with one strong arm. "Because you went through with it. We made beautiful love. I came inside you. That's as beautiful as it gets, baby."

She sighed and deeply inhaled his scent, letting it surround and comfort her agitation.

He kissed the top of her head. "I love you, Kylie. My love isn't conditional on how we have sex or *if* we have it for that matter."

"I'm glad," she said, her voice muffled by his body. "I want to be normal, Jensen. I just don't know how to be."

He laughed softly, a slight ache in his voice. "Fuck normal. We've already had this conversation and you already know my feelings on the subject."

She sighed and closed her eyes, enjoying him wrapped around her. Solid. So strong. Her rock.

For several long moments silence fell between them. A comfortable silence neither sought to end. And then she felt him tense slightly against her, as if he were preparing to say something.

She reared her head back, seeking out his gaze.

"Are you ready to talk to me, baby? About your past?"

His dark eyes swept her face intently, concern and love reflected in his expression.

Her breath hitched and her pulse sped up, as did her respirations. It was stupid, really. It was just words. Memories. They couldn't hurt her unless she let them.

And this was the last barrier between them. The last piece of the trust puzzle.

"Yeah," she quietly whispered. "I am."

He squeezed her again and pressed an encouraging kiss on her forehead. "Take your time. I'm not going anywhere."

She hugged his body to hers. It surprised her, that she wasn't on the verge of a panic attack over the idea of relating something so deeply personal. Something she had never confided in anyone. Not even Carson. She realized she wanted—needed—to unburden herself. Finally.

"I don't even know where to start," she said. Tears burned the edges of her eyes and she swallowed back the knot already forming in her throat.

"At the beginning. Or wherever you like. I'm here to listen."

"He was always abusive," she said, her voice trembling. "I don't ever remember him not being. I can barely remember my mother, so I don't know if she was any better than he was. My feelings are influenced by the fact she left me and Carson with that asshole. How does a mother just leave like that?"

Jensen tensed and she bit into her lip, sorry that she'd made that remark so soon after Jensen had confided his own mother's desertion. She'd never really considered just how much she and Jensen had in common. Two halves to a whole.

"I'm sorry," she said in a distressed voice. The last thing she wanted was to pull Jensen back into his own past. Hers was bad enough.

"No, baby, no. Don't apologize. You need to talk about this with someone who loves you. Someone who will listen. Tonight isn't about me. It's about you."

She nodded and then squeezed her eyes tightly shut. The rest was . . . hard. Shame and a sense of degradation burned through her memories.

"He raped me for the first time when I was thirteen."

Jensen went rigid next to her. She curled her fingers into his chest, needing something solid, tangible. He slid his hand between them, splaying over hers.

"And there was violence. So much violence," she whispered. "Nothing Carson and I ever did was right. When he was drunk, he always targeted Carson. But it was when he was completely sober that he directed his ire toward me. I could almost understand, well not really, but it would make more sense if he was just a mean drunk and he only became abusive when he was drinking. It was the vengeful targeting of me when he was fully cognizant of what he was doing that frightened me the most. It seemed so *personal*.

"At least with Carson it always seemed to be a case of Carson being in the wrong place at the wrong time. It's a sad testament that I felt safer as long as he was drinking."

Jensen kissed the top of her head, leaving his lips there pressed against her hair.

"I've never told anyone this," she began. She started shaking, no longer able to keep the memories at bay. Manageable. They poured through her mind leaving inky darkness and pain in their wake.

"What, Kylie?" he gently coaxed. "What haven't you ever told anyone?"

"There was a time when I seriously considered suicide."

Jensen sucked in his breath and then expelled it in long, shaky puffs. "Oh God, baby. I'm so sorry. That's a heavy burden to carry by yourself. Why have you never told anyone?"

"Because it demonstrated just how weak I am," she said wearily. "Just another shortcoming on my list. It was only the thought of leaving Carson behind by himself that kept me from doing it. Not that I didn't want to die. I did. So many times it would have been so easy to make it all stop. I was angry at my mom for leaving us and yet there I was thinking of doing the exact same thing to Carson."

"Kylie, you aren't weak. It took a hell of a lot of courage and guts not to do it. To remain in that situation with no hope of getting out of it. You were just a child who thought you'd never get out of your hell. I can't say I blame you for contemplating suicide."

"It broke Carson to know what our father was doing to me. I suppose he felt like you in some ways. Helpless to make it stop."

"I know that feeling only too well," Jensen murmured.

She didn't want to discuss every sordid detail. There was no need to do that to either herself or Jensen. It was enough that he knew. That she'd told him.

"When and how did it end?" Jensen asked, after her long silence.

"Carson worked odd jobs and he saved up enough money for us to run. We left in the middle of the night while our father was passed out. I was so worried about Carson because our father had beaten him worse than usual. He had bruises, broken ribs. God only knows what else. But he got us out of there."

"Where did you go?" Jensen asked softly. "How did you make it? How did you end up going to college, even?"

"We were homeless for a while. While we had some money, we couldn't afford to use it for rent and who would rent something to two kids? We would have been turned over to the police and then sent back to our father. We had to eat and we used the money sparingly. Carson worked his way through college and I worked odd jobs to help. When he started working, he in turn helped me through college."

"And you call yourself weak," Jensen said in bewilderment. "How could you ever think so? Do you even realize the kind of strength it took to survive, and then being homeless with no one to look out for you except each other? I don't know of many people who would have had that kind of resolve."

"I wish I could see it the way you do," she said wistfully.

"You're a brave, courageous woman, Kylie. Never doubt that."

"I love you," she said.

"I love you too, baby. Did you or Carson ever see him after that?"

Kylie shook her head. "No, but Carson looked for him years later. I think he wanted revenge."

"Can't say I blame him," Jensen muttered. "Did he find him?"

"He never would say. I only found out because I saw the file he left open on his desk. When I asked him about it, well, you can imagine I freaked. That shouldn't surprise you. It's no wonder he wouldn't tell me anything. He likely worried I'd go off my rocker and do something stupid. Who knows. Maybe I would have.

"But the kind of revenge Carson wanted wasn't the kind that would land you in jail on a manslaughter charge. He wouldn't have risked his marriage to Joss. He wanted to see if our father was living well because he wanted to ruin him. He wanted to take away everything he had, if he had anything at all. And he wanted our father to *know* who ruined him and why."

"I disagree that he shouldn't have given you the information," Jensen murmured. "It was your right and you wouldn't have done anything stupid. What Carson was negligent in realizing is that you might have gained some closure if you knew he wasn't a threat to you any longer."

She frowned. "I hadn't thought about it that way. I think it's the uncertainty that gets to me sometimes. Like I'm afraid he'll pop up out of the blue. He could be dead by now for all I know."

"I could find out for you if you ever truly wanted to know," Jensen said quietly.

She froze, a curl of fear winding its way through her chest.

"Maybe one day," she hedged. "Maybe never. I just know I don't want to know right now."

"When you're ready, let me know. I'll make damn sure he knows nothing about you. And perhaps I can just verify whether Carson was successful in his quest for vengeance."

"Thank you," she said.

She felt . . . deflated . . . all of a sudden. Like a huge weight had been lifted, leaving her sagging. She was emotionally wrung out even though she'd barely scratched the surface of her abuse. Maybe she'd never tell Jensen the entirety of it. Or maybe one day she'd be ready to completely rid herself of the poison that had infected her for so long.

"You're more than welcome, baby. I love you. And I'm so damn proud of you. Now you just have to be proud of yourself and see what a huge accomplishment it is for you to be where you are right now and for not letting your past overtake your future."

She grimaced. "It wasn't all that long ago that I was doing just that."

"You're too hard on yourself, Kylie. Lighten up. The only one knocking on you is you. Everyone else around you sees what I see. A resilient, fearless woman."

"I like that," she said with a smile. "Fearless. Definitely at the top of the list of words I would have never used to describe myself."

"Then revise the damn list and remove all the derogatory words about you," he growled.

She yawned, exhausted from the day's emotional events.

"Maybe we can make that list together one day. At the very top, the most important word to describe me, is *loved*."

"Always. And you are loved, Kylie. By more than just me."

"I know that now," she said, snuggling farther up against Jensen.

"Think you can sleep?" he asked, concern in his voice. "I worry what this will do for you. I know what it did to me when I told you of my past."

"As long as you're here, I can sleep," she said.

He hugged her to him. "Then sleep, baby. I'll hold you for as long as you want me to."

TWENTY-SIX

FEARS of Kylie being tormented by nightmares kept Jensen up long after Kylie settled into a fitful sleep. And when he finally followed suit, it wasn't Kylie who had nightmares.

Jensen stood, paralyzed, unable to move, unable to do anything but stare as his father struck Kylie again and again. His dreams, often of his mother being abused while Jensen was unable to prevent it, were now of Kylie in his mother's stead.

He was watching through the eyes of an adult but trapped by a child's limitations.

"No," he croaked out. "Oh God, no. Stop hurting her. Please."

His father lifted his head and stared directly at Jensen, his mouth twisted into a cruel smile. "You're worthless. You can't protect her. You've failed her just like you failed your idiot mother."

And then Kylie called his name. It was a plea for help, one he couldn't ignore even in his dream.

Finally, finally he was able to move. No longer was he encased by lead. No longer was he in the body of the child he was. He let out a roar and launched himself at his father as his adult self with all the strength he'd lacked when he was just a boy.

He knocked his father away and then lunged for him, wrapping his hands around his father's throat. He'd stop him this time. He'd never hurt another woman. Jensen was no longer the helpless child he'd been for so many years.

All his hatred and anger poured from him in black waves, giving him even more strength.

He wouldn't fail his mother this time. He wouldn't fail Kylie.

He squeezed, watching his father's face go purple, his eyes bulging at the strain.

Kylie called out to him again, her voice desperate. Hoarse sounding. She was pleading with him. To stop?

Shock froze him. Why would Kylie beg for his father's life?

This time when she said his name, it was barely distinguishable and was accompanied by a whimper of pain. He struggled through the haze of the nightmare, confused by Kylie's actions.

And then, as if he'd been doused by cold water, he roused from sleep.

Horror swept through him with agonizing speed. His hand was wrapped around *Kylie's* neck, his fingers digging into her skin. Tears streamed down her face as she struggled helplessly in his grasp. Desperately pulling at the hand around her neck.

Oh God, he was going to be sick.

He released her instantly and she fell away, holding her throat and gasping for breath. She coughed and choked, hunched over, her hair in disarray around her shoulders. She huddled on the very edge of the bed, pulling her legs up to her chest protectively. She rocked back and forth, her broken sobs ripped horrific wounds in his soul. Wounds he might never recover from. How could he?

"Kylie!"

His agonizing cry of her name sounded much like a noise a wounded animal would make.

What had he done? How could he have done something so horrible? He'd become the very monster both their fathers were.

"Kylie, oh my God, are you all right, baby?"

He hovered over her, still shaking from the dream. He was afraid to touch her, but he had to offer her comfort.

He pulled her into his arms, tears wetting his cheeks as he rocked her back and forth.

"I'm so sorry," he choked out. "Oh God, baby, I'm so sorry."

Despair settled over him, turning everything to black. Sorrow and regret weighed him down, hammering into his mind.

He'd done the one thing he'd sworn never to do. He'd hurt her.

He was no better than his father. All the things he'd said, all the things he'd never imagined doing to another human being now battered him. The whispers in his mind, the ghosts from his past, taunted him. Mocked him and told him what a hypocrite he was.

He closed his eyes, his thoughts bleak as he realized the magnitude of what he'd done. As he realized the *consequences* of what he'd done.

Tears blurred his vision. Grief for what he'd lost in the space of a few moments.

He had to let her go.

Kylie was stiff in his arms. She hadn't made a sound other than the low whimpers of fear. He wondered if she was even capable of speech after he'd nearly choked her to death.

She'd wear bruises tomorrow. Marks that he'd put there.

He would never forgive himself for this.

"I'm okay," Kylie whispered.

Her hoarse words jerked him to awareness, away from the blackness of his thoughts.

He loosened his hold on her and pulled away, not meeting

her gaze. He couldn't. There was nothing to say, no apology sincere enough for what he'd done. No way for him to make this right.

"I'll pack your things and then I'll take you home," he said gruffly.

Kylie flinched and her head flew up so he could see her wide, frightened eyes. Only now confusion had replaced the fear and uncertainty.

"*What?*" she whispered.

He winced every time she spoke. She could barely talk in a loud enough tone for him to hear.

"I'm taking you home," he said, his gaze sliding away from her. He couldn't sit here and look at what he'd lost. Couldn't face what he'd done. It was a knife to his heart.

"I don't understand."

Her voice trembled and tears crowded her eyes, making them go glossy and wet.

"We can't be together, Kylie."

He hadn't meant the words to come out so forcefully. Or with such heat. But he was dying slowly, with every breath. All his pain came out in those damning words.

"You're giving up on us?"

The hurt in her voice poured more salt on his exposed wound.

"I love you, Jensen. And you're just quitting? Just like that?"

"Goddamn it, Kylie. Look at what I did," he all but roared. "How can you even consider being with a man like me? I could have *killed* you—I *tried* to kill you."

"It was a dream," she said. "You didn't mean it."

Bile rose in his throat. God, she was trying to rationalize his behavior. His thoughts went to the woman he and Kylie had seen in the parking lot the other night. How she'd explained away her husband or boyfriend's actions. And now Kylie was doing the same thing for him.

He wouldn't allow it. She deserved better than him.

"Listen to yourself, Kylie," he said in a cold voice. "Listen to you explain away my abuse. How you rationalize it. Get dressed while I get your stuff together. I'll take you home tonight."

"You said you loved me," Kylie whispered, tears running down her cheeks. "You promised . . ."

"Yeah, what did I promise?" Jensen demanded. "I promised never to hurt you."

Kylie turned away, presenting her shoulder to him. A shoulder that heaved with her quiet sobs as she began to dress.

It took Jensen half an hour to pack up all of Kylie's belongings. He shoved them into the trunk of his car and then went back for Kylie, who was now sitting on the sofa in the living room.

Her face was pale, her eyes red and ravaged by tears. Her hair was in disarray, tousled not only from sleep but from what he'd done. His fingerprints shone on her neck, a stark reminder of how close he'd come to killing her.

"Let's go," he said shortly.

Kylie rose shakily on her feet. She still wouldn't look at him, something he was glad for. He had enough regret for both of them.

He got into the driver's seat as she slid in on the passenger side. The drive to her house was silent, the quiet oppressive and stifling. With every minute that ticked by his sorrow and self-loathing grew until he was certain he would be consumed with it.

He finally pulled into Kylie's driveway. He got out and headed to his trunk to retrieve all of her things. Stuff she'd brought to his house. Stuff he'd gotten used to being strewn all over his house.

He set everything inside her door, wanting to get this over with as quickly as possible. When he turned to go back to his car he nearly collided with Kylie. He put his hands on her shoulders to steady her and she wrenched herself from his grasp.

With a sigh, he headed toward his car, turning his back on her for good.

"I would have never given up on us like you're doing," she called out.

He stopped in his tracks, the accusation halting him.

"Don't do this, Kylie. Don't make it even harder than this is."

"I love you," she choked out.

He closed his eyes as his wounds began to bleed all over again. "I love you too, Kylie, and that's why I have to go."

He fled toward his car, not waiting for her response. He couldn't take any more. He had to get away before he completely fell apart.

The drive home was a blur. Images of Kylie with his hand wrapped around her neck bombarded him left and right until he was dizzy. The huge knot in his gut grew.

He'd never love another woman. Not the way he loved Kylie.

As soon as he pulled into his driveway, he threw open the door, bolted out and heaved his guts all over the front yard.

TWENTY-SEVEN

KYLIE watched the sun creep over the horizon as she sat in a chair on her back deck, wrapped in a blanket. It was plenty warm, and yet a bone-deep chill had settled in. She had the fleeting thought that she might never be warm again.

Jensen gave her warmth with his smiles, his tenderness, his love. And now it and he were gone.

She wished she could muster the emotional strength to hate him. But all she could see was the desolation and horror in his eyes. The loathing and self-recrimination for what he'd done.

She rubbed absently at her still sore throat where the bruises, shaped into fingerprints, had spread across her skin.

He could have killed her.

It was what he said and what she'd pondered and yet she couldn't bring herself to believe it. As soon as he'd come out of the dream, he'd released her. He wouldn't consciously ever hurt her. She believed that with all her heart. So why didn't he?

He'd nagged at her about her self-confidence and yet he appeared not to have any himself. Or at least when it came to her.

She sighed and stared down at the paper in front of her. Her resignation letter, addressed to Dash. She wouldn't stick the knife deeper by including Jensen in her resignation.

Her laptop and phone lay on the table next to the letter. She'd spent most of the night Googling and looking up mortgage companies and Realtors. She didn't need to get a mortgage. She had enough invested to buy a house with plenty left over. Besides, who would give her a mortgage when she was unemployed?

It was hours yet before any of the businesses would open. She hesitated a moment as the idea gripped her. She should go now and place the letter on Dash's desk. Before he or Jensen would come in this morning.

The weekend was a blur. She'd done nothing but lie in bed, covers up to her chin. In between bouts of crying. She hadn't eaten, hadn't slept. She'd barely managed the feat of dragging herself to the bathroom to take care of the essentials.

Then her mind had sprung into recovery mode. She couldn't hide in her house forever. People got their hearts broken every day. She wasn't special in that regard. Life went on. The question was whether she was going to move on or be like she'd always been in the past. Timid. Afraid. Stick her head back in the sand, adopting the mantra of "ignorance is bliss."

She knew two things. One, she couldn't continue working for Dash and Jensen. And two, she needed to move. It was an idea she'd entertained in the past, but she'd never wanted to expend the energy to do it.

Now the letter was typed, and she had the phone number of a local real estate company. It was time to act and to stop being so passive when it came to her life.

Her muscles protested as she hauled herself to her feet. But she pushed back the discomfort, picked up the letter and went back inside the house to get dressed and grab her keys to the office.

Thirty minutes later, she placed the letter on Dash's desk along with today's to-do list. She felt a brief moment of guilt for doing this to Dash. He'd never been anything but patient and understanding with her. He was a dream to work for. And quitting abruptly when they hadn't yet found her replacement wasn't fair to him. But she couldn't come in to work where Jensen would be and pretend her heart hadn't just been destroyed.

She then walked into her office and began packing up her belongings and personal effects.

When she was done, she turned, taking one last glance at the business her brother had built. The place she'd worked ever since graduating college. Yes, she was good at her job. She would have made a damn good partner too. But there were other jobs out there. It was time to cut ties and let go and move on.

Carson was gone. He wasn't ever coming back. She wouldn't be anyone's burden any longer.

With a sigh, she trudged toward the elevator. In the lobby, she waved at the night guard who looked at her curiously as she hoisted the box she was holding higher so she wouldn't drop it.

When she got home, she left the box in her car, uncaring if it came in or not. All she wanted was to go back to bed and stay there for a week. Maybe she would. Or at least until word spread about what happened and Chessy and Joss hunted her down.

She should call them. Tell them herself. But she couldn't make herself do it. There was nothing her friends could do anyway, other than give her a shoulder to cry on and tell her it was okay and that there were other fish in the sea.

Yeah, whatever.

She might not have a ton of experience in love and relationships, but even she knew that she'd never find another love like Jensen.

She walked past the things Jensen had carried back into her house and into the kitchen. She glanced at the bottle of wine on the counter and shrugged. Why not?

She poured herself a generous glass and started for the bedroom when she turned back and grabbed the bottle. It would save her a trip back later, and once she got into her bed, she wasn't coming back out for anyone.

TWENTY-EIGHT

"YOU mind telling me what the hell this is about?" Dash bellowed.

Jensen looked up tiredly as Dash waved a piece of paper in front of his nose. Jensen was in no mood for guessing games. He hadn't slept since Friday night. He had a hangover from hell, after doing something he never did. He'd gotten rip-roaring drunk, and he'd stayed that way the entire weekend.

Just more evidence that he was more like his father than he thought. Apparently the apple didn't fall too far from the tree.

"Christ, you look like shit," Dash said in disgust.

"Fuck off," Jensen growled.

"She quit," Dash bit out as he put his hands on Jensen's desk and leaned forward.

He shoved the letter of resignation where Jensen couldn't help but see it.

Despair blanketed Jensen, suffocating him. Blackness swirled, drowning him in sorrow.

"Don't let her," Jensen said bleakly. "I'll go. I'd never do anything to make *her* go. I can work out of another office and leave the two of you here."

"Joss went by her house today, worried sick when I told her

Kylie had resigned. Kylie wasn't home. No one knows where the fuck she is. And she's put her goddamn house up for sale," Dash roared. "What the fuck did you do to her?"

Jensen closed his eyes. Tears burned his eyelids like acid.

"I hurt her," he whispered. "I swore I never would."

Dash sent him a puzzled look. "Hurt as in how?"

Jensen shook his head. "It doesn't matter. What matters is that you not let her do this. Tell her I'm cleared out. Do whatever you have to. I'll clean out my desk today. She can have my office or remain in hers."

"Jesus Christ, am I even going to have a business after all this?" Dash demanded.

"I don't give a fuck about the goddamn business," Jensen growled. "All I care about is Kylie."

Dash shook his head. "For someone who says he hurt her, I'd say you still care an awful lot about what she does."

"Of course I care," Jensen raged. "I love her. I'll never goddamn love anyone else."

"Then why the fuck are you here and not over there at her feet begging for forgiveness?" Dash roared back.

Jensen surged to his feet, planting his palms down on the desk. He leaned forward so he was eye to eye with Dash.

"Because some things are unforgivable," Jensen choked out. "Some things can't be taken back, can't be redone. No matter if she forgives me—she likely would. I can't forgive *myself*. Do you understand that?"

Dash sighed. "Yeah, man. I get that. But Jensen? Here's a clue for you. You said you hurt her. What the hell do you think you're doing now?"

Jensen sank back into his chair and ran a hand through his hair. God, he was so tired. He wanted one night where he wasn't swallowed by the demons of his past. When he wasn't seeing his hands around Kylie's throat or hearing her calling his name.

He just wanted . . . peace. Was it too much to ask for?

But then how could he ever truly be at peace when the woman he loved was gone from his arms?

"Don't let her quit, Dash," Jensen said, his weariness evident in his every word. "Whatever you have to do in order to convince her. Do it. I'll be out by the end of the day."

TWENTY-NINE

KYLIE patiently sat and listened to the dozen voice mail messages from Chessy, Joss *and* Dash. She sipped the strong coffee as she sat in the small café in the neighborhood she was house hunting in.

Amazing how much more productive she was when she wasn't shitfaced drunk from all the wine she'd consumed this week.

The lightbulb had gone on when she discovered she was completely out of wine. Then she'd surveyed the bottles littering her kitchen in disgust. Enough of that already. A week was long enough to wallow in her misery. It was time to get on with the rest of her life.

She cringed when she listened to Dash's message. Jensen had cleared out his office and would be working out of another. Dash wanted Kylie to get her ass back to work and to call Joss before she lost her mind.

Guilt crept over her. She'd avoided her friends—everyone—for the entire week. She'd listened to the incessant ringing of the doorbell and the pounding. She bet the pounding came from Chessy. She was rather persistent when she put her mind to something. But the alcohol haze had made it impossible for her to do anything more than lie sprawled on her bed staring up at the ceiling, praying Joss and Chessy would give up and go away.

Though her house had gone on the market Monday, it wouldn't start showing until the following Monday. That—and the realization of how much wine she'd consumed—had given her sufficient motivation to sober up and get her ass out of the house.

She listened to the rest of the messages but winced when she heard Joss begging her to call. There were tears in Joss's voice. Dash would kill Kylie for upsetting Joss this way. And she couldn't blame him.

She had to face them at some point. She couldn't hide forever. Jensen wasn't an integral component of her circle of friends. He'd mainly become a part through Kylie. So it wasn't as if she had to worry about running across Jensen when she visited with her friends. She may have lost him, but she'd be damned if she lost her friends too.

Her head ached vilely, the result of all the wine she'd drunk. She could barely even remember the last five days.

What she wanted to do was run by the store, stock up on more wine and then retreat to her house and drink. A lot.

But what she *needed* to do was text Joss and Chessy and get it over with.

Sighing, she typed in a quick message to both.

I'm ready to come over and spill. Any chance wine could be involved?

She hit Send and set her phone back on the small table. She knew she looked like hell. She'd received more than one cursory stare by the other customers in the café. How was she supposed to look when she'd been dumped by the man she loved and then spent the rest of the week in an alcoholic stupor?

Her phone chimed and she hesitantly reached for it.

Get your ass to my house stat. And yes, wine will be here. Can you come now?

That was from Joss. Before she could respond, Chessy chimed in.

I'm coming right over! Give me fifteen at the most. Joss, you got enough wine or you want me to bring some?

Kylie smiled, some of the weight shifting from her heart.

I've got it covered. Just get over here!

She punched in her response and hit Send.

I'm on my way. Twenty minutes, depending on traffic.

She grabbed her keys, downed the last of her coffee and then headed for the door.

She was terrified. She wouldn't lie to herself about that. The idea of pouring out all of her despair to *anyone* made her stomach tighten. But she had to remember her promise to herself about being more open with her friends. Her *best* friends. They weren't just anyone. They were special.

She drove in tense silence. She'd nearly put her fist through the dash when one of those sappy breakup songs started playing on her satellite radio. Silence, however unbearable, was still preferable to listening to her problems being sung in real time.

Twenty-two interminable minutes later, Kylie pulled into Joss's driveway and sat there a long moment, mustering the courage to go in. If she didn't get out soon, Chessy and Joss would both come out and drag her in by her hair.

She made herself get out of the car and walk to the door. She was almost there when the door flew open. Dash. Double ugh. Facing the girls was bad enough. Facing her boss too? Why hadn't she made it clear to Joss that this was a girls-only event?

Dash's stare was fixed on her and as she drew closer, he paled.

"He said he hurt you but I thought he meant emotionally," Dash said through clenched teeth. "What the fuck did he do to you, Kylie? I'll kill him for this."

Her hand fluttered upward in an effort to hide the bruising on her throat. But it was too late. Dash had seen the marks on her pale skin.

Joss flew around Dash and plowed into Kylie just as she reached the top step. She wrapped her arms around Kylie and hugged her for dear life.

Kylie glanced up at Dash over Joss's shoulder to see him smoldering with rage.

"It's not what you think," she said in a low voice.

"And just what is it then?" Dash asked in an icy tone.

"Leave her alone, Dash. She'll tell me and Chessy and then if anyone needs their ass kicked we'll sic you on it," Joss said.

Kylie nearly wilted in relief. God she loved her friends. Why had she avoided them all week? She could have been here days ago, wrapped in the love and support of her best friends instead of being at home drunk off her ass, alone and miserable.

Joss took Kylie by the hand and dragged her past Dash and into the house. Dash didn't look pleased, but he bit back any response and allowed Joss to have her way. Thank God.

"Stay out of our hair for a while, darling," Joss called back to Dash. "This is girls' night and the girls' code is 'what happens in the circle stays in the circle' and 'no men allowed.'"

Dash rolled his eyes. "I'll be in the bedroom watching TV. But I expect a report later. I'm not letting it drop, Joss. If that son of a bitch put his hands on her, I'll take him apart."

"I love it when he gets all alpha," Joss whispered to Kylie. "It makes me want to go jump his bones right now."

Kylie groaned. "Seriously, Joss? I just got dumped and you're taunting me with Dash's alpha maleness. So not fair."

Joss's face wrinkled in sympathy. "He ended it?"

"Hey, no talking until y'all get in here so I can hear," Chessy complained as the two women entered the living room.

Chessy rose from her perch on the couch and ran over, throwing her arms around Kylie.

"Don't you *ever* scare us like that again," Chessy said. "Joss and I were so worried, Kylie. What happened, sweetie? You look terrible!"

Then she backed away, her gaze drifting over Kylie's face and neck. Joss and Chessy both gasped.

"Did he do that to you?" Chessy choked out.

Kylie sighed. "It's a really long story, guys. Can we sit down and open a bottle—or three—of wine? I'm going to need it for this."

"Coming right up," Joss said.

"I need at least three glasses in me before the bloodletting starts," Kylie muttered.

"Then drink up and make it fast because we want every single detail," Chessy warned.

Joss returned a moment later, a bottle of wine in both hands. Glasses were already sitting on the coffee table. Joss poured, filling all the glasses, and then she handed one to Kylie.

She drank thirstily, draining the glass in seconds. Joss arched one eyebrow but quickly poured Kylie another.

"It's times like these that I wonder if we shouldn't have something a little stronger," Kylie said.

"Well, if we're going to get shitfaced, I suggest we raid Dash's liquor cabinet," Chessy said.

Joss frowned. "If we are getting shitfaced, then neither of

you is leaving tonight. I'll give your keys to Dash and you'll have to go through him before you leave."

Kylie and Chessy groaned, but gave up their keys. Joss left to give them to Dash and then returned to the living room.

"Okay, so what shall it be?" Joss asked dramatically as she opened the liquor cabinet.

"What's the old saying?" Chessy mused. "Beer before liquor, never sicker? Liquor before beer, never fear? Does that apply to wine as well?"

Kylie frowned. She was already fuzzy from the two hastily downed glasses of wine she'd had. "Would wine be substituted for beer or liquor? And does that mean I'm going to puke my brains out because I drank liquor after wine?"

"Honey, we'll all be puking our brains out later," Chessy said dryly. "Come on, Joss. Just pick something so we can move on."

Joss shrugged and then reached in, pulling out two bottles of liquor. She plunked them down on the coffee table and then retrieved shot glasses from the cabinet.

"I vote we pour them all now," Chessy said. "If we're pouring after imbibing a lot, we're going to totally make a mess in Joss's living room."

"Good idea," Kylie said. "Pour them up, Joss."

Joss carefully lined up a dozen shot glasses and then began filling them all.

Chessy picked two up and handed one to Kylie. She handed the other to Joss and then retrieved another from the coffee table for herself. She held up her glass to Joss and Kylie.

"Here's to men are assholes," Chessy said.

"I'll drink to that," Kylie said.

"I'll drink as long as we exclude Dash from that statement," Joss said.

Chessy rolled her eyes. "He's been an asshole before. And he'll be one again before it's all over with. Just drink with us, damn it."

Joss laughed and then they clinked their glasses together.

Then they tossed the alcohol back.

Kylie's eyes watered, her nose burned, and she nearly choked as fire ripped down her throat and into her belly.

"God, that's horrible!" Kylie sputtered.

"You don't drink it because it's good," Chessy said. "You drink it for what it does. Give her another, Joss. We have to loosen up her tongue."

Joss thrust another glass into Kylie's hand and then Joss and Chessy directed her to drink it.

The second went down a little better than the first. Thank God.

She leaned back against the couch so her stomach would settle and to allow the alcohol to take control.

"I've spent the week shitfaced," Kylie admitted.

"Oh honey, I wish you would have answered your damn door," Chessy said. "You should never have to drink alone. I'm more than willing to be your drinking buddy."

"Couldn't," Kylie said lamely. "I had to work some things out."

"Like quitting your job and putting your house up for sale?" Joss demanded.

Kylie winced. "Yeah, those things."

"What on earth happened, Kylie? And how the hell did you get those bruises?" Chessy asked.

Kylie closed her eyes, trying to hold the tears at bay. They burned her eyelids. She thought she'd cried herself out and that she didn't have any more tears to shed. Apparently she was wrong.

Joss and Chessy descended, each taking a position on either

side of her. Chessy wrapped one arm around her while Joss gently pushed Kylie's hair from her eyes.

"Talk to us, Kylie. We've been so worried," Joss said in her sweet, loving voice.

"He didn't hurt me on purpose," Kylie said. "He'd never do that. I know it but he doesn't. Or at least he doesn't now."

"You're not making sense, hon. Slow down and start from the beginning," Chessy prompted.

Kylie sighed but did as her friends asked. She spilled the entire sorry tale starting from when she confided her past to Jensen to the present. She didn't spare herself any in the telling. She told them she'd spent the week in the wine bottle crying her eyes out.

"Oh wow," Joss breathed. "That's a tough one for sure, sweetie. Poor Jensen. I can't imagine how he felt when he woke up to see his hands wrapped around your neck. Dash would die if he ever did something like that."

"That's just it," Kylie said. "Jensen would never do anything to hurt me. It was a dream—a nightmare. He didn't know what he was doing. But he just shut me out. He couldn't dump me fast enough. How the hell do you convince someone they're wrong if they won't stick around to talk to you about it?"

They were all silent for a moment and Chessy reached for the bottle, pouring them each another shot.

Kylie gratefully downed it, hoping for the numbness to settle in soon. A balm to the ache in her soul. At least for a little while she'd feel nothing but the warm buzz of alcohol. And to think she'd always loathed the idea of getting drunk. This week had taught her a lot about her old ideas and ways.

She handed her glass to Chessy and motioned for another.

By the time the fourth shot had been consumed, Kylie was

definitely feeling the effects. So why the hell was she still crying and sniffling like an idiot?

She flopped back onto the couch again and stared up at the ceiling, waiting for it to spin.

"I should have known," Kylie said, despair creeping into her voice once more. "I've never been an optimist. I was conditioned at a very young age to expect the worst. It's certainly all I ever received. And yet I didn't see this coming and I should have. I was so sure that Jensen was the one. I was so caught up in the joy of overcoming so much and being able to be in a relationship that I never even gave thought to the idea that we wouldn't be together. And that was so stupid of me. Maybe later I'll be able to blame it on being in love for the first time in my life. No wonder I never dated. Who the hell would want to go through this every time you split up with someone?"

"Amen," Chessy muttered.

Kylie turned her head so she could see her friend, even though at the moment there were two Chessys.

"How are you and Tate?"

Chessy made a face. "Fine. Not fine. I don't know."

"I feel guilt for being so damn happy," Joss said mournfully.

Kylie reached over to squeeze her hand. "Don't. You deserve to be happy. You've certainly had your share of hell."

They drank another shot. And then another for the hell of it. Somewhere in the midst of finishing the first bottle, they ended up on the floor in front of the fireplace.

"Do you know your ceiling is spinning?" Chessy asked Joss.

"That's not the ceiling. It's your brain," Kylie said sagely.

"What are we going to do about Jensen?" Joss said, pushing the topic back to Kylie's situation.

Anger surged through Kylie. It was the first time she'd felt pissed. Really pissed. She'd experienced a lot of varying emotions the last week. Mostly sadness, grief, but not true anger.

It hit her like a freight train, clouding her mind until all she saw was red.

How dare he just give up on them? He was willing to put up with her issues and give her as long as it took to get over them. To work through them. Did he expect her to back off the minute his issues overrode hers?

"I'm pissed," Kylie said, though it sounded like it came from someone else across the room.

"You should be," Chessy said.

"I agree," Joss said solemnly.

"Wait. What are we pissed about?" Chessy asked in a puzzled tone.

"Jensen," Kylie supplied.

"Oh, that's right," Chessy said.

"What gives him the right to just give up on us like that?" Kylie demanded.

"That's the spirit," Joss encouraged.

"He was all willing to tie himself to the bed for me. To give me as long as it took to work past my issues. Does he expect me to tuck tail and run the minute his issues rear their head?"

Kylie sat straight up and promptly regretted it. The room spun crazily around her and she had to close her eyes so she wouldn't throw up.

"That's it!" she exclaimed when she got her bearings. "Oh my God. I'm such an idiot."

"What's it?" Joss and Chessy chorused.

Kylie smacked herself on the forehead and then sagged backward with a groan.

"Maybe you should be careful there," Chessy said. "You may knock yourself out."

"Care to share your epiphany with us?" Joss prompted.

"I'm going to tie his ass to the bed," Kylie announced. "Wait. First I'm going to make him make love to me. Without the damn rope. But after? When we're ready to go to sleep? That's when I'll tie him up," she said triumphantly.

"I'm confused," Chessy said. "But that could just be the alcohol talking. You're going to have to explain, hon. I'm a little stupid when I'm drinking."

Joss and Kylie both chuckled.

"He made this big deal out of me tying him to the bed when we make love. So I'd know he couldn't hurt me. So I'd know I was safe. Okay, so the reason he dumped me, or at least the reason he gave me for dumping me, was because he was afraid of hurting me. So if I tie him to the bed while he's asleep and he has a nightmare, voila! He can't touch me," she said smugly.

"You're a fucking genius," Chessy said in admiration.

"I'll drink to that," Joss said.

"Uh, maybe we should let up on the alcohol," Chessy advised.

"Yeah, I have to sober up now," Kylie said.

"How come?" Joss asked.

Kylie pushed herself upward again, holding herself up with one hand so she didn't keel over onto Chessy.

"Because when I sober up, I'm going over to his house. If he thinks he can just dump me for my own good and make me miserable in the process, he's got another think coming!"

"Uh, ladies? Not to interrupt what has to be scintillating conversation, but do you realize what time it is, that you've been drinking for the last several hours and that you're all lying on the floor?"

Heads turned in the direction of Dash's voice. Joss sent him a dazzling smile.

"Hello, darling," she said in a dreamy voice. "Have you come to take me to bed?"

Dash chuckled. "Since I don't imagine any of you are going to make it to bed unless I carry you, I think it's safe to say I have come to take you to bed."

Kylie scowled. "I can't go to bed now. I have a seduction to plan. Hey, Dash. You're a guy."

"I hope to fuck so," Dash said in amusement.

She pointed a finger at him. "So if a woman throws herself at you—naked—you're not going to say no, right?"

Dash chuckled. "I think that depends on which woman throws herself at me."

"Damn straight," Joss said. "I'll kick someone's ass if they ever throw themselves at you!"

"Calm down, honey. It's not going to happen. Now, are you girls done for the night? Kylie, perhaps you should get some rest so, uh, your seduction plan doesn't go awry. You may also want to revisit the issue when you're sober. You may decide that was the alcohol talking."

Kylie made a face. "What a downer you are, Dash."

"Sorry, sweetheart."

Joss sighed. "Are y'all ready for bed? Chessy, you and Kylie can share the guest bed. It's a queen so y'all will have plenty of room."

Chessy said glumly, "I spend so many nights alone these days that having someone in bed with me will be a novelty. Even if it is just Kylie."

Dash leaned over Kylie and slid his arms underneath her body. He hoisted her up, and her stomach lurched. Oh God, please, please don't let her puke all over Dash. There was only so much humiliation she could take.

"I'll get Kylie settled in. I think she's a little more shitfaced than the two of you are," he said to Joss. "I'll be back to get the rest of you once I get Kylie to bed."

Joss waved her hand in the air like she didn't have a care in the world. And why would she? She had a wonderful husband who loved her to pieces.

If she didn't love Joss so much it would be so easy to hate her.

Dash walked into the guest bedroom and deposited Kylie onto the bed. Then he went into the bathroom and returned with a plastic basin that he set on the floor beside the bed.

"If you need to puke, just lean over the bed," he said gently. "You might have trouble getting to the bathroom in time."

"You're the best, Dash," she murmured. "Joss is such a lucky bitch."

Dash's chuckle was the last thing she heard before it was lights-out and she was out cold.

THIRTY

KYLIE'S head felt like someone had hit her with a sledgehammer. Her mouth was dry and the mere thought of alcohol made her want to vomit.

At the time it had seemed like a good idea. Now? Not so much.

Dash had let them all sleep in and when they got up and stumbled into the kitchen looking like death warmed over, Dash served them breakfast and some foul-tasting concoction he swore would cure a hangover.

He so lied.

She slowly got out of her car, glancing over again for the reassurance that Jensen was here because his car was. Lucky for her, she still had a key, so she didn't have to worry about his doing what she had done and not answering the door.

It was Saturday. No work. And it was early enough that Jensen could still be in bed.

That thought considerably cheered her. It would certainly make her planned seduction easier to pull off.

She shook her head at that crazy thought. Her a seductress? Someone was probably laughing their ass off in heaven over that.

She paused at his front door and waffled on whether to use the key or knock.

The element of surprise was important, so the key it was.

She slid it into the lock, trying to make as little noise as possible. Then she eased the door open and peered inside.

So far so good.

When she got to the entrance to the living room, she froze, taking in the scene before her.

Jensen was sprawled on the couch, head back, either sound asleep or passed out. Judging by the bottles lying around, passed out was probably a good bet.

If it wasn't such a familiar sight, Kylie might have mustered some outrage.

How pitiful they both were. Obviously miserable apart. It was a damn good thing one of them had sense. This crap was going to end right now.

"Jensen. Jensen!" she said louder. "Wake your ass up."

She walked closer and then bent down to get in his face. "Wake up, Jensen!"

His eyelids fluttered sluggishly and then he seemed to realize who was standing over him in his living room.

"Dream," he muttered. "Too much to drink. Fuck me."

"I'm not a dream. More like a nightmare, but we'll work on that," Kylie said in amusement.

He blinked again and then rubbed an arm across his eyes. Then he frowned.

"What the fuck are you doing here?"

"Nice. Good to see you too, Jensen. How's life been treating you? Wait, don't answer that. I'd say it's pretty obvious judging by all the empty liquor bottles."

She leaned in closer so she was right over his face and she scowled big.

"So help me God, if you aren't able to get it up because you're too hungover, I'll kill you."

His mouth fell open and she caught a whiff of his breath. Okay, she could work with his. It wasn't too strong, so she imagined it had been hours since he drank. Possibly even last night and then he'd slept it off.

"What the hell are you talking about?" Jensen demanded. "You aren't supposed to be here. We're over, Kylie."

"Keep talking," she said with a sneer. "You might even convince yourself before it's over. But I know it's a lie and you damn well know it too."

"What do you want from me?" he asked in bewilderment.

She touched his cheek and stared him directly in the eye so he'd see how serious she was.

"Do you trust me, Jensen?"

"Of course," he said gruffly. "It's not you I don't trust. It's me. Goddamn it, Kylie, why are you making this so fucking hard? Was it so you could see how miserable I am? Well, take a good look. This is me without you."

Her heart melted on the spot. The aching vulnerability in his voice undid her.

"Prove it," she challenged.

"Prove what?"

He was sounding more irritated by the minute and she had to act fast before he threw her out of his house. Again.

"That you trust me," she said softly.

"There's nothing to prove. I trust you more than anyone else on earth."

"Then come into the bedroom with me," she said.

He closed his eyes. "I can't do this, Kylie. Please don't ask me to."

"I'm asking you to trust me, Jensen. You said you did. Now show me. Please," she added, the word sounding strangled.

"Fine. We go into the bedroom. Then will you leave me the fuck alone?"

"Are you so desperate to get rid of me, Jensen? Does your version of love mean forgetting someone you love, or supposedly love, so quickly?"

He surged up from the couch, his eyes glittering dangerously. Before? Such an action would have her terrified and dissolving into a panic attack. But now? She was so relieved to have at least a part of the old Jensen back and not this pathetic, grieving man who'd drunk himself into oblivion.

She'd done the same. If she hadn't had her head stuck so far up her ass she could have had her epiphany a hell of a lot sooner and neither one of them would have had to be miserable all damn week.

"Don't ever question my love for you," he seethed. "It's because I love you that I want you as far away from me as possible."

Ignoring that particular outburst, and happy to have him on his feet so she didn't have to try and get him up by herself, she took his hand and led him toward the bedroom.

When they got there, she turned, placing her hands on his chest and looking him in the eye.

"Remember what you said. About trust."

"I remember," Jensen said in a tight voice.

She nodded and then turned back toward the bed and began stripping out of her clothes. She whispered a short prayer that this worked out the way she hoped.

"What the hell are you doing, Kylie? You—"

He broke off, his mouth falling open when she turned to him, fully nude.

He closed his eyes and let out a groan. "Why are you torturing me like this?"

She slid her fingers down his chest and down to the fly of his jeans. Then she leaned up and pressed her mouth to his.

At first, he didn't respond. He held himself rigidly as she explored his mouth. Then his lips parted, a rush of air escaping. Slowly his arms crept around her, anchoring her in place.

She ripped her mouth away, gulping for breath. Then she kissed the lobe of his ear and whispered softly, "Make love to me, Jensen. Really make love to me. No rope. Just you and me."

A groan escaped his mouth. The sound seemed to come from his very soul. It was a sound of agony—and need.

"You said you trusted me," she said quietly. "Give me this, Jensen. Trust me. Make love to me."

He walked her backward toward the bed, ripping at his own clothing until he was as naked as she was. He certainly wanted her. His body couldn't lie about that. No matter what he said or thought, he was as desperate for her as she was for him.

The backs of her legs bumped into the bed and then she toppled back, landing on the mattress with him on top of her.

"Be sure this is what you want, baby," he said breathlessly. "If you don't want it at any time, say stop. I'll stop, no matter how hard it is."

She stroked a hand over his face, tracing the hard lines of his jaw.

"I don't want you to stop, Jensen."

He let out a groan and then dipped his head to kiss her. He kissed her hungrily, all of his need pouring out in a heated rush.

His body was hard and heavy on top of her and she reveled in the feel.

His erection was lodged between her legs. She could feel him hard and pulsing against her clit. She shifted restlessly, wanting, needing. She didn't want to wait. She wanted him inside her. She wanted to feel complete and whole for the first time in a week.

"Jensen," she whispered. "Make love to me. Now, please."

He ignored her demand and kissed a line down her body. He licked and tongued her nipples, coaxing them to aching, straining peaks. He took his time, tasting and sucking until she was out of her mind with need.

Then he continued down her body, stopping at her navel to tease and torment her with his tongue. Her fingers dug into his shoulders and she pushed him downward, hoping he'd get the point.

He laughed softly but complied with her silent request. He pressed a kiss to the top of her curls at the apex of her legs. Her thighs automatically loosened and spread, inviting him to explore her most sensitive region.

He petted and stroked with his fingers before finally spreading her soft folds. His breath huffed out, making her twitch. Her entire body tightened in anticipation, waiting for when he would give her what she wanted.

Then his tongue flicked over her clit and she arched up, a gasp escaping her lips. He lapped again before gently sucking the nub into his mouth.

She moaned helplessly. Sobs spilled from her throat. Desperate sobs of need. So much need. She'd missed him. Never had she felt this kind of connection to another human being. She was lost without him. She had an ache in her soul only he could assuage.

He put his mouth over her entrance and then slid his tongue inside, fucking in and out of her with his tongue. He kissed and sucked until she was mindless. She called his name over and over, a broken plea for him to make love to her a litany on her tongue.

Finally, finally, he rose above her, fitting his body to hers as he stared down at her with those intense dark eyes. She searched his gaze for what he was feeling. If he was as desperate as she was. If he'd missed her even half as much as she'd missed him.

What she saw burning in the depths of those eyes took her breath away and filled her with hope.

She saw love. Still love. It hadn't left. He still loved her. They could work this out. He loved her and she loved him. She refused to countenance any other possibility.

They belonged together.

"Are you okay?" Jensen asked, still poised at the rim of her entrance.

"I want this," she breathed. "I want you, Jensen. I've been so lonely and empty without you."

"Oh God, baby. Me too. If you only knew how miserable I've been."

"Then do something about it," she said softly. "Make us both whole again."

He gathered her in his arms, holding her close just as he pressed inward. She moaned in delight as he pushed even further. She tilted her hips upward as much as she could, inviting him deeper.

His entire body was tense. His muscles coiled and twitched with the agony of holding back his control.

She dug her nails into his shoulders and then lifted her head to whisper in his ear, "You won't hurt me, Jensen. I trust you. I love you. Don't hold back. Not with me. Show me who you really are. Because that's the person I love."

Her words shattered what control he had. An agonized groan tore from his mouth just as he thrust forward, sinking himself as deeply as he could go.

His body arched over hers, cupped protectively over and around her. He held her tightly, their bodies undulating in perfect rhythm. She lifted her legs to wrap around him, holding him close to her so no distance separated them.

He rose and then sank, over and over, her body clutching greedily at him each time he withdrew. She was slick around him, there was no doubt that she wanted him every bit as much as he wanted her.

Their passion grew to a fever pitch. It was quick. But then they'd been without one another for far too long. Their bodies and souls were on fire. Two halves to a whole, finally back together. She would never let him go. No matter what he said or what he tried to do, she wouldn't let him go. If she had to follow him to the ends of the earth, he was hers and she wasn't letting go. Never.

She kissed him desperately, her rising orgasm making her crazy with need. Their mouths worked hot over one another's, tongues sliding deep, dueling and then tasting. The sounds of their bodies and mouths slapping together were the only sounds in the room. They moved as one in perfect synchronicity.

They were one.

Better together than alone.

"Are you there, baby?" Jensen asked gruffly. "I want you there with me."

"Oh yes," she said, expelling a long sigh. "I'm there. Take us both over, Jensen."

He slipped his hand between them, sliding his thumb over her clit as he thrust hard and deep. A kaleidoscope of color and feeling exploded in her vision and through her body.

Her gaze locked with his, not wanting to miss a single thing in his eyes as he orgasmed. The eyes didn't lie. They were an open window to his soul.

And what she saw in those dark depths filled her with joy and relief.

He loved her. He wanted her. He missed her with his every breath.

He wrapped himself around her and then hurled them both over the edge, carrying her as they fell. She felt like a leaf in autumn, windblown and scattered here and there. Blowing with the wind.

She drifted slowly downward, dizzy and content, until she settled back onto the bed, Jensen's warm body covering hers protectively.

He buried his head in her neck and she could feel him trying to catch up, his breaths ragged, his chest heaving.

She ran her hands up and down his back, idly caressing him as he pulsed deeply within her. Finally, she felt complete. After so many days of being lost she was finally home. Right where she belonged.

But she still had one thing left to do.

She turned, trying to move Jensen's weight off her and to the side. When he realized her intent, he swiftly rolled them both onto their sides.

"Sorry, baby, was I hurting you?" he asked in concern.

She put a finger to his lips to shush him.

"I'll be right back," she murmured. "Don't move."

Ignoring his inquisitive look, she crawled out of bed, her

heart beating violently. This was the moment of truth. If he refused her, she didn't know what to do. This had to work. She had to convince him of her faith.

She pulled the rope out of his drawer and returned to the bed, ignoring his look of confusion. Before she could chicken out and before he realized what she was doing, she quickly looped the rope around his left hand and secured it to the bed.

Satisfied with the knot, she settled back onto the bed and curled back up against him, utterly sated and content. And she waited for the inevitable question to come.

"What's going on, Kylie?" Jensen asked, a perplexed look knitting his forehead.

She breathed out a deep breath and looked him directly in the eyes.

"No one trusts you more than I do," she said. "But you have to trust *yourself* with me. I don't need you tied to the bed in order to make love to you. I just proved that to you and myself. However, I propose that at least until *you* are as certain as I am about you never hurting me, that we tie you to the bed while we *sleep*. That way even if you have a nightmare, you can't possibly hurt me."

Jensen looked utterly overcome. Tears glittered brightly in his eyes. Eyes full of love and . . . relief.

"Come here," he said in a choked voice.

She snuggled into his arms and he threw his right arm around her, holding her as tightly as he could. He buried his face in her hair and his body shook. Tears burned her own eyes as she held on to him fiercely. Relief was so profound that she was weak with it. They were going to be okay.

"I love you," he said rawly. "I love you so much, Kylie. I'll never love anyone as much as I love you."

"I love you too," she whispered.

He finally let her go only enough so he could see her face. She reached up to wipe the tears from his face and he did the same to her.

"You really think this can work?" he asked hesitantly. "You have to understand, Kylie. That night . . . Oh God, that night was the best and worst night of my life. The best because you trusted me enough to open up about your past. And then the worst . . . You can't imagine how I felt when I woke up to see my hand around your neck, to know I was hurting you, something I'd sworn never to do. It *sickened* me. All I could think about was getting you as far away from me as possible so I could never hurt you again. I'd die before ever doing that, baby."

She stroked his face lovingly. "Oh yes, this will work. We'll make it work. We'll do what we have to do." She sucked in her breath and gathered her courage. "You once told me I should get help, and you were right. But I think . . ." She let out another long breath. "I think we should both get help—counseling— together. We'll work through it together. Take it one day at a time. And we'll see how things play out. But what I won't do is stay away from you over some ridiculous fear of you hurting me. I only feel safe when I'm with you. I know you'd never pur- posely hurt me, Jensen. Now you have to believe it too."

He caught her hand, pulled it to his lips and pressed a kiss into her palm. His breath puffed out erratically over her hand as he tried to regain his composure to respond.

"No one has ever had as much faith in me as you," he said, his voice breaking with emotion.

"And no one has ever believed in me as much as you do," she returned. "It only stands to reason that since we're both such fucked-up individuals that we stick together and be fucked-up together. We understand each other, Jensen. Who else would ever understand us and love us as much as we do?"

He laughed softly, relief rolling off him in waves.

"I like that. Fucked-up together."

"Are we back together then?" she asked hesitantly.

He squeezed her tightly and then kissed her on the mouth. "Hell yes we're back together. I guess I just needed you to kick my ass for me. And I agree. I think we would both benefit from counseling. I don't want to ever be in a position to hurt you again, so I'm willing to do whatever it takes to ensure that."

Relief surged through her heart and soul until she was weak with it.

"I'm only better when I'm with you," she whispered. "You make me believe, Jensen. You make me believe I can have a normal life and a normal relationship. You make me have so much hope for the future. But only with you. I don't want those things except with you."

"I can't believe I found you," Jensen said in awe. "You're so fucking perfect for me."

"You sacrificed a lot for me, Jensen. The unselfishness of your actions still blows me away. You denied an essential part of yourself for me. How can I do anything but fight for you—for us—with my dying breath?"

He gently caressed her face, love glittering warmly in his eyes. "It was no sacrifice, Kylie. The reason I was never willing to give up control before was because I'd never met a woman who made me *want* to. I want to do this for you. It's an honor and a gift and I mean that from the bottom of my heart. I will always put you and your needs above my own. Always."

"I love you," she said, her heart swelling until she felt near to bursting.

"I love you too, baby. Thank God you had enough strength and resolve for both of us. Thank God you didn't give up on us as I was willing to do. This last week has been the most miserable of my entire life. I never want to go through the pain of losing you again."

She grimaced wryly. "I have a confession to make. There are as many empty wine bottles in my house as there are liquor bottles here. And well, Chessy, Joss and I put a serious dent in Dash's liquor cabinet last night. I'm as hungover as you are, maybe even more."

Pain filled his eyes. "I'm sorry, baby. In my effort not to hurt you, I only hurt you more. I'm sorry for that. If you give me the chance, I'll prove to you that I'll never willingly hurt you again."

"It's over," she said softly. "For both of us. It's in the past. Now all we can look forward to is a future brighter than the sun. Giving in to you was the best thing I ever did and I'll never regret a single minute of it."

"I'm glad you feel that way, baby."

His expression grew more serious as he stared at her.

"Can you tolerate my dominant ways? Because they will assert themselves, Kylie. When it comes to you and your protection and care I simply don't know any other way to be. But in bed? I will always give you control for as long as you need it. But when we're out of bed, I'll want to take over. Can you handle that?"

Her heart softened at the uncertainty in his eyes. "Oh yeah, I can handle that," she breathed. "I like your bossy ways. You and they have grown on me. And one day . . ." She sucked in a breath before plunging ahead. "One day I hope to give you control when we're in bed."

Fire lit in his eyes. He caressed her cheek with his free hand.

"If that ever happens, just know that I will cherish you and treat you with the utmost care and tenderness. I never want to make you regret giving me such a precious gift."

Their mouths met, their tongues tangled and Jensen rolled to his back, taking Kylie with him.

"What are you doing?" she whispered.

His eyes gleamed and he kissed her again.

"I'm bound and helpless so I think it's time you took full advantage of your man and made love to him."

She laughed, the sound joyous and carefree. So much love filled her heart, banishing the darkness of the past week. Jensen was hers and she was his. They still had a lot to work through, but she knew in her heart that they'd get through it together.

With his love, she could be the person she'd always wanted to be and have the life she'd always wanted to live. What could be better than that?

And then she proceeded to do exactly as Jensen had asked. She made love to her man.

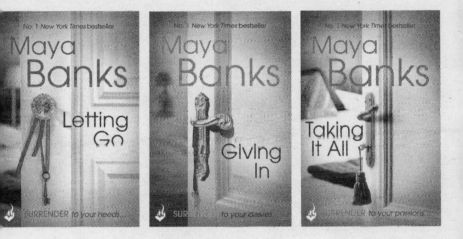

Letting Go

Josslyn had perfection once and, when her husband died, she was sure she'd never find it again. Yet now she cannot resist searching for the one thing her beloved husband couldn't give her – dominance and the chance to let go. Entering a hedonistic fantasy club, Joss never imagines she will find inside the one man who's long been a source of comfort – her husband's best friend.

Dash has been in love with Josslyn for years, but unwilling to act on that attraction, even long after his best friend's death. But when Joss explains in detail what she needs, Dash knows *he* has to be the man to introduce her to that world, touch her, cherish her . . . love her. And that he'll be the only man she will ever submit to . . .

'I can give you all that you want and need and so much more.'

Surrender to your passions . . .

Taking
It All

In the beginning, Chessy and Tate's passionate marriage was everything she wanted. She offered her submission freely and Tate made her feel safe and loved. But as the years have passed, and Tate's business built, their marriage has taken a back seat and Chessy knows that something has to give or they stand to lose it all.

Tate loves his wife and providing for her has always been his first priority. Worried that she is unhappy, he arranges for a night together to reignite the fire that once burned like an inferno between them. But a business call at the wrong time threatens everything he holds dear. To win back his beloved wife's love, Tate determines to show her that nothing is more important than her – and that he will do and give whatever it takes to get back the passion and trust they once had.

'You're it. And I want it all, but I want it with you.'

headline
ETERNAL